DEBATING WITH THE DUKE

Second Sons of London
Book Two

Alexa Aston

ARE YOU SIGNED UP FOR DRAGONBLADE'S BLOG?

You'll get the latest news and information on exclusive giveaways, exclusive excerpts, coming releases, sales, free books, cover reveals and more.

Check out our complete list of authors, too!

No spam, no junk. That's a promise!

Sign Up Here

www.dragonbladepublishing.com

Dearest Reader;

Thank you for your support of a small press. At Dragonblade Publishing, we strive to bring you the highest quality Historical Romance from some of the best authors in the business. Without your support, there is no 'us', so we sincerely hope you adore these stories and find some new favorite authors along the way.

Happy Reading!

CEO, Dragonblade Publishing

To Save a Love
To Win a Widow

The Lyon's Den Connected World
The Lyon's Lady Love

King's Cousins Series
The Pawn
The Heir
The Bastard

Medieval Runaway Wives
Song of the Heart
A Promise of Tomorrow
Destined for Love

Knights of Honor Series
Word of Honor
Marked by Honor
Code of Honor
Journey to Honor
Heart of Honor
Bold in Honor
Love and Honor
Gift of Honor
Path to Honor
Return to Honor

Pirates of Britannia Series
God of the Seas

De Wolfe Pack: The Series
Rise of de Wolfe

The de Wolfes of Esterley Castle
Diana
Derek
Thea

PROLOGUE

Vitoria, Spain—June 1813

EVERETT JOINED HIS friends just outside Wellington's tent, which served as the command post for every campaign.

"About time you got here," Owen said, punching him in the arm as Percy and Win nodded in recognition.

Other officers milled about, speaking in hushed tones as the group awaited entrance. It was just after one o'clock in the morning and Everett thought they would be given their orders to engage at dawn's light.

"Today could be the day," Win said, echoing Everett's own thoughts. "The beginning of the end for the French."

"We've certainly slogged through enough of Portugal and Spain," Percy noted. "I would love to finish off the enemy this day so we could head toward the Little Corporal."

All four men had been with Wellington since they had been commissioned into His Majesty's army six years ago. Missing from their group was their longtime friend, Major Spencer Haddock, who had left the military upon the death of his father last autumn. Spencer was now the Earl of Middlefield, safely ensconced in England. The last letter he had sent to their group had been several months ago. At least the last letter that had reached them. Correspondence arriving during wartime to a soldier, even an officer, was unreliable at best.

"Did you hear Jourdan had a fever all yesterday? The French troops remained idle all day," said Owen. "I heard it from a scout who just returned and is with Wellington now."

"I heard some rumors, as well," Percy shared. "That a convoy left Vitoria last night but a slew of siege artillery had to be left behind."

"Why?" asked Win.

Percy grinned. "Because it seems the French couldn't find enough draft horses to pull their cannons."

Everett knew Bonaparte had recalled a huge number of French soldiers to France after his failed invasion of Russia, giving the British and their allies a leg up in Portugal and now Spain. He wondered if that had included animals, as well.

Suddenly, men began moving forward and he fell in line, accompanying his friends inside Wellington's tent.

Over the next half-hour, their commander laid out his battle plans. The ambitious attack would originate from four directions, with the British having fifty-seven thousand soldiers fighting alongside sixteen thousand Portuguese and eight thousand Spaniards. The action would center on the Zadorra River, running from the east to the west. The hairpin turn that changed the course of the river to the southwest would become instrumental during the attack.

He learned that his regiment, along with those of his friends, would be part of General Rowland Hill's right column, a force that would push the French on the south side of the river. While they engaged with the Hill's troops, Wellington's right center column would cross from the north bank of the Zadorra near the hairpin, which would put them directly behind the French troops' right flank. That meant three of the columns—those from the south, north, and west—would attack the French while the remaining column would seemingly appear from nowhere at its rear.

The plan was bold and yet strategic, typical of Wellington. As

Everett left with his friends, they discussed it as they returned to their own men.

Before they parted, Owen brought the group to a halt. He thrust out a hand and the others covered it with theirs.

"To second sons," Owen said and the others echoed his words.

Peeling off in different directions, Everett returned to his men, thinking of how second sons in *ton* families almost always went into the army. A few entered the navy but it was a military way of life for them. All his close friends were the second born sons in their families. Only Spencer had left the military life behind, thanks to the death of his older brother, the heir apparent. At least his old friend was safe back in London. Everett chuckled, thinking that the most dangerous things Spencer now navigated were ambitious mamas seeking a titled gentleman for the daughters they paraded about on the Marriage Mart.

He awakened a few men, who did their job and roused the others. Every soldier knew being roused in the middle of the night meant imminent battle lay ahead. These were seasoned veterans who had fought at Salamanca and Burgos with Everett. He trusted them and they did the same, knowing he would lead them into battle with grit and determination.

It was a twenty mile march by the time they reached their fighting position and Everett worried about the men, having little sleep and already tired. Still, they were His Majesty's army of redcoats, the best trained forces in the world. He knew today they would taste victory.

The fighting proved fierce as he shouted several times for his men to regroup and push forward. He moved up a slight hill and as he topped it, he came face to face with the enemy. A French bastard, taken by surprise, jabbed Everett in the shoulder with his bayonet. A hot pain seared through him as he brought his sword full force, arcing high overhead, striking his enemy at where the man's neck joined his shoulder.

Surprise filled his attacker's face, the blade embedding deep.

The Frenchman tried to turn but it only forced the sword further into him, almost severing his head.

Everett lifted a booted foot and kicked the man hard in the chest. As he fell to the ground, his rifle went with him, effectively removing it from Everett's shoulder.

He continued to fight, feeling the blood gush from the wound. When a brief break came, he bent, dizziness overwhelming him a moment. He took a deep breath and gripped the shirt of a fallen soldier, pulling hard. It ripped away and he folded it several times, stuffing the remnant inside his own shirt, hoping to stanch the bleeding.

He was a bit shaky on his feet, nevertheless he continued to fight. To shout commands. To give encouragement and praise.

Then, hours later, it was over. The French had been defeated, thanks to squabbling among their officers and unanswered calls for help to reinforce those in precarious positions. Unfortunately, many of the enemy soldiers escaped, falling back to the Zuazo ridge, where they had stockpiled large amounts of field artillery. The place only fell to defeat when Gazan and d'Erlon couldn't agree on a united front and soldiers under both French commanders fled the battlefield, leaving cannons behind. The road became jammed with abandoned wagons, allowing too many of the enemy to make their escape. Even if they had tried to pursue, the allied forces were exhausted from the long march in the early morning and the battle itself.

Everett's left shoulder ached fiercely now and he knew he needed to have it cleaned and stitched if he was going to have any chance at survival. He shouted to gather his men and became utterly disillusioned at what he witnessed. British soldiers everywhere ignored their commanding officers, turning away to plunder the many French wagons which had been left behind. Everett's voice grew hoarse trying to get his men to return to their duty. He saw he wasn't the only officer confronted with the impossible situation.

Owen found him. "You look like a ghost, Ev. You've lost a lot of blood. I'll take you back."

"No, I must get—"

"There's no getting these fools to do anything," Owen said, his disgust obvious. "We have lost control of the situation. Our objective has been met. The French are in retreat. Now, we get you to a doctor."

He staggered a moment, swaying as if blown by the wind. Owen caught him, slipping one arm about Everett's waist. They passed dozens of looting soldiers before Owen stopped and thrust him onto the back of a horse. Swinging up behind Everett, Owen dug his heels into the mount and took off.

They reached the medical tents and being an officer helped put Everett near the front of the line. Owen stayed with him as the army physician cut away Everett's uniform coat and pulled the crumpled shirt off, tossing it to the ground.

"A nasty wound, Major," the doctor said, cleaning it with water so he could examine it better.

"He needs stitches. Now," Owen ordered.

"Patience, Major. I will tend to your friend."

"Use wine," his friend cautioned. "Brandy if you have it."

For some reason, the British had learned on the battlefield that if wounds were rinsed with spirits, the likelihood of infection lessened.

The doctor did as Owen requested and, soon, the threaded needle went in and out of Everett's shoulder, knitting the wounded skin together. He gritted his teeth as Owen tried to distract him, talking of the things they would do when the war was over and they returned to Kent. But Everett knew they would never really return. The army was their life now. Bonaparte would eventually be defeated—and then they would be off to somewhere else in the world. North America. India. The Far East.

Once the wound was sewn closed and bandaged, he thanked the doctor and Owen, who had been joined by Win, led Everett back to his tent.

"Has anyone seen Percy?" he asked.

They all shook their heads, no one voicing their fears that one of them might have fallen in today's action.

Reaching his tent, he collapsed on top of the cot.

"I'll stay with Ev," Win volunteered. "You might need something. Someone should be here with you."

"I'll go look for Percy," Owen said, determination filling his dark brown eyes.

Owen left and Win pulled Everett's boots off and swung his legs onto the cot. He closed his eyes, the sounds of battle still ringing in his ears. The cannons firing. The cries for help.

"Too many died today," he said quietly, looking over at his friend.

Win had taken a seat on the next cot. "Too many from both sides," he agreed. "But not Percy. Never Percy," he said fiercely.

Win and Percy were cousins and best friends since childhood. If Percy had died in action, a part of Win would die, as well.

"Why did the men break ranks like that?" he asked after a long silence.

"The temptation of all those goods was too great," Win replied. "Regular soldiers aren't like us, Ev. They come from hard backgrounds. Their pay is a fraction of ours—and you know ours is a pittance. They saw what they had never had and they wanted it. Felt as if they deserved it."

Everett shook his head. "Wellington will be furious. Discipline is foremost with him. To have the majority of his soldiers break ranks as they did, completely ignoring their commanding officers while the French retreated, won't be easily forgotten. Or forgiven."

"Wellington is hard on himself and harder on his officers. This will be unthinkable," Win said. "Let us hope that today's battle at Vitorio is the proverbial straw that has broken the backs of the French here in Spain."

Everett fell into a troubled sleep, dreaming of images of war. He awoke in a cold sweat.

Win came toward him, placing his palm on Everett's brow.

"Warm but not the heat of fever. That's a good sign."

"Tell that to my aching shoulder," he joked, relieved that no fever had set in. His shoulder was extremely tender but his gut told him he would recover. Already, he felt stronger and knew once he ate and got a bit more rest, he would recover fully.

His friend removed a flask and handed it over. "Drink," he advised. "I wanted you to do so earlier but you fell asleep."

Sipping from the flask, Everett felt the fire of brandy scorch his throat, burning with heat as it moved to his belly.

"More," Win urged. "Wellington won't be moving any troops for a few days at least."

"Have you heard about casualties?" he asked, glancing toward the tent flap, which was pushed open to help catch a breeze. He saw night would soon fall.

"Bad. Over five thousand is the estimate."

Everett winced at the number and then asked, "Have you heard any other news?"

Win nodded. "Percy is back."

Relief swept through him. "That is good news."

"And it looks as if today's battle may be the final blow. There will be a few other cities that we will need to take. San Sebastián. Pamplona. But once that is accomplished, we will most likely move toward France."

"So today marks the beginning of the end," he noted. "At least, if we can get our men back under control."

Percy and Owen entered the tent. Both men immediately broke out into smiles at seeing Everett awake and talking. They took a seat on the cot next to him and each shared what they had heard.

Then Owen glanced over and retrieved a letter sitting on the ground beside Everett's trunk.

"This has your name on it," he said, passing it to Everett.

When an officer wasn't in his tent as mail was being delivered, it was usually placed atop his cot. The soldier leaving it apparently hadn't done so. It was good thing Owen had spotted it or the letter might have been swept aside and lost.

He gazed at the writing, expecting to see Spencer's neat, precise hand. Instead, he didn't recognize the handwriting.

"Who is it from?" Percy asked. "Spence?"

"No." He frowned. "The hand is unfamiliar."

"Open it, Ev," Win urged. "We need something to talk about besides the battle."

Flipping it over, he broke the wax seal and unfolded the single page. It contained only a few lines and was signed by a Mr. Scofield. The name rang a bell but he couldn't place it. He raised his eyes to the top, noting the date was over five weeks ago.

Dear Major Wayland –

I will be brief. You are the new Duke of Camden.

Your brother suffered grievous injury and died from his wound. Since he had not yet wed, he had no legitimate heir.

Please sell your commission as soon as possible and return to England. You have a myriad of responsibilities to assume. Come to my offices so I might apprise you of the situation.

Sincerely,
Mr. M. Scofield

Stunned, Everett handed the letter to Owen, who read it aloud to the others. Silence filled the tent.

Then Percy spoke. "You will finally leave this hellish life, Ev. Or should I say *Your Grace?*

He shook his head, no words coming. "I never expected this," he said, dazed. "It . . . can't be right. Mervyn . . ." His voice trailed off.

"Mervyn was a fool. Who knows what trouble he got himself into?" Owen asked. He placed a hand on Everett's shoulder. "I'm certain Lawford was with him. If this Scofield won't give you the entire story, go and demand it from my brother."

He and Owen had grown up on neighboring estates and had

been friends since their earliest memories. Their older brothers, heirs apparent to the titles, were also close friends. You never saw one without the other.

"You're right. Perhaps this Mr. Scofield was aiming to be diplomatic by committing none of Mervyn's sins to paper. If he refuses to give me the truth, I'll make certain Lawford divulges the circumstances."

"You better go see General Hill now," Percy urged. "It's late but you cannot tarry. You're a duke now. You are needed at home."

Everett looked at his friends, his throat thick with emotion. Once Hill had been informed, everything would unfold quickly.

"This might be the last time we are together," he said.

Thrusting out his hand, the others covered it. "To the Second Sons of London."

His friends repeated the phrase.

Win helped him to rise. Though a bit unsteady on his feet, he insisted on making his way to General Hill's tent on his own. As he arrived, he realized that he was the second member of their close-knit group of second sons to leave—and assume the duties and title of a firstborn son.

CHAPTER ONE

Stoneridge, Kent—August 1813

EVERETT CLIMBED FROM the farmer's cart and thanked him.

"No, Major," said the farmer, "I must thank you for your service to king and country. It's fine men such as you that keep our hopes alive and keep our country from falling under the hands of Bonaparte and the French."

The farmer gazed at him questioningly. "Are you sure I can't take you the rest of the way?"

He shook his head. "No, I think I will enjoy stretching my legs. Thank you again for your kindness in taking me this far."

Everett gave a wave and the farmer clucked his tongue, the cart horse starting up again. He watched the cart roll away for a moment and then turned to start up the drive to Spence's house.

England was in all its glory at this time of year. The lane leading up to Stoneridge was lined with full, mature trees and Everett could see the main house in the distance. He wondered what Spencer would think with Everett turning up unannounced this way. He had missed his friend, one he had made on their first day of school almost twenty years ago. Along with Owen, the three of them had been a tightknit brotherhood during those school years. They had added to that brotherhood at Cambridge when they met Percy and Win. Everett wasn't bothered by leaving the war behind but he did hate walking away from his men and his other three friends. At least he would now be back with Spence for company.

His old friend had settled in at Stoneridge. Hopefully, he would be able to help Everett understand more about his responsibilities as a peer. He had still been a bit muddleheaded when he reached England and met with Mr. Scofield. Everett knew he should have gone directly to his country seat at Cliffside but he was terrified to do so.

He had no idea how to be a duke.

Since Spencer was now the Earl of Middlefield and had held the title for almost a year, Everett hoped his friend would be able to show him the ropes. His head still spun at the number of properties he held and the vast amount of wealth that accompanied them. Mr. Scofield had told him there were only a handful of dukes in all of England—and that Everett was among the wealthiest of that select group of peers. He wanted to do right by his people on his many estates.

He also knew he must provide an heir.

He vowed to himself once that heir did arrive that he would teach the boy everything he needed to know to be a good duke.

The idea of marriage, however, terrified him. He was not simply reserved, as Spence and Percy. Everett was incredibly shy. Owen had been the one who had drawn him out from himself but Everett still felt uncomfortable around people, especially in a social situation.

It struck him as he walked briskly toward the house that Spence might not even be in residence. If his friend had ideas of fathering an heir of his own, he most likely would have attended the London Season. All Everett knew was that it started immediately after Easter but he had no clue as to when it ended. Spence might still be in London. He should have thought of that before he left town and came directly to Stoneridge.

He slowed his pace, uncertainty filling him. If Spence wasn't here, he supposed his friendship would be enough to have the butler grant him a night's respite. Hopefully, the stablemaster might even lend him a horse in order for him to travel to Cliffside, his country seat fifteen miles away.

Anxiety filled him as he approached the front door and knocked. It was answered by a butler who looked at Everett's uniform and smiled.

"Welcome, Major," the butler greeted. "I am Callender. Might you be a friend of Lord Middlefield's?"

Everett nodded. "I am, Callender. Is Lord Middlefield at home or is he still in London for the Season?"

"His lordship is at Stoneridge and I am certain he will be pleased to see you, Major. Shall I take you to him?"

"I would like that very much, Callender."

"Follow me, Sir," the butler said, leading him to a side parlor. "If you will wait a few minutes, Major, I will tell Lord Middlefield you are here. Might I give him your name?"

Everett said, "Please tell him the Duke of Camden is here to see him."

Callender's brows rose a good inch. "Of course, Your Grace. Please excuse me."

The butler vanished and Everett paced about the small room, wondering if he should have used his title. It was the first time he had done so. He knew servants always announced a visitor by his or her title and name. He had resigned his commission so, strictly speaking, he was no longer Major Wayland. If he was going to be the duke he wanted to be, he must start thinking of himself as one.

Then he realized that Spence would think it was Mervyn who had come to call upon him. Unless Spence had heard of Mervyn's ghastly murder. Either way, Everett was looking forward to seeing the look on his friend's face.

The butler returned and said, "Lord Middlefield will see you now, Your Grace. Please come with me."

Instead of leading Everett up the stairs, the butler went down a corridor and entered a room which looked to be Spence's study.

Callender went to the French doors and said, "His lordship is taking tea outside, Your Grace. I will bring another cup."

Everett moved toward the door and the butler opened it for him. He grinned, eager to see how Spence reacted, and stepped through the doors.

As expected, his friend's face was wary to start. Then he realized it wasn't Mervyn at all. Spence leaped to his feet, closing the short distance between them, throwing his arms about Everett.

"Ev!" Spence exclaimed, slapping him on the back and then looking into Everett's eyes. "It really is you, isn't it?"

Spence hugged him tightly again. It was then Everett saw the woman sitting at the table. She had golden hair and was a true beauty. Spence must have wed without his friend's knowing.

Spence pulled away and said, "You must meet Tessa." He turned as Lady Middlefield rose and smiled warmly.

"It is wonderful to meet you, Your Grace," she said.

He merely looked at her blankly.

"This would be the part where you take my hand and tell me that you, too, are happy to make my acquaintance," she said teasingly.

Everett shook his head and reached for her hand. Raising it to his lips, he kissed it and lowered it again, releasing it.

"Forgive my ill manners, Lady Middlefield," he apologized. "I had no idea my old friend had married."

Spence laughed heartily. "Well, I wrote you and the boys. I suppose that letter did not reach you before you left the Continent. Just like the letter telling me you were now the Duke of Camden somehow went missing."

Before he could reply, Lady Middlefield said, "Come, Your Grace. Have a seat. Would you care to join us for tea?"

Callender appeared at that moment with a cup and saucer. "I thought His Grace might wish to partake in tea."

"Thank you, Callender," the countess said. "That was most thoughtful."

"Come and sit," Spence urged and the three sat as Lady Middlefield poured out and asked Everett how he took his tea.

"I haven't had tea in so long, I will take it any way you give it to me, my lady."

She smiled at him. "You are back in England, Your Grace. It is time to spoil yourself a little bit," and she added two lumps of sugar and a generous splash of cream, handing the saucer to him.

Then she added, "I feel as if I know you because Spencer has spoken of you and his other friends often," she confided.

"You need to tell us everything, Ev," Spencer said. "What happened to the despicable Mervyn that made you Camden?"

"How long have you been at Stoneridge?" he asked. "And how long have you been wed?"

Spence said, "Tessa and I met before the Season began. I will tell you for me, it was love at first sight."

Everett contained his surprise. To hear his friend had wed—much less making a love match—shocked him.

His friend continued. "We wed shortly after the Season was underway. In April. Because neither of us is much for town life, we decided to forgo the Season and a honeymoon and come straight to Stoneridge. We have been here since May."

Spence reached for his wife's hand and laced his fingers through hers. The gesture was intimate and loving. It told Everett all he needed to know.

He said, "You are happy then."

"Very," the couple answered in unison, laughing.

"But tell us about you," Spence urged. "And Mervyn."

"Since you have been gone from London, you would not have heard the news," he began. "My brother was murdered. His throat slashed by a footpad."

Lady Middlefield shuddered. "What an awful way to die."

"Mervyn frequented the stews," he explained. "His solicitor, Mr. Scofield, gave me a little background as to what my brother had been up to in the years I have been gone from England."

"When did this occur?" Spencer asked. "And was Owen's brother with yours? I cannot recall his name."

Everett said, "Mid-May. Mr. Scofield wrote to me but Wellington's army was on the march and it took until after the Battle at Vitoria for the missive to catch up to me," he explained. "Once informed of Mervyn's death, I knew I had to sell out and return home. As for Lawford, Owen's brother? You're right. He was with Mervyn that night. They always were inseparable."

"Was he, too, murdered?" Lady Middlefield asked.

"He might as well have been. Lawford, who became Earl of Danbury two years ago, was stabbed and his head slammed into the ground. I visited him after I met with Mr. Scofield to see if I could learn anything further about the incident. Danbury has no recollection of that night—or much of anything—due to his head injury. He also has fought numerous infections. Looking at him was like viewing death itself," Everett revealed. "And you know we have seen more than our share of that, Spence."

Lady Middlefield's eyes filled with sympathy. "You have seen much, Your Grace," she said quietly. "As has Spencer. Please know you are among friends. You need never speak of the war or your brother's death again."

"Thank you," Everett said, feeling a bond with this woman. "I have never been around women before, my lady. I had no sisters. My life was spent at school—and then war."

She touched his sleeve. "My husband views you as his brother. I do the same. Would you consider calling me Tessa? Lady Middlefield sounds so formal and distant. I hope we will see you often."

A feeling of peace descended upon Everett. "I was right to come here first. I have no family beyond my close circle of friends. Mr. Scofield dumped so much upon me that I couldn't even think. I have been frightened to take up my ducal duties. In fact, I have yet to go to Cliffside. I came here, to Spence. To seek his guidance."

Everett placed his hand atop hers. "I now see I will need yours, as well, Tessa. Please, help me begin. I have no idea where to start. I never thought to be a duke. I have no training in the ways of a titleholder."

"Neither did I," Spence said. "You know that. As second sons, we had fathers who ignored us. They thought the army would take care of us." He gave Everett a wry smile. "Instead, we have inherited unexpectedly. I have learned a great deal since I returned to England last autumn and will share with you everything I know. Tessa can help you see that your house is organized and that you have efficient and effective servants."

"I adore organizing a household," Tessa said, her eyes sparkling. "Spencer and I would be happy to go with you now to Cliffside and help you get on your feet as far as your country estate goes."

Everett chuckled. "You would earn my gratitude if you did so. Of course, besides my country seat, I have half a dozen other properties scattered about England, not counting the London townhouse."

Tessa's face filled with determination. "Then we will start at Cliffside and see that it is in order. We can leave tomorrow morning, can't we, Spencer?"

"Of course."

Tessa rose. "I will go consult with Callender and see that a room is prepared for you, Your Grace."

"What? You can't call a brother that," he teased. "I am Ev. Or Everett."

She looked pleased at his words. "You shall be Everett to me. Oh, how I look forward to having a brother. My two cousins, Adalyn and Louisa, are like sisters to me and my closest friends. Spencer now looks upon them as his sisters. You will have to meet them."

A slow smile spread across her face and she said, "Please excuse me. I'll also let Cook know we have a guest for dinner and I'll tell Abra and Rigsby to pack for us."

After she left, Spence started laughing.

"What is so funny?" Everett asked.

"Did you not see that smile my beautiful wife gave you before she left?"

"Yes. What of it?"

Spence chuckled. "She is planning something. Not only will she make certain your households are in good order, but I have the feeling my darling girl has something else in store for you."

"What?" he asked, clueless.

"I suspect Tessa has in mind to find you a wife, Ev."

CHAPTER TWO

London—March 1814

L ADY ADALYN GOULDING made her way downstairs to her
sitting parlor, knowing Louisa would arrive in the next half-
hour. They had arranged to go together to visit Tessa, who had
arrived in town yesterday afternoon. The three cousins were
closer than sisters and Adalyn couldn't wait to hold little Analise
again. Tessa had given birth to her first child two months ago.
Adalyn had been present, holding Tessa's hand and encouraging
her as Analise made her appearance in the world. She had helped
clean the baby and presented her to Tessa and Spencer, who had
been alerted of his daughter's arrival.

The earl had sneaked into the bedchamber and sat on the bed
next to his exhausted wife, his arm about Tessa as he kissed her
brow and told her how much he loved her. When Adalyn
brought the baby to them, Spencer had claimed his daughter,
tears in his eyes. For a moment, she had watched the threesome,
a new family coming together, and an ache formed within her.

She wanted a baby. And that meant she needed a husband.

A husband had never been a priority for her. She had gone
into her come-out Season unlike most other young women. They
sought to make a quick match with the highest title they could
land. Adalyn merely wanted to enjoy her youth. She had spent

several Seasons doing just that, thanks to her parents indulging her as they usually did since she was their only child. The years had seen her become a leader in fashion, with ladies wishing to copy her style of gowns. She attended every social affair on the calendar. She danced and saw plays and went to garden parties and Vauxhall outings. She had collected numerous suitors who, when they realized she wasn't interested in marriage, became loyal friends and confidantes.

Somehow, matchmaking became her forte and she had helped bring several couples together by the close of every Season. She had thought to try and match Tessa to a gentleman when her cousin finally came to London last year after being buried in the country nursing her ill parents for five years. Adalyn hadn't needed to find Tessa a husband, however. Lord Middlefield had pursued Tessa all on his own and Adalyn had heartily approved of the match. She now looked upon Spencer as the brother she had never had and was delighted Tessa had such a fine man who loved her completely.

But seeing Tessa's happiness last year had changed something in Adalyn. She began to want what Tessa had. She wanted a man to look at her the way Spencer did his wife. And after holding Analise, Adalyn craved a child of her own.

She had decided this would be the Season she would take a husband. If she couldn't find a gentleman to fall madly in love with, then she would choose the best candidate available and make him her husband. He would be someone who placed a priority on having a large family. A man who would treat her well but absolutely adore their children. At four and twenty, Adalyn was older than the majority of brides on the Marriage Mart. Still, her mirror told her she was attractive. She had sky blue eyes and thick, straight, honey-blond hair. Her skin was smooth and her smile bewitching.

Her huge dowry would also tempt more than a few bachelors. At least she had been out in Polite Society long enough to know which ones to avoid. She might be friends with several rogues but she wanted to find a husband who would be faithful to his vows. Perhaps with Bonaparte about to be deposed, if the newspapers could be believed, it might mean an influx of new gentlemen returning from war and attending *ton* events. No matter, she determined to wed at Season's end and would be ecstatic if this time next year she had a babe of her own.

Adalyn entered her private parlor and took a seat. She saw her correspondence had been placed upon the table as usual and picked it up. It did not surprise her to find two requests from bachelors she knew well, asking for an audience with her in the next few days. Both gentlemen had recently come into their titles as viscounts and had sown their share of wild oats. She suspected each had now decided to claim a bride and wanted her help in doing so.

It was unfortunate that neither gentleman would make a good husband for her. Lord Pierce gambled far too much for her tastes. She had observed that once bitten by the gambling bug, many men were lured to their downfalls. She would not see her dowry—much less her future and that of her children—gambled away. As far as Lord Bayless went, he was a handsome devil and knew it. While he would wed and produce the needed heir and spare, he would never be faithful to his wife.

Oh, dear. She already was becoming choosy. But she must stand up for herself and make the best match possible if she were finally to wed. She hadn't waited all these years to simply agree to wed the first bachelor who asked. No, she would compose a list of the characteristics she would seek in her spouse. Perhaps Tessa and Louisa might help her in this endeavor.

Rainey, their butler, entered and said, "Miss Goulding is here, my lady."

She chuckled as her cousin entered and they greeted one another. Even after all these years, Rainey insisted upon announcing Louisa. Her cousin only lived two doors down and they were constantly at each other's houses when Adalyn and her parents were in town.

Louisa smiled cheerfully. "I am so eager to see little Analise. I am jealous that you have already met her."

"She is adorable, I will give you that," Adalyn said. "I am happy that Tessa and Spencer decided to come to town so we can enjoy seeing them. Having just given birth two months ago, I thought they might stay at Stoneridge this Season.

"Tessa wrote to me and said there is a reason they have come to town for the Season," her cousin said. "Hopefully, she will reveal to us why when we visit with her today. Are you ready to leave now?"

"I am if you are."

Adalyn rang and Rainey appeared again. "Please have the carriage readied," she told the butler. "We are going to visit Lord and Lady Middlefield."

"At once, my lady," the servant said and exited the room.

Half an hour later, they disembarked from the carriage and were shown into the drawing room by Marsh, the Middlefield butler. Tessa sat with Analise in her arms, cooing to the baby. Once again, the tug on Adalyn's heart told her she would actively pursue a husband this Season. The two cousins went to Tessa and Louisa said, "Please, don't get up, Tessa. We will just sit here and gaze upon you as you look like the Madonna with her child."

Tessa chuckled. "Being a mother is something that has changed my world. I am so blessed to have Spencer as my husband. Analise has added a dimension to our lives which I heartily recommend."

"Might I hold her?" asked Louisa.

Tessa nodded and Louisa went and lifted the babe into her arms. As Louisa gazed at the infant, envy filled Adalyn. She didn't like experiencing such an ugly feeling, especially because she loved Tessa with all her heart and was happy for her cousin.

Tamping down the hateful feeling, she asked, "Are you going to tell us now why you have decided to come to town? I had thought you would prefer to remain in the country since you've so recently given birth."

Tessa said, "We did not talk about this when you came for Analise's birth but Spencer's good friend, the Duke of Camden, will make his first appearance in Polite Society this year. I aim to help him find his duchess."

"The Duke of Camden!" Louisa exclaimed. "Oh, that was such a huge scandal last spring. I believe you had already left for the country when it occurred, Tessa. The duke being murdered like that and his close friend, the Earl of Danbury, also attacked."

"I hear Danbury still hovers between life and death all these months later," Adalyn said, shuddering.

Tessa nodded. "Yes, Camden shared with us what happened to his brother. He, like Spencer, is a second son who now assumes a title he did not know he would ever hold. I like him quite a bit," Tessa continued. "Spencer and I went with him to Cliffside, his ducal seat in Kent, and helped him get things in order when he first arrived in England from the war."

"What is he like?" Louisa asked.

"He is friendly once you get to know him," Tessa said, "but I believe in society he will be quite shy."

Adalyn chuckled. "He will need to overcome his shyness or else. With a new duke in town, the Marriage Mart will be thrown into a frenzy."

"I was hoping that the two of you might come to dinner tomorrow evening and meet him," Tessa said. "Neither of you have yet to wed and I believe one of you could be his future wife." She looked at Louisa, who had grown still. "You told me last Season that Uncle did not want you to wed because he needed you as his hostess, especially with the war going on. That war is almost over now. It is well past time for you to look for a husband, Louisa. Holding Analise, you look so natural. You need to fulfill your destiny as a wife and mother."

Louisa stood and brought the baby to Adalyn, handing her over. Adalyn gazed down at the infant, who stared up at her with large, blue eyes, studying her intently.

Louisa seated herself. "I would like to wed," she said quietly.

"I have yet to discuss this with Papa but I agree with you, Tessa. Now that the never-ending war is all but over, I hope to participate in more of the Season's activities than in the past and entertain any offers of marriage which come my way."

"That is good to know," Tessa said. Looking to Adalyn, she asked, "And what of you? I have wed. Louisa intends to. What about you, Adalyn?"

"I have never hidden from you what is in my heart," she began. "You are my sisters. I have reached a point in my life where I am ready to settle down." She swallowed and then admitted, "I want what you have, Tessa. Holding Analise only confirms that."

Tessa clapped her hands in delight. "Then I hope to see both my cousins wed this year," she proclaimed. "And possibly one of you might end up with Everett."

"Is that Camden's Christian name?" Louisa asked.

Tessa nodded. "It is. Just as the two of you have adopted Spencer as your brother, I have done the same with Everett. I hope one of you might grow to love him. He is a fine man."

"Well, I hope Adalyn and I don't wind up fighting over him," Louisa joked.

"It won't come to that," Adalyn said. "If you find you have feelings for this duke, you are more than welcome to have him."

"Then will you come to dinner tomorrow night and meet him?" Tessa asked. "Even if neither of you finds him to your liking, then between the three of us, we should be able to help bring him together with an appropriate woman."

"That is Adalyn's specialty," Louisa said brightly.

Tessa frowned. "What are you talking about?"

"I thought I had told you I have a bit of a reputation as a matchmaker," she said. "I have successfully brought together several couples over the last few years."

"If I knew this, I have forgotten it," Tessa said. "So, you are a matchmaker? A matchmaker who now needs to make her own match."

"Now that you mention it, I thought to ask the both of you for your advice," she began. "I have thought I should compose a list of the qualities I might seek in a husband."

Tessa burst out laughing.

"What is so funny?" Adalyn asked, surprised by the outburst.

"Love isn't like that," her cousin said. "You can make all the lists you want but your heart will loudly proclaim to be heard. I know mine did. You know I didn't even like Spencer when we first met."

"That's true," she said. "But Louisa and I did like him. So did Abra, who was responsible for the two of you meeting. We could all see the earl was mad for you and agreed to support him in his efforts to win you over." She paused. "I said I wanted what you have, Tessa, but I am not certain that includes love."

"Why else would you wed then?" her cousin asked, perplexed.

"Because I want children," she explained. "And companionship. Rarely does anyone in the *ton* make a love match. You are an exception. Please, help me with my list."

Doubt filled Tessa's eyes. "I will help with this list but I hope that Cupid's arrow strikes your heart."

"I am more practical," Louisa announced. "I don't expect love at all. But I, too, would like to compose a list. It will help me evaluate any suitors that come to call upon me."

Adalyn knew that Louisa had put off suitors long ago because of her father's wish for her to remain by his side. She was delighted her cousin would now pursue what was best for her and not allow her father to cling to her as he had ever since Louisa's mother passed.

"I think our lists will have much in common, Louisa," she said. "But we should each write out our own so we will have a copy for ourselves. We might wish to add to it—or even strike through some of it—as the Season unfolds."

Analise began to fuss. "It is time for her feeding and nap. Come up to the nursery and see it and then we will work on your lists together."

The three women went upstairs and handed the babe to her wet nurse. They toured the nursery and Adalyn was filled with eagerness to create her own nursery for her children.

They returned to a small parlor where Tessa kept a desk for correspondence. She retrieved two pieces of parchment.

"I will sit at my desk and record your suggestions. Remember that your lists might change as the Season progresses but this will be a good place to start."

Adalyn watched as Tessa labeled each list with her cousins' names and then looked up expectantly.

"I want someone who likes to laugh and will make me laugh," she said.

"A sense of humor is important to some," Tessa agreed, scribbling away. "Do you wish the same, Louisa?"

Her cousin frowned. "Perhaps. Put it on my list but it is not the first thing I think of."

"Then what is?" she asked. "Of course, many other things are important to me. I do know that laughter keeps happiness in a relationship and helps keep people young. That is why I thought of it first."

"A good point," Louisa agreed. "I do want it on my list but it would not be a deciding factor for me."

"What would?" Tessa asked.

"I want respect," Louisa said firmly. "My husband must think highly of me."

"Write that on my list, as well," Adalyn said. "I want my husband to hold me in esteem."

The three discussed their lists for over an hour. What made for a good husband and a solid marriage. Attributes such as patience, kindness, fidelity, and intelligence appeared on both lists. Tessa also started a second list at the bottom of both women's pages for the things they specifically did not want in a future mate. On that list went gambling, excessive drinking, and being a braggart. Adalyn adamantly opposed wedding a man in financial need, while Louisa didn't mind if her fiancé sought a huge dowry.

"I have seen more than one gentleman inherit an estate worth next to nothing," Louisa claimed. "Due to the negligence of his father. Why should a man be punished for the sins of his father? If my dowry can help bolster the family's finances, I am not opposed to seeing it used in that way."

Adalyn disagreed, silently thinking if gambling ran in a father's blood it was a strong possibility the son would inherit the same lust for it. Still, she would wait and only voice an objection if she believed Louisa was making a dreadful mistake in her choice of husband.

The only other thing they disagreed upon was a man's nature. Adalyn was adamant that she wanted someone sociable and unreserved. She herself was gregarious and forthcoming and thought her best match would be a man possessing those traits. Louisa, on the other hand, didn't mind if her betrothed was quiet and a bit guarded. Because of that, Adalyn thought the Duke of Camden would be a good candidate for her cousin. Tessa seemed to think a great deal of Camden. Adalyn decided the man would be too reserved for her tastes, though.

Tessa sighed. "I am still upset that neither of your lists includes love."

"Just because you are deliriously happy with Spencer doesn't mean we will be able to find love," Adalyn pointed out. "The qualities we have pondered and included are more than enough for me. If a man is affable, I might even grow to love him over time."

"I agree," Louisa seconded. "You were most fortunate, Tessa. You found an exceptional man—and you both fell in love. I believe Adalyn and I will be happy if we can find a mature bachelor with several of the characteristics which we seek."

"Let me say this then," Tessa said. "You simply must kiss any man you are considering as a husband."

"Why?" Louisa asked, baffled.

"Because physical attraction and desire for one another is very important in a marriage," Tessa shared.

Adalyn scoffed at that notion. "I have been kissed more than a few times over the years. I don't think it's important at all."

Tessa gave her a knowing look. "You simply haven't been kissing the right men, Adalyn."

"I haven't kissed a man at all," Louisa lamented.

"Truly?" she asked.

Louisa shrugged. "You know I only go to a few social events. Mama, before she passed, pounded into my head that I was never to kiss a man before we wed. It would ruin me."

"Your mother was a fine woman," Tessa said, "but she was wrong about this, Louisa. Promise me—the both of you—that if you do find a suitable man that you are seriously considering as a husband that you will find a way to kiss him without being discovered. I don't want either of you forced into a marriage if caught in the act."

"I refuse to be ruined," Adalyn declared. "But I will take a married lady's advice and find a way to encourage a man I am considering to give me a kiss or two in private."

Louisa sighed. "Something tells me I'm not going to be good at this at all."

"Just be yourself," Adalyn told her cousin. "You are marvelous as you are. Don't change for any man. He will like you for you. If he wants you to behave differently, then he is not the one for you. For either of us."

"So, do you both believe your lists are complete at this point?" Tessa asked.

They agreed and Tessa handed them their copies and smiled. "We accomplished much by composing your requirements for a husband. Perhaps I can help both of you in your search to find the right man to serve in that role. In the meantime, your search starts tomorrow evening at dinner. With the Duke of Camden."

Adalyn would leave the duke to Louisa.

But at least the list in her hands gave her a better picture of the husband she would seek this Season.

CHAPTER THREE

"HOLD STILL, YOUR Grace," Roper pleaded.

Everett closed his eyes and willed himself to quit wiggling as the valet worked on tying the cravat that threatened to strangle Everett.

Tonight was simply a dinner. With Spence and Tessa.

And two ladies . . .

He had marched into battle. Surely, marching into a dining room shouldn't be such an abominable chore. After all, Tessa had told him quite a bit about her cousins so that they wouldn't seem as such strangers to him.

Miss Goulding, a year younger than Tessa, was the daughter of Sir Edgar Goulding, one of the wizards of the War Office. Tessa said Miss Goulding's mother had passed away several years ago and Miss Goulding acted as hostess to her father and the many people he entertained, especially working dinners at home. Tessa said her cousin was soft-spoken and mature for her years and the kindest person she knew.

Lady Adalyn Goulding was the same age as Tessa and the only child of the Earl and Countess of Uxbridge. She was, according to her cousin, quite lively and never seemed to have met a stranger. Lady Adalyn was a known leader of the *ton*, both in fashion and patronage. If Lady Adalyn liked a person, so did all of Polite Society.

He shuddered just as Roper finished.

"There, Your Grace," the servant said soothingly.

Everett opened his eyes and stood, walking toward the mirror. It was odd to see himself in anything but his officer's uniform, much less clothing so expensive and intricate. Part of being a duke meant dressing as a duke. Spence had taken him to a London tailor who charged so much for a single coat that Everett thought the cost might feed a family of four in London for a year. And it wasn't merely a single coat he'd purchased. After the tailor consulted with Spence, Everett found himself the owner of dozens of coats of varying cuts and colors. He had also been fitted for trousers and waistcoats and shirts and boots and more than a dozen hats. Why, his dressing room in this townhouse was larger than what many families lived in.

He doubted he would ever become accustomed to his immense wealth.

At least his friends had helped him establish an orderly household at Cliffside. Mervyn rarely went to the country and the staff had been trimmed to a minimum. They had also become a bit lax with their employer's prolonged absence. After Tessa finished her work, Cliffside now gleamed as much as Everett's Hessians did. She had hired a new butler and housekeeper and a bevy of servants. Spencer had convinced Everett to replace his elderly steward and now he had an efficient man in the role, one he trusted and admired.

It had taken several weeks but Everett had visited every tenant at Cliffside, wanting to show his interest in them and reaffirm his commitment to the estate. Many of the tenants had never laid eyes upon Mervyn. Mr. Painter, the new steward, had accompanied him on these visits, taking notes of everything Everett wanted done about the property. As a result, many of his farmers wound up with new roofs and painted cottages.

Eventually, he would journey to all the properties he held. Already, he had written to each of those estate's managers and would stay in close contact with them, thanks to Mr. Johnson, the secretary he had hired. Johnson helped to oversee all Everett's holdings and would work as his personal secretary, as well. With the Season on the verge of starting, a deluge of invitations had already been delivered. Johnson would oversee Everett's calendar and coordinate with Roper as to the events Everett would be attending.

The thought of having to make an appearance at so many social affairs turned his gut inside out. He was already a bundle of nerves attending a small dinner party tonight with only two ladies.

What would it be like walking into a ballroom containing several hundred people?

"Are you pleased, Your Grace?" Roper asked. "Is there anything else I might do for you?"

The valet had proved his worth. Though Everett had not thought he needed a valet since he was perfectly capable of bathing and dressing himself, Spence convinced him otherwise. Roper would coordinate the various outfits each day, keeping track of which had been worn and where so that he wouldn't repeat something too often. Supposedly, that was a cardinal sin of the *ton*, one affecting women more than men. He was more than willing to allow Roper to keep the wardrobe up to snuff. Buttons in place. Shirts and cravats ironed. Boots polished. As well as noting the various combinations which had been worn.

"I look my best," Everett said. "I cannot ask for anything more."

Roper grinned. "Wait until the Season starts, Your Grace. You will be the best dressed peer in the land."

He gave the valet a stiff smile, resisting the urge to tell Roper that he had no desire to attend any social events. But he wanted a family. Especially now that he saw how happy Spence and Tessa were with little Analise's birth. His strapping friend was but a gentle giant when holding his newborn daughter, cooing softly to her. Spence had chosen Analise's name, which meant graced with God's bounty. Everett only hoped he, too, would be graced with numerous children.

He desired both sons and daughters. And that meant taking on a wife. Tessa had told him she was there to guide him in finding his duchess. He would get practice tonight in a small setting with her two cousins. Perhaps one of them might even appeal to him and he could forgo the Season altogether. Of the two, Miss Goulding sounded more to his liking. He would see tonight if the two of them might suit.

"Shall I call for the carriage, Your Grace?"

"No, Roper. Lord Middlefield lives but a block away. I shall walk to dinner."

"Walk?" the valet asked blankly.

"Yes. It is done with two feet and highly effective in getting a person from place to place, especially when only a short distance is involved."

When Roper continued to stare at him, Everett said, "I have what is termed a dry sense of humor. I can say something in a serious tone which is meant to be humorous."

"Of course, Your Grace. I will wait up for you."

The valet left and Everett figured his little joke had fallen flat. It would probably be the same in Polite Society. Though his friends always understood his sense of humor, many outsiders did not. Perhaps he would refrain from making any type of humorous remark in the company of others. Better to be thought quiet and serious than be completely misunderstood.

He did believe being a duke was serious business. He had so many others he was responsible for. So many people's lives in his hands. Investments to oversee. Holdings to manage. He supposed the time for joking was past.

Heading downstairs, he found Bailey hovering in the foyer.

"Your hat and walking stick, Your Grace," the butler said, handing both over.

"Thank you, Bailey."

"Are you certain you don't wish for the carriage? I could send it later so that you might use it when you return home from Lord

Middlefield's."

"That isn't necessary. Good evening, Bailey."

"Good evening, Your Grace."

Everett stepped out the front door and found the March air brisk. He set out at a quick pace and arrived at Spencer's residence in just over two minutes. It was nice to have his friend so close by.

Marsh greeted his knock and led Everett to the drawing room upstairs. As the butler announced him, he drew in a deep breath and stepped into the room.

The first thing he noticed was he was the last to arrive. Spence and Tessa stood near the fireplace with two women, whom he assumed to be the cousins invited to dinner this evening.

The second thing he observed was how beautiful the two women were.

As Everett approached, he took in each, assessing their looks quickly, a holdover from his army days.

The one directly across from Spence had hair so blond that it was almost white. Large sapphire eyes stood out in her elfin face. She might be a couple of inches over five feet and had ample breasts. She had beautiful posture and a maturity about her.

The other had eyes the color of a summer sky and rich, honeyed hair. She was a few inches taller than her companion and was on the thin side, with an average bosom. Her generous smile, though, spoke of mischief.

"Your Grace," Tessa said, a smile crossing her lips. "How good of you to come."

"Did you give me a choice?" he asked, taking her hand and kissing it.

"May I introduce my cousins to you?" she continued. "My mother had two brothers and they are the offspring of those brothers." Tessa indicated the elfin blond. "This is Miss Goulding. Her father, Sir Edgar, serves in the War Office."

He took her hand after she curtseyed to him. "Miss Goulding.

I am enchanted."

She studied him carefully and then smiled politely. "It is a pleasure to meet you, Your Grace."

Yes, she had a maturity about her and seemed a bit reserved. He would have liked her for that alone but knowing she was Tessa's cousin and how much Tessa thought of her, Everett found himself liking Miss Goulding quite a bit.

Releasing her hand, he turned to the second cousin, whose lips seemed to twitch in amusement.

"And this is Lady Adalyn Goulding, daughter of Lord and Lady Uxbridge," Tessa continued.

The taller blond also curtseyed and Everett took her hand. "It is good to make your acquaintance, my lady."

Lady Adalyn contained her mirth and said, "Oh, Your Grace, I am happy to meet you. Spencer and Tessa speak so highly of you."

"Do I amuse you, my lady?"

Laughter spilled from her now. "You just are so very serious, Your Grace. I thought Spencer was quiet and grave but you make him seem rather outgoing."

He released her hand, realizing he still held it. "I am a duke. Dukes are supposed to be solemn."

"Says who?" Lady Adalyn challenged.

"Says . . . society," he blurted out, feeling his neck grow hot under his cravat.

It wasn't the only thing that heated.

"Would you care for an aperitif, Your Grace?" Marsh asked, a tray of drinks in his hands.

"Yes, thank you," Everett said, glad that he had something to hold to keep his hand occupied.

And hoping he wouldn't spill it as nervousness set in.

The butler left once the drinks had been dispersed and Spencer said, "We were just discussing news Louisa—Miss Goulding— brought us. Tell him."

Miss Goulding said, "Bonaparte's victories in the Six Days'

Campaign have not made a difference. Papa has received word that the leaders of Paris have surrendered to the Coalition."

He sighed in relief. "That is incredibly good news."

"Uncle Edgar said spies have sent word that the French advisory body will now turn against the Little Corporal," Lady Adalyn added. "That he will most likely be deposed since the Allies fight against Bonaparte—not France."

"Papa believes France will offer the country honorable peace terms if Bonaparte is removed from power," Miss Goulding continued. "It seems that the Bourbon monarchy would once more be restored."

"That would mean the war would finally be over," Spencer said with glee. "The Second Sons could come home."

"The Second Sons?" Lady Adalyn asked, turning her gaze upon him.

"It is a nickname our little band of friends came up with," Everett explained. "We five were all the second child to be born in our families. Tradition has second sons entering the army though occasionally one will join the navy."

"I am aware of that practice," she said. "Would that mean your friends would be free to part ways with the military with the war ending?"

"I am afraid not," he shared. "Second sons don't inherit their fathers' titles or wealth. For them, the military is a lifelong commitment. Spence and I are exceptions since our older brothers died without leaving an heir."

"But surely they will return to England once the threat of Bonaparte is gone," Tessa said, looking dismayed. "Even if they do remain officers."

"For a time," Spencer said. "Then they will ship out for other parts of the world. North America, most likely, since we are still engaged at war with our American cousins." He slipped an arm about his wife's waist. "But I do hope Owen, Win, and Percy will be home long enough for you to meet them, love."

"I hope so, too," she said. "I know how much you think of

them."

Marsh appeared. "Dinner is served, my lord."

"Will you see my cousins into dinner?" Tessa asked him.

"Of course." Everett offered his arms. "Ladies?"

They each took one and he led them into the meal. With such a small group, the conversation was easy to follow and quite lively. Miss Goulding proved to be highly intelligent and could carry on about any topic with ease. She even mentioned how she had been around adults most of her life and felt comfortable around older people. She also seemed open-minded about a good number of things.

Lady Adalyn, on the other hand, was incredibly opinionated. About everything. Everett thought her a bit overwhelming. She was vivacious and constantly changing the subject. A man would have to be on his toes to keep pace with her.

He wondered what she would be like in bed.

Again, heat seemed to ripple through him. He had no idea why she caused him to think such wayward thoughts. Perhaps it was her plump lips. They seemed to beg to be kissed.

He shook off the thought. Lady Adalyn was a whirlwind. Miss Goulding was more to his taste though he felt no physical attraction to her. It didn't matter. In the end, he would couple with his wife—whether it be Miss Goulding or someone else—and they would produce the agreed upon number of children. He hoped for four but would settle for two or three. He would have to ask Spence about how to negotiate that kind of thing with a wife.

Looking to his friend, though, he saw that would be pointless. Spence was besotted with Tessa. They probably made love once a day and would gladly accept however many children resulted from their couplings. There would be none of the going their separate ways, as he planned to do with his wife. That was the way of Polite Society. He knew that from his own parents. He had never seen an affectionate gesture or heard either speak a kind word to the other. At least he would be civil to his wife and see that she had everything she needed once they parted for good.

He felt eyes upon him and met Lady Adalyn's gaze.

"You are awfully quiet, Your Grace," she pointed out.

"It is my nature," he admitted. "You should meet my friend Owen. We grew up on neighboring estates. Owen talked enough for the both of us."

"Owen brought both Ev and me out of our shells," Spence shared with the ladies. "I am merely reserved. Ev can be downright bashful."

"Unless on a battlefield," Lady Adalyn said. "I can't see you being shy around your men or the enemy."

Spence grinned at him. "Ev is a beast when it comes to war. You wouldn't recognize the quiet, refined duke if you saw him on a battlefield."

"I was never a duke on the battlefield," he pointed out.

"But you are one now," Spence said. "And you will be a good one. I know it."

"Shall we leave the men to their port?" Tessa asked and rose, as did her cousins.

Spence glanced to him. "Shall we skip the port and cigars and head straight to the drawing room?"

"Yes."

Everett had never cared much for cigars. He had also found the conversation stimulating and would prefer to remain in the ladies' company.

Louisa linked arms with Tessa. "Perhaps we can entertain His Grace with a few songs. What should we perform?" she asked and the two women left the room, Spencer trailing after them.

That left him with Lady Adalyn.

She gave him that mischievous smile, as if she knew he were uncomfortable at that thought. "Are you willing to escort me to the drawing room, Your Grace?"

"Of course," he said stiffly.

She placed her hand on his sleeve and they left the dining room. They reached the drawing room and found Tessa already seated at the piano, her husband by her side, ready to turn the pages of music for her.

Everett led Lady Adalyn to a settee and took a seat beside her. Tessa played an introduction and then Miss Goulding began to sing.

"She is remarkable," he told his companion after the first song concluded.

"Louisa has all the vocal talent in the family. And Tessa plays beautifully."

"What of you, my lady? Do you sing or play?"

She snorted. "Frogs sing better than I do, Your Grace. If I practiced my pianoforte, I might—just might—be passable. Barely."

"You don't practice?"

She grinned cheekily. "Not if I can help it."

Miss Goulding was consulting with Tessa on what to sing next so his companion said, "You will need to exhibit courage when you hit the ballrooms, Your Grace. The same as when you led your troops onto the battlefield."

"What do you mean?" he asked, his brow furrowing at her odd statement.

"Only that you are an incredibly eligible bachelor. The rare duke who will be perusing the Marriage Mart. All those eager mamas will be thrusting their darling daughters into your path. If you don't stand up for yourself, you will be crushed by their ambitions."

Everett shuddered. "You are saying they seek a title for their daughters who are of marriageable age."

"Exactly. The higher, the better. At least, that is the usual attitude. Land a gentleman with the loftiest title. The most wealth. The largest number of estates. And don't look back—unless you are gloating."

"You make it sound so . . . repulsive."

"It can be. It can also be wonderful." She closed her eyes and a dreamy expression crossed her face. "There is the dancing. The music. The wonderful food and company." Her eyes slowly opened. "Spencer will help you navigate things. So will Tessa. If you have taken a liking to Louisa, I can assure you she would make for a perfect duchess."

He wondered why she left herself out of that equation." And what of you, Lady Adalyn? Are you willing to help me swim through the shark-infested waters of the *ton*?"

She studied him a moment thoughtfully. "I could do that. I can even help you find a bride, Your Grace. You see, my hobby is matchmaking. I help bring couples of the *ton* together."

CHAPTER FOUR

EVERETT HAD NEVER heard of such a thing. Yet it didn't surprise him. Nothing about this woman did.

Disgust filled him as he regarded her. "You actually run a business that places eligible couples together?"

Lady Adalyn's laughter tinkled as bells. "No, Your Grace, not a business. I would never charge for my services or advice. In fact, I don't consider them services at all. Merely helping friends and acquaintances in Polite Society to make the best match possible."

"I think that is repulsive."

Her eyebrows arched. "And why would you consider that repulsive, Your Grace? The parents in Polite Society have always done that very thing, arranging for their children to wed someone of their liking. Sometimes, they match their children to the offspring of an old family friend. More often, they choose a spouse who will elevate their own family's standing. It isn't often two people meet and fall in love as Tessa and Spencer did. I have seen too many unhappy unions and merely wish to help others find a partner they won't become miserable with."

She could have been speaking of his parents. Everett knew theirs had been an arranged marriage.

"I realize you have never been involved in the Season in previous years but I can assure you what I do for others, by putting them together, gives them a fighting chance to actually enjoy their marriages."

He regarded her with suspicion. "Why do you say so?"

"Many times, a couple becomes betrothed when they barely know one another. An unwritten rule of the *ton*—which you should become familiar with those, Your Grace—is that a man is only to dance with a woman once per evening. If he dances twice with her, it is a sure sign to others of his interest. Even that he is staking his claim to her."

"Dancing twice in an evening indicates that?" he asked in disbelief.

"Oh, yes, Your Grace. And if you danced thrice with the same young lady? Why, it would be a downright scandal." She grew serious. "But what I am saying is that with such limited contact, many young ladies receive an offer of marriage from a gentleman when they have barely been in that man's company. Even if she has danced with him half a dozen times, I will tell you that most dances are not conducive to conversation. Unfortunately, conversation in the *ton* is usually limited to the weather."

"The weather? What does the weather have to do with anything?"

"That is the point, Your Grace. The weather is an inane but safe topic. No controversy involved. And because of that, most couples who become betrothed know little to nothing about one another. Even if a gentleman has called upon a lady in her home, it has always been with other visitors around. A chaperone must always be in the room. One or both of her parents. An elderly aunt. Even younger sisters or brothers, watching and listening."

Adalyn paused before continuing. "Having been out in society for so long, I am friendly with many gentlemen in the *ton*. I also keep a watchful eye on the new girls who make their come-out each Season. Because of this, I have a better idea as to which couples might suit one another. Gentlemen, in particular, come to me and ask for me to help choose their brides every Season."

He looked at her incredulously. "But you have yet to wed yourself, Lady Adalyn," he pointed out.

She shrugged. "It hasn't stopped anyone from asking me. I am happy to comply with their wishes. As a matter of fact, I have already received contact from two such gentlemen this week. Both have recently come into their titles and know their carefree bachelor days are behind them. It is time for them to select a wife and provide an heir to the title. I will admit that both of these gentlemen are rogues and have chased skirts since they were wet behind their ears. They have no idea what to look for in a wife. Because of that, and our association with one another, they trust me to advise them."

"So they turn over the biggest decision they will ever make to you?"

Lady Adalyn grinned triumphantly. "Yes, Your Grace. You now understand my role." She eyed him with speculation. "Because I have proven to be not only reliable but even talented in this area, you might wish to place your trust in me, as well. You are new to Polite Society. Having been in the military so long, Spencer is most likely the closest friend you have who is in society. He didn't bother to look at any women last Season because he met Tessa before it even began and knew he wanted to make her his countess. Therefore, you have no male friends or family members who could advise you in this matter. I, on the other hand, am merely a third party and would give you fair advice as I evaluate brides for you. Of all those who wed in the *ton*, it is dukes who must be the most careful."

"Why do you say that?"

Lady Adalyn's laughter tinkled again, like music to his ears. "Because dukes lead all of Polite Society. There are but a handful of you and your peers look to you to set the tone and pace for everything from politics to what is the most fashionable drink. Consequently, your duchesses are the same. They are the women who lead the other women of Polite Society, be it in matters of fashion or ways to influence their husband's ear on loftier matters. I would say it has been more than one duchess who bent the ear of her duke and influenced his vote in the House of

Lords."

She smiled brightly at him. "Because of my experience in these matters, it would be ideal if you put yourself in my hands and allow me to select a bride for you."

"That is the most outrageous statement anyone has ever made to me, my lady. Choosing a wife will be the most important commitment I ever undertake—and I plan to make this decision on my own with no help from you."

She nodded sagely. "I admire you for your effort, Your Grace. I do wish you the best of luck in your endeavor. Remember, though, that I have warned you. Just as unattached females are paraded about on the Marriage Mart by hopeful mamas, you will be in a category all your own. The *ton* will scrutinize your every move, with assertive, overbearing mamas trying to convince you to wed their daughters. I wouldn't put it past your peers to do the same."

She smiled warmly at him, causing a tingle to ripple through him. "If you change your mind, I am available and would be more than happy to help you. Tessa is a sister to me and I absolutely adore Spencer. Because they also think of you as family, I will do the same and be happy to aid your search. It would require spending a bit of time with you. I would need to learn your likes and dislikes. See what you value and what might be important to you in a marriage. Just let me know what you decide."

By now, Everett realized Miss Goulding had been singing and he had missed most of the song she had performed because it ended moments later. He studied her carefully, noting her poise and the grace in which she held herself and decided he needed no help from this busybody beside him in finding a bride. Miss Goulding would do nicely.

All he had to do now was to figure out how to offer for her.

He would talk it over with Spence, of course, and also Tessa if it came to that.

But he had no intention or desire to consult Lady Adalyn

about anything. She might be Tessa's beloved cousin but he had taken a dislike to her. She was far too forward and he abhorred the idea that she dabbled in matchmaking. She would be the last person he would consult regarding a bride.

Yet as her vanilla-scented perfume wafted over to him, he once again tamped down the urge to lean over and inhale her. In no way would he ever consider a woman such as Lady Adalyn for his duchess. He believed her to be a hoyden. Far too opinionated and unlikeable. He might not seek a love match as Spence had but Everett knew he wanted a quiet, docile woman to wed and bear his children. Lady Adalyn was the last woman to be his duchess.

He turned his attention once more to Miss Goulding, who began to sing again. She was incredibly talented and seemed to be a sensible type of woman. He would ask Spence about what it took to woo a woman and then Everett planned to make Miss Goulding his duchess.

When she finished singing, he rose and went to her.

"I was touched by your voice, Miss Goulding. Though I know little about music, I can tell you are most talented."

"Thank you, Your Grace," she said, demurely gazing down.

"Might I call on you tomorrow afternoon?" he asked spontaneously.

A blush stained her cheeks. "Why, certainly, Your Grace." She provided him with her address.

He noticed Tessa beaming at him as the entire group returned to the area where Lady Adalyn sat, an amused look upon her face.

They conversed for another hour and Everett believed his decision to court Miss Goulding was a sound one. She was well spoken and entertaining yet she never sought too much attention.

If only he weren't so aware of Lady Adalyn.

That woman was wrong for him in every possible way.

The evening ended and the hosts accompanied their guests downstairs, seeing them out. A carriage awaited the two women and he noticed a servant had joined them in the foyer and now waited to climb into the carriage. He supposed she would be considered a chaperone for the two women. Everett realized he had a lot to learn about this society he now joined and was expected to help lead.

"Goodnight, Your Grace," Miss Goulding said and allowed a footman to aid her into the carriage.

"Goodnight, Miss Goulding," he called after her.

Lady Adalyn turned to him. "It was an interesting evening, Your Grace. I can see you have decided upon Louisa. She will make for a wonderful duchess. She has experience in entertaining and is thoughtful and mature." Pausing, she added, "Don't be a dolt and offer for her right away. Louisa has waited a long time before considering to wed. She should be wooed and allowed to enjoy all the trappings of the Season. And then I expect you to cherish her when she becomes your wife. If you stray—if you cause her any kind of heartache—I will cut off your balls."

With that, she gave him a beautiful smile and stepped into the carriage.

>>><<<

ADALYN KNEW SHE was in deep trouble as she seated herself in the carriage. It boiled down to two things.

First, the tall, handsome, forbidding Duke of Camden had decided to make Louisa his duchess.

Second, she was utterly enamored by the duke.

This wouldn't do at all. Not at all.

Looking to Louisa, she asked, "What did you think of Camden?"

Her cousin shrugged indifferently. "He seemed very nice."

She snorted. "Come now, Louisa. Give me your true opinion."

Louisa sighed. "He is quite handsome, with that black as coal hair and deep gray eyes. He is a little too physical for me, though. Too tall and a bit too muscular. I found that intimidating."

"I will give you that he is handsome. But he is interested in you, Louisa, else he would not have asked to call upon you tomorrow."

Louisa twisted her hands in her lap. "I didn't want to agree to him coming to call but I didn't know what else to say. How do you tell a duke no? You don't."

"Why would you not wish him to call?"

Louisa hesitated and then said, "As I said, he is most amiable. But I keep thinking about what Tessa said. How if I were truly interested in a man, I should allow him to kiss me." Frowning, she added, "I just don't see myself kissing His Grace. Ever."

Adalyn had thought of nothing *but* kissing the duke ever since he had appeared in the drawing room.

Why did he appeal to her so? It wasn't because he was a duke. She had no interest in titles. And then there was his attitude toward her matchmaking. He had made it obvious he did not approve of that practice. Also, he seemed too sober and solemn for her taste. While he did appear intelligent—an item on her list—nothing else about him seemed right for her. Except those sensual lips. Every time he spoke, she found herself watching them, fascinated by them. Wanting to press hers against his and see if Tessa was right and there really was something about kissing.

This was madness. She hadn't thought looks were important at all and therefore hadn't put it on her list. But all she could think about was Camden's looks. His broad shoulders. How well his coat fit him. How the tight breeches he wore emphasized his muscular legs.

It was frustrating to now realize that she was only attracted to his looks and nothing else about him. He was judgmental. Taciturn.

Most important, however, was that his interest had turned to Louisa.

Swallowing the bitterness that threatened to escape, she said, "Let him call. See if your opinion of him changes. If an opportunity arises to kiss him, take it."

"Take it!" Louisa cried in horror. "How can you say that, Adalyn? We have only met him this evening."

"He would not be Spencer's longtime friend if something was wrong with him. You know how Tessa has always been a good judge of character. Give him a chance, Louisa. Then if he isn't for you, he isn't. There will be plenty of gentlemen for you to look at this Season."

Looking glum, her cousin said, "I haven't even spoken to Papa about wanting to find a husband. Something tells me that he will not approve."

"*I* will set Uncle Edgar right on this matter if I must," Adalyn said confidently. "He has had you long enough. It is time you lived for yourself." She reached for Louisa's hand and squeezed it.

Glancing across at Bridget, Adalyn saw her maid nod in approval.

"Let me say something to him first," Louisa said. "I will have to let him know the duke is coming to call tomorrow." She paused. "Would you come over and be there when he arrives, Adalyn? Then I might not be so frightened."

"You? Frightened? Not in a thousand years, Louisa. Besides, I don't think it's a good idea that I am there."

"Why?"

Because I would want to kiss the duke myself.

"He wants to visit with you. Not me. I found him a bit boring though perfectly nice and I think he believes I am too outspoken."

"Because you are?" Louisa said, grinning.

"Perhaps."

The carriage came to a stop and the footman opened the door.

"I will talk to Papa tomorrow morning," Louisa promised. "I will send for you if reinforcements are required."

"I will be happy to speak with Uncle Edgar regarding your

future but I have no intention of staying and interrupting your time with His Grace. I will be long gone before he arrives."

She kissed her cousin's cheek and Louisa exited the carriage.

Once the door closed, Bridget said, "It's about time that girl wed. Sir Edgar has been selfish keeping her to himself."

Adalyn chuckled, thinking her maid as outspoken as herself.

And wondered what the Duke of Camden would make of them both.

CHAPTER FIVE

Everett showed up at the Middlefields' doorstep in time for breakfast the next morning. He had done so the last few days since Spence and Tessa had come to town. Marsh took him into the breakfast room and his friends greeted him enthusiastically.

"I suppose this is becoming a habit," Spence said with a twinkle in his eyes.

"Don't listen to him," Tessa told Everett. "He is delighted to see you, as always." She looked at him hopefully. "Are you here to discuss last night?"

"I did want to thank you for having me to dinner and introducing me to your cousins," he began. "I also got the impression that I need to learn more about these unwritten rules of the *ton*."

Tessa laughed. "There are a plethora of them," she admitted. "The best person to walk you through those would be Adalyn. She knows everyone and everything about Polite Society. I am certain she would be happy to fill you in." Tessa paused, her eyes widening. "Oh, dear. I had not thought to ask you this but do you dance, Everett?"

"No. What of it?"

"You simply must learn to dance," Spence advised. "You will be attending many a ball and balls mean dancing."

Tessa fretted. "It may be too late to hire a dance master. Do you mind if I teach you the basics? Just a few of the country dances that are typically danced at balls. And the waltz, of course."

"The waltz?" he asked.

"It is the most important dance," Spence told him. "It is one of the few times in which you can engage a young lady in conversation for any length without being interrupted." He smiled. "The waltz is also what I would term an intimate dance."

Everett felt himself flush. Immediately, his thoughts went to Lady Adalyn and holding her close in a dance, inhaling the vanilla that seemed to cling to her skin. He tried to erase the ridiculous image from his mind. He was not interested in her, he told himself.

"We should start today if you can spare the time, Everett," Tessa suggested. "I do know that you are calling upon Louisa this morning at eleven. She was kind to agree to see you at that hour but if you get with Adalyn, she will explain to you the hours in which it is appropriate to call upon young women."

"There is no reason to meet with Lady Adalyn," he said stiffly. "I merely wanted to know a little more about these rules of Polite Society. I am certain you or Spence can clue me in."

A shadow crossed Tessa's face. "You don't like Adalyn," she stated. "I understand she can be a bit much, especially for someone as quiet as you are. She has a good heart, though, and she can introduce you to many people in Polite Society. But what of Louisa?" Tessa asked. "Obviously, you asked to call upon her because you wish to know her better. Is that correct?"

"Your cousin is a most intelligent woman," he said. "She also has a quiet beauty about her and a maturity which I appreciate. Although I have not met any other ladies of the *ton*, I believe Miss Goulding to be a prime candidate to be my duchess."

There. He'd said it. Aloud.

Everett looked to Tessa, seeing the pleased look on her face.

"You don't have to make up your mind so quickly," she told him. "Although I adore Louisa and would be thrilled if the two of you suited one another. I do think it wise, though, that you attend a good number of *ton* events and meet other young ladies, as well."

"You think it too soon for me to offer for her?"

Tessa looked at him intently. "I will say two things to you, Everett. One, Louisa has only attended a handful of society events each Season since she came out. She is ready, however, to seek a husband this year and I want her to enjoy a full slate of *ton* events since she hasn't been able to in the past."

"If that is the first, what is the second?"

"You barely know Louisa," Tessa pointed out. "She is not going to accept an offer of marriage from you after one meeting. It would not be fair to her—or you. Marriage should never be undertaken lightly," she explained. "I think you would do both of you a disservice if you did not get to know her better before deciding to extend an offer of marriage."

Spence cleared his throat. "Tessa has yet to ask you what I believe is the most important question, Ev."

"And what would that be?"

"What is your reaction to Louisa?"

"What an odd question to ask, Spence," Everett noted, feeling uncomfortable. "I am not certain I even understand what you mean."

Spence and Tessa exchanged a look that said volumes between them. Everett supposed a couple as close as they were—especially a married couple—would have ways to communicate between them without having to use words.

Spence's gaze was direct as he said, "Are you physically attracted to Louisa Goulding?"

Everett frowned at the question. "I have told you I admire Miss Goulding's intelligence and find her quite beautiful," he said stiffly. "I wish to call upon her today in order to get to know her a little better, as Tessa has suggested. I don't see what a physical reaction has to do with offering marriage to a woman."

Again, Spence and Tessa immediately glanced at one another.

Tessa rose and said, "I will leave this conversation to you

gentlemen. It was good to see you, Everett, as always. After your visit with Louisa today, please stop by here again. We only have a little more than a week before the Season begins and I must start your dance lessons in earnest if you are to be a success."

She paused as she passed his chair and placed a gentle kiss upon his cheek, and then she left the breakfast room.

Spence flicked his wrist and the two footmen and butler followed Tessa from the room.

"I will only say this once, Ev," Spence began. "I asked about your physical reaction to Louisa because a solid marriage is based upon two things. Desire and love."

Everett moved uncomfortably in his chair. "I do not wish for you to lecture me about marriage, Spence. Especially about love. You are incredibly fortunate to have made a love match. Having met Tessa, I can see you with no other woman. But to expect the same for me, especially as withdrawn as I am, is asking too much. Yes, I know my duty is to sire an heir and I will do so. In fact, I hope I will arrange with my duchess to have several children.

"You must understand that I saw what it was like between my parents. Love never entered the picture. My mother did her duty by providing an heir and a spare and they went their separate ways. I know this is the way of the *ton* and expect to follow this pattern accordingly."

"No," Spence said flatly. "That is not good enough."

"You can't make me fall in love, Spence. Frankly, I doubt it exists. At least for me."

"I want the best for you, Ev. I also know that Tessa and I want the best for Louisa. If you do not feel attracted to her, you should not pursue her."

Everett countered with, "What if I like her? Isn't that enough? What if we do actually wed? Become friends. We could fall in love, you know."

Spence shook his head stubbornly. "No, that is unacceptable. You need a reaction within you. When you meet the right woman—the one you want to marry—your heart will know it.

Your mind will know it. Your body and soul will know it."

Everett felt the flush growing along his neck and was grateful his cravat hid it from his friend.

He had reacted strongly. Physically.

To Lady Adalyn.

She was totally wrong for him. Even she must be aware of that, as well. It would be madness to pursue any type of relationship with her, much less wed her.

He could be as stubborn as Spence if not more so and said, "I have always valued your advice, Spence, but you need to keep matters of the heart to yourself."

"I see." The set of Spence's jaw let Everett know his friend was angry with him. It was not Spence's way, though, to confront Everett with that anger. He would give Spence time to cool his heels and all would be right with them once again.

"Thank you for breakfast," Everett said. "And most of all, for your friendship. I hope no matter who my bride is that you will support my choice."

With that, Everett rose and took his leave.

➤➤➤❮❮❮

ADALYN ANXIOUSLY WAITED for word to arrive from Louisa the next morning. When it didn't come, she composed a note and sent Bridget to deliver it.

"Be sure you put it in Louisa's hand yourself," she instructed the maid. "Do not leave it with the butler or even her personal maid."

"Yes, my lady. I know what I'm doing," Bridget said confidently.

She paced about her bedchamber for three-quarters of an hour until Bridget returned.

"Well?" she demanded.

The servant handed over a letter. Quickly, Adalyn broke the seal and skimmed the contents.

"Louisa wants me to come to her now before Camden visits her," she murmured. Looking to Bridget, she asked, "Did she say anything?"

"No, my lady. She read your note and then took time to compose one of her own for me to bring to you."

"Why did it take so long?"

"Your cousin was with her father. I waited for her on the bench in the foyer. I saw her come out and called to her." Bridget paused. "Her eyes were red."

"She was crying?" Distress filled her.

"Not at the moment. But I think she had been," the maid said with certainty.

"Damn Uncle Edgar," Adalyn said furiously. "He doesn't understand what he is doing to his own daughter."

Bridget looked at her. "Then you'd best set him straight, my lady."

"I bloody well will. Come. We will go there now."

Adalyn donned her spencer and bonnet. Bridget already had on her shawl.

The pair went downstairs and she saw Rainey. "Where is my mother?" she asked, thinking it might be smart to bring reinforcements.

"At the modiste's, my lady. Your father dropped her there and then went to his club."

"Thank you. I will be at Miss Goulding's," she informed the butler, disappointed she wouldn't have Mama's support as she addressed her uncle.

"Very good, my lady."

Rainey opened the door for her and they hurried down the pavement to her uncle's townhouse. The butler admitted them and took Adalyn to the drawing room where a distraught Louisa sat chewing on her nails.

Rushing to her, Adalyn jerked Louisa's hand away. "Don't do that."

"Why?' Louisa asked bitterly. "Because I am too proper and

mature to do so?' Her hand went to her mouth again.

Gently, she tugged on her cousin's wrist, lowering it. "No. Because you don't want to have bleeding stumps when His Grace comes to call. And the Season starts in eight days. They would never have time to grow out by then. Nails bitten to the quick would not make a good impression on this Season's bachelors."

Fire lit Louisa's eyes but her cousin blinked and it was quickly distinguished. "Papa says that it is too soon for me to think about a husband. That he still needs me."

"Balderdash! I will go see him now."

"It won't do any good," Louisa said sullenly.

Adalyn took her cousin by the shoulders. "Go wash your face. Dab on a bit of scent. Get ready to visit with His Grace. And kiss him, for goodness' sake."

She stormed from the room, hurrying down the stairs and barging into her uncle's study without knocking.

Unfortunately, another gentleman was sitting across from Uncle Edgar.

"What is the meaning of this, Adalyn?" her uncle asked sternly.

"I needed to speak with you about something very important," she said, not meekly but with deference.

"It will have to wait."

"I don't mind doing so," she said politely. "I can visit with you once your meeting is over."

Before he could say anything, she exited the room. Across from the study was a chair. Adalyn took it.

And waited.

She had never been patient, neither as a child or as an adult. The sitting with nothing to do exacerbated her anger. Knowing anger would do her no good, though, she breathed deeply and formed her argument in her mind. Uncle Edgar was known for his brilliance. She would have to be logical and organized when she confronted him. In fact, she now looked upon this respite as a blessing because it gave her time to collect her thoughts and solidify her arguments.

She wagered almost an hour passed before the door opened and the visitor stepped from the room. He spied her and smiled.

"I wish you good luck, my lady."

"Is he in a good mood?"

"He should be. Bonaparte has no standing any longer. Within a week, he should have abdicated his throne."

"What will happen to him?" she asked, finding it hard to believe the day everyone in England had waited for had finally arrived.

"The forthcoming treaty structured by the Allies will decide that, my lady. You can trust that Lord Castlereagh will see things through for the British and maintain our best interests."

"That is wonderful news." She rose. "Do you think I dare venture in now?"

The man smiled. "I would hurry. Sir Edgar will probably be leaving soon for the War Office."

He took his leave and Adalyn went to the door. She knocked briskly but didn't wait for a reply. Stepping inside, she saw her uncle placing documents from his desk into a satchel.

Glancing up, he asked, "What is it, Adalyn?"

"Sit down, Uncle Edgar."

"I don't have the time," he said gruffly, slipping some papers into a satchel.

"Then make it."

He frowned but stopped what he was doing and took a seat at his desk. She stepped into the room and sat opposite him.

"I know you are in a hurry to leave for the War Office. Your visitor explained that Bonaparte will soon be history. I know you will have a lot to discuss with various officers and diplomats. But I must say something important—and you must listen, Uncle. Because you are a good man who is making a mistake."

"Mistake?" he scoffed. "This must be about this nonsense of Louisa wanting to wed."

Adalyn looked at him sternly. "It is not nonsense, Uncle. It is her life. You have your life. You had a life with your wife. Once she died, work consumed you. You drew Louisa into that work. I understand how important it was. It involved the security of our nation. Louisa has done her part, Uncle Edgar. She has supported you. Taken responsibility for many things in order to free you to go about the work of our government. But that is over now."

"The work is just beginning," her uncle complained. "I will be busier than ever with the aftermath. There will be the treaty to enforce. Lord Castlereagh has informed us that a congress will take place, most likely in Vienna. Diplomats from all across Europe will attend. I will need Louisa to go with me to it."

"No," Adalyn said flatly. "You will not. There will be women there who will look after your needs. You will be gone long hours at the negotiating table. Leaving Louisa in a hotel room by herself for hours and days on end is no life for her. She has sacrificed so much for you, Uncle Edgar. She loves you deeply. But this must stop. She is three and twenty now. Past the time when most women have wed. She deserves a life of her own. With a husband and children."

She rose. "I am not pleading with you. I am telling you. Quit being so selfish. Release her. Let her remain in London while you go and represent Britain's interests abroad. Let her find happiness. She had to grow up very quickly when her mother died suddenly. You have depended upon her for too long now. Keep loving her—but let her go."

He gazed at her a long moment and then tears formed in his eyes.

"Have I really been that awful?"

Adalyn went around the desk and leaned down, wrapping her arms about his neck. "Not awful at all. Louisa loved helping you. She told me how close your work has brought the two of you. But it is your work, Uncle. It is time for her to begin her own work. She longs for a husband and children. You owe it to her."

She kissed his cheek and stepped back. "You are one of the best men I know. You were a good husband and have been a wonderful father and uncle."

"Are you flattering me, Adalyn?"

She grinned. "I am telling you the truth. But if it takes flattery to complete the job, I will be your chief sycophant."

"You shame me, Niece. I feel terrible. I have been quite selfish, holding Louisa close to me the way I have."

"But you love her enough to realize that, Uncle Edgar. And now you can release her from any kind of promise you have had her make to you. Go do the work of a dozen men now. I know you do that every day. Just leave Louisa here. She can come stay with us if you are worried about leaving her behind."

"That would help ease my worries if I knew she was with you and your parents, Adalyn."

He rose and embraced her. "It took courage to stand up to me and speak your mind."

"I would do that for anyone I love. Especially Louisa."

"I must depart immediately but I promise I will speak to my daughter when I return this evening." He paused. "In the meantime, feel free to share the good news with her that her adoring papa wants her to enjoy the Season and find a good man to marry."

"Thank you, Uncle Edgar."

Adalyn left her uncle's study and flew up the stairs, eager to share the good news. She opened the drawing room door and rushed in, only to bump into Louisa.

Her cousin's face was bright red. "Oh! Adalyn! I . . . must leave."

Louisa hurried out.

She turned—and saw the Duke of Camden standing there.

Marching up to him, Adalyn shoved him hard in the chest.

He didn't budge.

"What the bloody hell did you do to my cousin?" she demanded.

CHAPTER SIX

E VERETT ARRIVED AT the Goulding residence, hoping he might have the chance to meet Sir Edgar. Most likely, though, the man was at the War Office and would not be at home at this time of day. He wondered who would chaperone Miss Goulding when he called upon her now. She had no mother. He knew of no relatives living with her and supposed like last night, a servant would serve as her chaperone, much like the one who had accompanied her and Lady Adalyn in the carriage last night.

He knocked on the door and was greeted by a butler, who said, "Ah, Your Grace. You are expected. Please accompany me to the drawing room."

Everett followed the servant up the stairs, telling himself repeatedly that Louisa Goulding was the ideal woman to become the Duchess of Camden, even as he thought he caught a whiff of vanilla in the air. It would help that he already was friends with Tessa because he knew the two couples could spend many happy hours in one another's company. Everett looked upon Spence and Tessa as his family and knew Miss Goulding felt the same toward them. He hoped their conversation now would not be stilted, especially since it would be just the two of them. Last night, conversation flowed freely, with no awkward pauses. He had high hopes Miss Goulding would think him appropriate as a husband.

He did understand from what Tessa said that Miss Goulding most likely needed to attend a full slate of events this Season. That meant he would show his interest in her and yet give her freedom to enjoy the social affairs she attended. It also meant seeing her talk and dance with other gentlemen.

He supposed he might be jealous of her doing so. At least the notion he should be jealous occurred to him. He shrugged off the lack of that feeling, not wanting to place too much importance on what Spence and Tessa had said about love and physical desire.

Clearing his mind, he paused at the door of the drawing room, allowing the butler to announce him. Once that occurred, the butler nodded at Everett and he entered the room.

As he crossed to where Miss Goulding sat, she rose and put a smile on her face. Immediately, he saw that she was distressed. He glanced about and noted no servant to act as a chaperone for her. He wondered if he should say something about the lack of a chaperone and her mood before deciding he would take his cue from her.

"Good morning, Your Grace," Miss Goulding greeted. "How delightful that you should call upon me this morning."

He took her hand and kissed it and then stared into her eyes. Despite what he had just decided, he asked, "Is something wrong, Miss Goulding? You seem a bit out of sorts."

She withdrew her hand and indicated where he should sit. Everett did so as she took a seat in a chair to his right.

"I received a bit of news I was not pleased with, Your Grace. Please, do not worry about it. Let us enjoy our visit instead."

"Should we be here in this room alone, Miss Goulding?" he asked. "From what I gather, this is not appropriate."

"You are correct, Your Grace. If someone were to come in and find us alone together, it would ensure a scandal. There would be two outcomes. One, you would be a gentleman and offer marriage to me. Or, you could excuse yourself and move on, never speaking to me again. The gossipmongers would rule and take the knowledge with them to every event that they attended. I would, in effect, be ruined and no gentleman would ask for my hand in marriage."

She gazed at him steadily. "However, we are inside my home, with no one from the *ton* to see us. Therefore, we can enjoy our conversation in private without worries."

Her words startled and intrigued him. "What happens when other gentlemen have called upon you, Miss Goulding? During the season, I gather that is common for bachelors to do so. Do you have a relative who comes to stay with you or even a servant who sits in the room?"

"I never have gentlemen callers, Your Grace."

Her words startled him. "Why?" he asked. "You are a most beautiful woman, well-spoken and thoughtful. I cannot imagine why you don't have a bevy of suitors beating a path to your door."

"After my mother died, Papa was despondent. I was the only one who could cheer him up. We became quite close and I began, even before my come-out, to serve as his hostess. Over the years, I have continued in that role, both as his hostess and confidante. He has many meetings here, instead of at the War Office. Bonaparte's spies are everywhere and, many times, Papa does not trust holding meetings where vital information will be given at his office. He told me he needed me and asked that I not pursue a husband when I made my come-out. Because of that, I have only attended a few events each Season and made it clear that I would accept no gentlemen callers."

Everett saw the sadness in her sapphire eyes. "I am sorry for that, Miss Goulding. With the war at its tail end, however, perhaps this would be the year for you to finally pursue a match."

She shot to her feet, wringing her hands, and he stood, as well. Desperation filled her face and she surprised him when she grasped his waistcoat in her hands.

"I must ask you something that I have never asked another," she said. Swallowing hard, she gazed intently into his eyes. "Would you kiss me, Your Grace?"

"K-kiss you?" he sputtered.

"Yes," she insisted. "Oh, I know I am mucking this up. That you took an interest in me last night and today was some sort of test that I would need to pass in order for you to decide if you wished to continue seeing me or not. Tessa insists that any man I am truly interested in must be one I kiss."

Her anguish was obvious as she continued. "I think you are very nice, Your Grace. You are friends with Spencer and I think the world of him. He has made Tessa so very happy and he is also a wonderful father to Analise. But . . ." Her voice trailed off.

"But what?" he prodded, uncomfortable that she still stood so close to him, her fists bunching his waistcoat so tightly that he couldn't draw away even if he wished to do so.

"I don't really want you to kiss me," Miss Goulding bemoaned. "You are perfect, Your Grace. A war hero. Handsome. Most intelligent. I know I should feel something—but I truly don't. I thought if we kissed then perhaps it would change things."

"I see."

Everett really didn't see anything at all. Miss Goulding was rambling and upset and the complete opposite of the woman he had met last night.

"I have never been kissed," she blurted out. "So I hope you know how to do this."

His neck burned in embarrassment. "I have done it on a few occasions, Miss Goulding. I should be able to shepherd you through it."

"Good."

He watched as resolve seem to fill her and, for a moment, he admired her pluck.

"Well?" she demanded, sounding most impatient. "How do we start?"

"Close your eyes," he said.

Her brow furrowed but she did as he asked. She even pursed her lips a bit, which almost made him chuckle. That would be the last thing she needed to hear, though. Her self-esteem was already on shaky ground.

Everett brought his hands to her face, framing it. Her skin was soft and warm. The faint scent of lilac swirled about him as he lowered his lips to hers and pressed his mouth to hers.

And felt nothing.

No spark.

No desire.

Absolutely nothing.

He lifted his lips and softly kissed her again, hoping something might stir within him. It wasn't as if he were inexperienced. Despite being shy, he was far from unworldly. In fact, the women he had made love to all seemed to agree that he excelled in the act.

Everett brushed his lips slowly against hers a few times and then broke the kiss. He gazed down at her as she opened her eyes. She released his waistcoat and took a step back.

Gazing up at him, she said, "I didn't feel much of anything, Your Grace. Did you?" She bit her lip. "Perhaps I was doing it wrong."

"No, you did everything perfectly, Miss Goulding," he assured her, remembering it was her first kiss. "I feel, however, that we are destined to be friends and not husband and wife."

Relief filled her face and then her cheeks turned bright red.

"Oh, dear," she fretted. "I actually had the audacity to ask you to kiss me. What was I thinking? This is incredibly embarrassing. Excuse me, Your Grace."

She raced across the room, only to run headfirst into her cousin, Lady Adalyn.

"Oh!" Miss Goulding cried. "I . . . must leave." She rushed through the doors.

Lady Adalyn turned and caught sight of Everett. She crossed the room with purpose and slammed her hands into his chest, pushing hard against it.

Anger simmered in her eyes when he didn't move and she

cried, "What the bloody hell did you do to my cousin?"

"I . . . didn't do anything," he stammered, wanting to protect Miss Goulding's privacy.

"That is an outright lie. Louisa's cheeks were flushed with embarrassment." Lady Adalyn paused. "Oh, my heavens. You took advantage of her, you bastard."

She slapped him hard, totally catching him off guard, and he stumbled back a step.

"I will kill you, Camden!" she shouted, raising both hands.

Everett knew she meant to claw his face or attack in some manner. He grabbed her wrists and forced them down. She tripped and fell into his chest but quickly recovered, jerking free and raising her hand to strike him again.

"No, you don't," he said, wrapping his arms about her so that her arms were bound to her side.

The trouble was that she was now flush against him. Her soft breasts pushed against his chest. She wriggled, trying to escape, moving against him so that his manhood began to stir. That wonderful, intoxicating vanilla scent enveloped him, going straight to his head.

Her beautiful face contorted with rage. "You are a bloody scoundrel. You aren't fit to speak to Louisa, much less touch her. Don't think you will wed her. I won't allow it. Do you hear me? Now, let go of me, you bloody oaf. Or I'll—"

Everett slammed his mouth down on hers.

He didn't know what else to do in order to quieten her. She wasn't the kind of woman who would listen to reason. She already thought him guilty of some terrible sin against her cousin.

Instead, he quickly realized he wanted to sin.

With her.

CHAPTER SEVEN

S HOCK FILLED ADALYN, enraging her. That the duke had the audacity to put his hands—much less his mouth—on her drew her ire. She struggled against him a moment, too close to knee him in his groin as Louisa had taught her and Tessa to do in case a man became too forward.

As she struggled, though, her senses were overwhelmed by this man. The spice of his cologne enveloped her as much as his strong arms did. The feel of his hard, muscled body against hers affected her in a way she couldn't explain.

And his lips crushed against hers stirred new feelings which puzzled her. Frightened her.

Thrilled her.

She had been kissed before, unlike Louisa, probably half a dozen times over the years since she'd made her come-out. None of these kisses had stirred anything within her.

Until this kiss now with a man she decidedly loathed.

A few of her previous kisses had been light, the man's lips barely touching hers. Twice, they had been sloppy, with both men drooling on her.

Adalyn couldn't say what this kiss was, only that there was power behind it. A force that seemed to drain her will and bend her to his.

She opened her mouth to protest. To tell off this dolt. Before she could begin to express to the Duke of Camden exactly what she thought of him, her open mouth allowed him to slip his tongue inside. She wanted to protest his actions, but found a delicious warmth wrapping about her, warming her from the inside. Suddenly, she realized she liked his kiss. His hold relaxed and Adalyn realized if she truly wanted to escape, now was the time to do so.

She didn't.

Instead, as if they had a will of their own, her hands slid up the wall of his chest and entwined about his neck.

The duke took that as a sign of encouragement and deepened the kiss. His tongue explored every crevice of her mouth, like velvet stroking her. Somehow, she found herself responding. Pulling him down closer. Wanting him and this kiss. Her tongue began to mate with his in a playful dance. He would retreat and she followed. She would pull back and he charged forth, seeking her out again.

Adalyn grew dizzy with the assault and clung to him even more, her aching breasts pushing against him. His arms had gone about her and his hands moved up and down her back, causing delicious tingles to ripple through her.

Then he broke the kiss, his lips still hovering just above hers. She could feel his breath and hear how uneven it was, much like her own.

Instead of releasing her, his mouth touched hers again. This time, his lips softly brushed against hers, causing a deep yearning to fill her. He continued a series of soft kisses which were as lethal as his others had been.

Adalyn fought to control her body. To assert herself and break the kiss. But that would mean forgoing these delicious feelings. She had never thought herself weak. Her father accused her of being the most hardheaded person he had ever known. Yet now, when she should exercise her own will forcefully, she shrank, giving this man control over her.

Camden gave her one final kiss, so gentle and promising. He

pulled away and she opened her eyes. She saw his intense gray eyes staring at her. They were dark with desire.

And she had put that desire there.

A surge of awareness filled her as she found the feminine power within her for the first time.

Adalyn realized his hands now gently clasped her waist and she tried to step back. His fingers tightened.

"I did not hurt Miss Goulding," the duke said solemnly. "I would never hurt any woman. Yes, she was a bit upset when she left me but I believe we now call one another friend. I will admit I had thought she might be a good match for me but we both understand that will not come to be."

"And what of me, Your Grace?" she asked, her heart racing.

"I . . . I don't know, my lady." He released her and took a step back. "You did not give me permission to kiss you and, for that, I do apologize."

"You better be glad no one saw this," she said, her hackles raising.

Camden gave her a rueful smile. "I understand," he said quietly. "Tessa has told me that you are the person who could share with me the many rules of the *ton*. I do know if we had been seen together in an embrace that I would have done the proper thing and wed you."

"Who says I would have wished to wed you?" she challenged. "When I marry, it will be for love," Adalyn told him, even though love had not been on her composed list. "I believe you to be arrogant and foolish, two things I cannot abide. Regardless of what Tessa said, I wish to spend as little time with you as possible."

She crossed her arms protectively and added, "I know you are dear to Spencer and Tessa and that we will be forced to see one another in social situations. However, do not expect a repeat of what just occurred between us," she said haughtily.

"I understand, my lady. I promise I will never seek you out in that manner again. I . . ." His face flushed with color, endearing him to her for a moment. "I don't believe I have ever done anything that bold before and certainly don't plan to repeat my actions."

"You better not," she scolded. "Although you are a duke. Polite Society forgives a duke almost anything."

He shook his head. "Perhaps that is why my brother was able to engage in despicable behavior. All because he was a duke."

Sympathy filled her, remembering how wild Camden's brother had been and how he was murdered. It had been the talk of the *ton* but the previous duke was this man's brother. Adalyn doubted the new Camden was anything like the old.

"I am sorry for your loss, Your Grace."

His brows rose and he said with venom, "I despised my brother and everything he stood for. I have spent my entire life trying to be the opposite of Mervyn," he declared. "Despite what just occurred between us, my lady, I view myself as an honorable man. I never asked to be a duke. I never wanted to be a duke. But I have promised myself to be the best man—and duke—that I can be. My behavior in your presence and society's from this moment on will be above reproach. I will find my wife and Polite Society will have nothing more to gossip of regarding my family. I will treat my new duchess with kindness and respect and allow her to go her own way once she has given me children."

His words surprised Adalyn. "You say children. Not an heir. And you mention separate ways."

The duke nodded solemnly. "I know love matches are rare and I do not envy Spence and Tessa for having one. My own parents loathed the sight of one another but my mother did her duty and provided two sons to her husband. They lived separate lives after she did so. I expect to do the same but I do hope my future wife will want several children. I look forward to having both sons and daughters."

For a moment, Adalyn felt pity for this man. A duke of the realm who had looks and wealth—and yet seemed so sad and alone.

"I have not meant to judge you harshly, Your Grace. I fear I was upset by the kiss but I did fully participate in it," she admitted. "I am as guilty as you of an indiscretion. I hope that won't color our future relationship."

One eyebrow shot up again. "I thought moments ago you said that you would merely tolerate me in social situations."

"I have changed my mind, Your Grace. I do see the good in you and I know how much Spencer trusts you. I also know you despise my matchmaking skills but I have been quite successful at it. If you do want help in finding your duchess, I will be more than happy to assist you in that endeavor."

"I will give it some thought, Lady Adalyn, though you know I disapprove of the notion. For now, I must take my leave. Give my regards to Miss Goulding."

It surprised her when Camden took her hand and tenderly kissed her knuckles.

He quit the drawing room and as Adalyn watched him go, she wondered what her true feelings were in regard to this man.

⇶⟫⟨⟨⟨

EVERETT LEFT THE Goulding townhouse, instructing his driver to proceed to White's. He didn't feel like going home and burying himself in the plethora of responsibilities that seemed to grow by the day. All he wanted was a little quiet time in order to think about what had just occurred.

And a brandy. Oh, how he needed a brandy! Even if he wasn't much of an imbiber.

Spence had told him about White's and Brooks's, gentlemen's clubs in which Everett held membership, and promised to take him to both. Everett decided he would investigate one of them now and asked his driver which club was closer.

"They're across the street from one another, Your Grace. Your brother, His Grace, preferred Brooks's."

"Then take me to White's," he ordered, climbing into his carriage and deliberately keeping his mind a blank as he watched the passing scenery.

Once they arrived, he entered the establishment and was greeted quickly.

"I am Camden," he said succinctly.

"Ah, Your Grace, I am delighted to welcome you to White's. I am Mr. Orr. Might I take you on a brief tour of the club to familiarize you with what we offer?"

Everett nodded brusquely and was shown the morning rooms, along with additional rooms for billiards, coffee, and cards. His escort returned him downstairs.

"Might I bring you anything, Your Grace? Newspapers? A drink?"

He noticed a large book on a table. "What is that?"

"Oh, it is the famous—or might I say infamous—White's betting book. Wagers of all sorts are placed within it, from anticipated births to the outcome of battles. You will also find numerous bets over trivial matters, as well. The men of Polite Society do find amusement in their bets."

It appalled him to think gentlemen in London had placed bets on the result of a battle as he and his fellow soldiers had fought for their very lives, as well as their country.

"I would like to look at this for a few minutes if I may."

"Certainly, Your Grace. I shall bring it to a table for you. Where would you like to be situated?"

"In the morning room to the left of the door."

That room only had a few men within it, all buried with noses in newspapers, no conversation evident.

"Very good, Your Grace."

Mr. Orr led him to the room and an area where there was seating for four members. He placed the betting book on the table.

"I'd like a brandy, as well," Everett informed him.

"At once, Your Grace."

The man left and Everett settled into a chair upholstered in rich, brown leather. He leaned forward and opened the book, which was much too large to hold comfortably in his lap. He began skimming, turning the pages, disgusted by the inappropriate nature of most of the bets. If this was indicative of the gentlemen who held membership at White's, he wanted nothing to do with the place.

Turning another page, he spied Lady Adalyn's name at the top and froze. Skimming it, anger simmered within him. The page had been created several years ago, with numerous wagers placed regarding when she would wed. He thought it outrageous for men to have placed bets regarding her unwed status and tamped down the bile that rose in his throat.

Everett closed the book and leaned back in his chair as a servant arrived with a brandy.

"Your Grace," the man said deferentially.

He took the snifter and thanked the servant. Bringing it to his lips, he took a sip. The brandy caused his lips to tingle and then burned as it went down his throat and settled in his belly. Closing his eyes, Adalyn's image shone clear in his mind.

What was he going to do about her?

Kissing her had been a terrible mistake. Worse than leading men into battle with no prior intelligence reports and seeing them sacrificed left and right. In this instance, Everett felt he had been sacrificed on an altar of his own making, gutted by Lady Adalyn. He could still taste her. Still sense the subtle scent of vanilla on his clothes from her. Feel those soft breasts pushing against his chest. He wanted to kiss her again. Do more than kiss her pretty pout. He wanted to kiss her breasts. Suck on them. Run his tongue along their curves.

He blinked several times, trying to dispel the erotic image of her, bare to the waist, his hands kneading her breasts, his mouth on them.

Taking another sip of brandy, he wondered how he could stop thinking about her when all he wished to do was rush back to her side and kiss her all over again.

She had been inexperienced in kissing. He figured she had most likely been kissed a few times but not to the extent he had imposed. His hand trembled as he thought of her response. How she had matched him. How everything had seemed so right.

She was reckless, though. Far too outgoing and bold for his tastes. He didn't know if the kiss had even affected her as much as it had him. She hadn't fawned over him afterward or showed any partiality to him. In fact, she had once more offered her match-making services to him to help him find a bride, which he construed meant she would not offer herself. Not that he wanted to marry her.

If only he could bed her. Once. Get her out of his head.

Laughter caused him to look up and he saw three men coming his way, drinks already in hand. Two looked to be in their late twenties, while the third seemed slightly older.

"Ah, it looks as though we have a new member, my friends," the oldest said, taking a seat without asking.

His companions did the same, irritating Everett. He took another sip of the brandy to fortify himself so that he might ask them to leave.

"I'm Lord Rosewell," the leader told him. "These two new viscounts are Bayless and Pierce."

"We have both recently come into our titles," Lord Bayless explained. "And who might we have the pleasure of addressing, my lord? You are new to town, I believe."

"It is Your Grace," he said stiffly. "I am the Duke of Camden."

The two viscounts looked suitably impressed. The earl chortled.

"I was friends with your brother," the earl said. "Camden was hilarious. Always in good spirits and eager for pleasure. Might you be the same, Your Grace?"

"I have come from the battlefields where men are dying every day."

Both viscounts swallowed uncomfortably and drained their

glasses. The earl merely gave him a sly smile and signaled for a servant.

"Bring a bottle," he ordered.

Lord Pierce glanced down. "Is that the betting book?"

"It is," Everett replied.

Lord Bayless reached for it, sliding it across the table and opening it. "I haven't wagered in a good two years. Need to see what's been going on."

Bayless and Pierce began thumbing through the book, pointing out items that interested them.

Everett felt Rosewell's stare and met it. "Are you a betting man, my lord?" he asked.

"I have been known to do so upon occasion. Not in the book. At the tables upstairs. Perhaps you care for a card game, Your Grace."

"No."

He finished off his brandy and set the snifter on the table, ready to leave. Then he heard Lady Adalyn's name coming from one of the viscounts.

"Lady Adalyn is going to find me a bride," Lord Bayless said. "I have an appointment with her tomorrow afternoon at two o'clock to discuss it."

"Why, I made one with her for the following afternoon," Lord Pierce said. "We should go together, Bayless. Let her talk with both of us at the same time. We don't want to compete for the same girls, you know."

"I wish Lady Adalyn was interested in a husband," Lord Bayless said. "For I certainly would be interested in dipping my wick in her."

The other three chuckled. Everett sat silently.

"We should place a bet on her, Bayless," Lord Pierce said. "She's bound to eventually look for a husband. We could make some real money at it."

"She's getting a bit long in the tooth for marriage," the earl said, flicking a piece of lint from his arm.

"I find Lady Adalyn to be quite beautiful," Everett said.

The earl sat up. "Oh. So you know her?"

"I do," he confirmed. "One of my closest friends, Lord Middlefield, is wed to Lady Adalyn's cousin."

Lord Rosewell nodded. "Yes, Lady Tessa. She made quite an impression on the Marriage Mart last Season. It was too bad that Middlefield swept her off her feet before anyone else had a go at her."

"Lord and Lady Middlefield are quite happy," Everett said firmly, daring anyone to challenge his statement.

Lord Rosewell steepled his fingers. "Perhaps this is the year that Lady Adalyn will receive my attentions."

Bayless barked out a laugh. "Rosewell, she isn't some lightskirt. That's the only kind of woman who interests you. Besides, I like her. I hope she does wed this year and produces the expected heir." He grinned. "Then she would be free to cavort with me."

Everett frowned. "But weren't you just mentioning how you wished for Lady Adalyn to find you a bride?"

"I'm the viscount now. Yes, I will do my duty and sire an heir. Once that is done, though?" His eyes gleamed with mischief. "I will return to the life I have always led."

"You merely want to move from strumpets to widows and see how randy you truly are," Lord Pierce joked. "How many did you—"

"I have an appointment," Everett interrupted, rising.

Lord Bayless said, "It was an honor to meet you, Your Grace."

"Likewise," Lord Pierce added.

Lord Rosewell said nothing.

"Will you be at the ball which opens the Season?" Lord Pierce asked him.

"I will see you there, Pierce," Everett said.

He left White's, nodding at Mr. Orr on his way out, and ordering his driver to return to Lord Middlefield's townhouse. He had forgotten Tessa had asked him to return in order to help him learn how to dance. She would be worried about him now. Hell, he was worried about him now. The kiss with Lady Adalyn had turned his world upside down and Everett didn't know if it would ever be righted again.

As he settled against the plush cushions in his carriage, he decided he would see Lord Pierce and Lord Bayless sooner than the opening ball.

Everett planned to stop by and visit Lady Adalyn tomorrow afternoon.

And ask for her to help him find his duchess.

CHAPTER EIGHT

EVERETT KNOCKED ON the Middlefield townhouse's front door. It swung open and Marsh greeted him.

"It is nice to see you again so soon, Your Grace," the butler said. "Lady Middlefield told me she is expecting you."

"There you are, Everett," Tessa said as she glided down the stairs. "I was becoming worried about you. I thought your visit with Louisa was at eleven o'clock. I thought that would put you back here by noon."

"I did see Miss Goulding at eleven as planned," he told her. "I had one other thing to do before I returned here. I hope I have not inconvenienced you, Tessa."

"You could never inconvenience me, Everett. Come, I will take you to our ballroom."

"The ballroom?" he asked.

"Yes, it will give us ample room to begin your dance lessons. Come along," she said, slipping her arm into his and leading him upstairs.

As they stepped into the enormous ballroom, a wave of nerves filled him. His heart sped up and his mouth grew dry. If he felt this nervous now in an empty ballroom, what would it be like when it was filled with the members of Polite Society?

Tessa led him to the center of the room and explained reels to him, both their structure and how the accent fell on the first and third beats of the music.

"Reels are very lively," she noted. "The music is played quickly, with dancers weaving in and out. A six-hand reel involves three couples. A four-hand Scottish reel includes two couples."

She showed him the footwork and they worked on it for several minutes, with Tessa calling out what foot to move and when to do so.

The English country dances made more sense to him. She said the most popular form was a longways set, where couples formed long lines and repeatedly executed a predetermined sequence of figures. Usually, this was done in couples but sometimes with a group of people. Everett came to understand how the figures involved interacting not only with your chosen partner but that you would progress so that eventually you danced with everyone in your set.

Her patience was endless and he began to anticipate what sequence came next and what figures would occur. Though he seemed a bit stiff at times, he now had the rudiments down.

"You really are getting the idea, Everett," Tessa praised.

"Even if I do lumber about with no rhythm?" he asked, grinning cheekily.

"Practice will help you become more comfortable with dancing," she said. "It is the same with my piano playing. When I begin to learn a new piece, it seems as though I have ten thumbs instead of two. After I spend time with the music, however, going over and over sections that prove difficult to play, it all comes together seamlessly. The same will be true of you with dancing."

Tessa glanced over his shoulder and Everett turned, seeing a servant standing against the wall, wondering how long she had been present.

"Abra," Tessa called, "please go fetch my husband."

The servant left and Everett asked, "Do you think I need to show off my new skills to Spence already? I fear I may forget everything you have taught me with an audience watching."

She chuckled. "No, I want Spencer and my lady's maid, Abra,

to join us. I have walked you through several things but it would be good to have another couple here to interact with. That will test your ability and memory."

Everett felt it unusual that Tessa would include her lady's maid in his dance lessons but then decided it could only benefit him. Anything that would help him from embarrassing himself in front of the *ton* would be welcomed.

Soon, Spence arrived and Tessa took charge as any good officer would, putting them through their paces and having them repeat steps multiple times. She was right, though. The more he went through the steps, the more at ease he felt. The few times he did make a mistake, he quickly realized what had gone wrong and was able to correct himself.

"You're doing well, Your Grace," Abra said. "You have caught on faster than his lordship did."

Everett hadn't thought to ask how Spence learned to dance.

Abra complimented him on one move but then told him he was doing something wrong and corrected him, showing Everett exactly what to do. His face must have betrayed he was a little taken aback by her forthrightness and ease in a duke's presence, for she grinned at him and said, "I'm not your typical lady's maid, Your Grace."

Abra led him back to Spence and Tessa and they commenced again. Everett actually found himself enjoying the lesson and was saddened when Marsh appeared and told them it was time for tea.

Spence looked to him. "I suppose you'll want to stay for tea, Ev. It seems you are eating me out of house and home," he teased. "Why, I believe you spend most of your waking hours here. Perhaps Tessa can have Mrs. Marsh assign a guest bed-chamber to you and then you won't ever have to go home."

Everett felt his face flush and Tessa quickly said, "Don't listen to him. We always enjoy your company."

They began moving to exit the ballroom and he said, "I must apologize for monopolizing your time. I know enough to get by at a ball now, Tessa. You do not have to continue my lessons."

"On the contrary, we are only getting started," she informed him. "You caught on quickly today and there are several more dances to learn."

"The waltz," Spence said. "Remember, I told you it is the one dance you must master." He grinned at his wife shamelessly. "I dance every waltz with Tessa."

An ache filled Everett, knowing he would never have what his friends did. Still, there had to be some young lady in Polite Society who would make for a good partner.

They entered the drawing room and the teacart was already present. Tessa poured out and he filled his plate, hungry after all the dancing he had done.

He knew he should address the topic of Miss Goulding and so he said, "I wanted to let you know how my visit with your cousin went this morning." He paused and then said, "While I find her to be a lovely woman, we have come to the conclusion that we would not suit enough to wed."

Disappointment flashed across Tessa's face but she quickly hid it. "That is a good thing, Everett. Hopefully, you and Louisa can remain friendly since I am certain you will see each other frequently in our home."

"I anticipate no problems, Tessa. I have, though, decided to take up Lady Adalyn's offer."

"Oh, are you going to spend time with her and learn about the customs of the *ton*?" Spencer asked.

"No. She has offered her matchmaking services to me," he revealed. "Tessa herself has told me that her cousin knows everyone in Polite Society. Lady Adalyn also told me that she keeps a close watch on the new girls making their come-outs. She believes she can find the perfect duchess for me. I am going to place myself into her hands. We start tomorrow."

Everett wished he could share with the pair that what they had spoken of—physical attraction—was present anytime he was in Lady Adalyn Goulding's presence. He still felt her entirely wrong for him, though, and he would make certain he never acted rashly and inappropriately with her in the future.

Hoping to draw their attention from the topic, he said, "I visited White's. I didn't like it one whit."

Spence burst out in laughter. "I doubt it was White's you don't like. The rooms are elegant. Well-furnished and comfortable. The help is superior and whatever you need appears almost before you can ask for it. I daresay it was the company that you found lacking. Am I correct?"

Everett nodded. "That's true. I met an earl and two of his sycophants. Two viscounts still wet behind the ears, having just come into their titles."

"Well," Spence said, "I fear you'll find many of the gentlemen of the *ton* not up to our standards, Ev. Who were these men that left such a poor impression upon you?"

"The viscounts were Lord Pierce and Lord Bayless. The leader of their trio was Lord Rosewell."

Tessa's nose crinkled in disgust. "Lord Rosewell's reputation is a nasty one. As for the other two, I think I danced with Bayless once last Season. That would have been before his father passed. If it is who I remember, he is quite good-looking and knew it. He was also most immature."

"Yes," Everett said. "That describes him perfectly."

Spence said, "I have met a few good men and plan on introducing you to them, Ev. Why don't we go to White's together tomorrow afternoon? Of course, no one will be a Second Son, but I have made a few friends in London."

"I can't tomorrow afternoon," he reminded. "I am meeting with Lady Adalyn."

"Why don't we go tomorrow morning then?" his friend asked. "Say, eleven o'clock?"

"I would like that."

Everett finished his tea and wondered how his unscheduled meeting with Lady Adalyn would go.

>>>>><<<<<

ADALYN ENTERED THE drawing room and saw her mother already present.

"Hello, dearest," Lady Uxbridge said. "Rainey told me you were expecting Lord Bayless. I can chaperone you for an hour but if he stays longer, you will need to send for Bridget."

"Do you have plans, Mama?"

"I am having tea with Lady Tealing." Her mother's eyebrows rose hopefully. "She does have two sons of marriageable age, you know."

Adalyn did know. Both men were not to her taste but she refrained from telling Mama that. Her mother, even at her mature age, was the most naive person that Adalyn knew. She would be horrified if her daughter told her about the reputations of these two eligible men in question. Adalyn didn't think them gentlemen at all and would never consent to a match with either.

She did owe it to her mother, however, to let her know of her intentions this Season.

"Mama, I do have news to share with you," she began. "I have decided that I have enjoyed my time as an unattached female but I am finally ready to settle down."

"Oh, Adalyn!"

Her mother threw her arms about Adalyn, holding her tightly. When she released her, she saw the tears in her mother's eyes and, for a moment, felt guilty knowing she had put them there.

"What changed your mind?" Mama asked. Then she looked sagely at Adalyn and said, "It was Analise, wasn't it?"

She nodded. "Yes, Analise has quite a bit to do with my decision. Every time I hold her, I yearn for a child of my own. I also see how happy Tessa is in her marriage. I only hope I can find someone who will make me half as happy as she is with Spencer."

A worried look crossed Mama's face. She took Adalyn's hand and said, "You have been out many Seasons now. Tessa was fortunate to only have one Season—and to find love." Mama looked at her in earnest and said, "Do you seek love, Adalyn?"

She didn't know how to answer the question and merely shrugged. "I cannot answer that, Mama. Not at this time. Since I am open to the idea of marriage, I am also open to the idea of love. Do I want to find it? It would be nice if I did. I cannot expect it, though. I do have a good idea of the traits I am looking for in my future husband. Louisa and I both made lists of what most appealed to us. We have thought of this carefully, Mama. I won't rush into anything."

Her mother's face glowed with happiness. "So, Louisa, too, will seek a husband. It is past time she did so. You know I think the world of your uncle but it is wrong of him to have tied Louisa to him for so long."

Adalyn did not mention that Uncle Edgar had not planned on allowing Louisa to pursue marriage. At least until she had intervened yesterday with him. Adalyn had found Louisa and told her cousin of the conversation the two had held. Louisa had burst into tears, grateful for Adalyn being her advocate in this matter.

She had also learned from Louisa why she was so distraught after her meeting with the Duke of Camden. It shocked Adalyn to hear that Louisa had boldly asked the duke to kiss her, based upon Tessa's advice.

Louisa had shared how nothing about the duke's kiss moved her and that she knew he was not the one for her. She explained to Adalyn that she was grateful knowing this, not having wasted any time on getting to know Camden better in order to evaluate whether he would be a good husband to her or not. Louisa said that while embarrassed about what she had done, she believed she and the duke would always be on friendly terms.

While Louisa had been open and honest, Adalyn had told her cousin nothing of her encounter with His Grace. She could barely admit to herself what had happened, much less tell Louisa what had occurred between her and the duke.

Sleep had taken a long time to come last night, thanks to

thoughts of the duke dancing in her head. She even found her body burning at the thought of the intimate kisses they had exchanged. The fact that she wanted more from him was beside the point. He was not for her. Though she did hope he would take her up on her willingness to guide him through Polite Society and find the right bride for him. it would be a kindness to him, something that Tessa and Spencer would appreciate her doing.

Yet the thought of helping the Duke of Camden find his duchess irritated her to no end. She feared she would be jealous of the woman he chose. Not that she wanted to be the duchess herself. Far from it.

Even Adalyn knew she lied to herself. She was besotted with the duke. She would have to do what she could to cleanse her mind of him.

And her body.

She could not keep wanting those kisses. Even though her thoughts had gone far beyond them. She could imagine him kissing her in places besides her mouth. Just the idea of that caused her cheeks to heat.

She turned from her mother and went to a chair, lifting her sewing basket from where it sat on the ground beside the chair. She really didn't want to embroider but she needed something to keep her mind off the duke.

Fortunately, the butler appeared at the door and said, "Lord Pierce and Lord Bayless are here to call."

Now, this was an interesting development. She had agreed to see Lord Bayless today and Lord Pierce tomorrow. Knowing, however, the pair was as thick as thieves, she supposed they had both shared with one another their plans to ask her to find them a bride and decided to do this together, as they did everything else.

Adalyn set the sewing basket back on the ground as she and Mama rose and greeted the two viscounts.

"It is lovely to see you again, Lady Uxbridge," Lord Bayless said smoothly, causing her mother to smile girlishly.

If only Mama knew that the viscount had an affair last Season with a woman more than twice his age.

Before Lord Pierce could also offer a greeting, she noticed Rainey coming through the door again.

"His Grace, the Duke of Camden."

The duke sauntered in and Adalyn's entire body caught fire.

CHAPTER NINE

A DALYN'S MOTHER TURNED to her. Quietly, she asked, "Why did you not tell me His Grace was coming today for a visit?"

Smiling even as she grit her teeth, Adalyn replied, "Because he had made no arrangements to call."

She then turned and gave the duke, now striding toward her, a tight smile. "Your Grace. What an unexpected pleasure."

She hoped he noticed she emphasized the word *unexpected*.

"It is so nice again to see you, Lady Adalyn," Camden said as if he hadn't a care in the world. He looked to her mother. "And you must be Lady Uxbridge," he added, capturing her mother's hand and kissing it. "I must say, Lady Uxbridge, that I would have taken you for Lady Adalyn's sister and not her mother."

Mama was all smiles now and coquettishly batted her eyelashes at the duke. "Your Grace, it is so very good of you to call upon us." Her eyes flicked to the other two visitors and back to him. "Won't you please have a seat?"

"Thank you, my lady. I believe I will."

The duke took a seat and Adalyn indicated for her other visitors to follow suit, wondering why the duke had ignored them.

Looking to Camden, she said, "Let me introduce you to our other visitors, Your Grace."

"Oh, no need to do so. I met Pierce and Bayless at White's

yesterday."

Adalyn looked at the pair and both nodded, perplexed.

Bayless said, "Yes, His Grace mentioned he was acquainted with you, my lady. That your cousin, Lady Middlefield, is wed to his good friend."

Pierce looked put out as he said, "We did not realize His Grace would be calling at the same time we were today. He did not mention it."

"Well, Lord Pierce, you were not scheduled to call upon me this afternoon," Adalyn noted. "I was only expecting Lord Bayless."

Lord Pierce shrugged. "We both decided since our visits with you involved the same purpose that it would be appropriate to discuss these delicate matters with us together." The viscount looked to the duke and back at Adalyn. "However, we would not want to take up His Grace's time."

The duke gave them a charming smile and said, "I am happy to sit and visit with Lady Uxbridge, gentlemen. That should give you time in which to discuss your business with her daughter."

Mama said, "Oh, that is too kind of you, Your Grace."

Immediately, she launched into a conversation with the duke, which gave Adalyn time to speak with the two viscounts.

The entire time she spent in conversation with Lords Pierce and Bayless, Adalyn sensed the duke listened to everything they said, even as he charmed her mother. When an hour had passed and she deemed she had sufficient information from the two young rogues, she told them she would think about all they had discussed and meet with them just after the Season began in order to share her thoughts.

"Of course, once the Season is in full swing, you will have met many of the girls I will recommend to you," she said. "It will also give me time to look over the new crop of young ladies on the Marriage Mart and get to know a bit about them myself. That will enable me to help you make the most amiable match."

Lord Bayless was the first to realize they were being dismissed and he rose. "Thank you, my lady, for your time today," he said graciously.

Lord Pierce echoed his friend's sentiments and the two bid her mother and the duke farewell, taking their leave.

Adalyn now turned her full attention to the duke, having no idea why he had come to visit today.

She asked her mother, "Isn't it time you were to going to Lady Tealing's for tea?"

Mama's cheeks pinkened and she explained, "There is no way I would leave His Grace here. He simply must stay for tea with us. I want Uxbridge to have the opportunity to chat with him. You wouldn't mind staying for tea, Your Grace?"

Camden smiled winningly, which tugged at Adalyn's heart. She didn't like the feeling. The duke was much too good-looking for his own good. She was not going to fall under his spell.

Unless she already had.

She watched her mother ring for Rainey and tell the butler to send a footman to Lady Tealing's residence, sending her regrets regarding their arranged date for tea.

"Merely say that I am unwell," Mama told the butler. "I do not want Lady Tealing's feelings to be hurt."

"Surely, Lady Uxbridge, you should see to your previous appointment," the duke urged. "I would not want to prevent you from visiting with your friend."

"I see Lady Tealing enough as it is," Mama declared. "I would not want to miss out on this time with you, Your Grace."

The duke smiled in delight at her mother, infuriating Adalyn.

Mama added, "Please let Lord Uxbridge and Cook know that we have a guest for tea today."

"Of course, my lady," the butler said and left the room.

Her mother brightened. "Now that those two have gone, we may all sit and visit. Won't that be pleasant, Your Grace?"

"I am always delighted to be in the company of two beautiful women," the duke said.

Adalyn wondered where this was coming from. When she

had met Camden, she had been told he was shy. He had been rather reserved and eventually seemed to come out of his shell as the evening progressed at Tessa's house. But this seemed to be a different man than the one she had previously met. He wasn't shy at all. He seemed determined to charm her mother.

He would not charm her.

"So, Your Grace, why did you come to call upon us today?" Adalyn asked sweetly.

"I did not want to say anything in front of Bayless or Pierce but I believe I will avail myself of your services, Lady Adalyn."

Mama looked confused. "Whatever do you mean, Your Grace?"

The duke focused his attention on her mother and said, "I am new to all of this, Lady Uxbridge. New to my title. New to Polite Society. Knowing only a handful of people, I am putting my trust in your daughter to help me find a bride this Season."

Her mother's cheeks blossomed with color. "Oh! But . . . you are a duke, Your Grace. You will have your choice of any available woman on the Marriage Mart. Why would you need Adalyn to help you in finding a bride?"

Then Mama's eyes cut to her daughter and Adalyn shook her head, knowing instantly what Mama was thinking.

"Your niece assures me that Lady Adalyn knows everyone in Polite Society," Camden continued. "I am merely a military man trying to find my way in the midst of a life I never expected to be living," he said apologetically. "From what I have been told, I understand dukes are powerful, influential members of the *ton*. That means my choice in a wife must be impeccable. I need a tremendous amount of help navigating not only the waters of Polite Society but how to choose the woman who will become my duchess. I trust Spence and Tessa implicitly—and they have complete faith in Lady Adalyn's ability to find my match. I am putting myself—and my future—in her hands."

Adalyn had thought she wanted to help this lonely man find a bride. Unexpectedly, misery filled her.

She wanted to be that woman.

But it seemed the duke and she had a contentious relationship. The fact that he was placing himself in her hands in order to help him find a wife was surprising as it was.

"So, how are we to go about this?" His Grace asked.

Rainey entered the drawing room and apologized for the interruption. "I am sorry, my lady, but Mrs. Rainey needs your assistance in a delicate matter."

Lady Uxbridge rose, as did the duke, who told her, "Please see to the crisis, my lady. Perhaps by the time you have solved it, your husband will have joined us and we can become better acquainted over tea."

Flustered, Mama said, "Thank you for understanding, Your Grace. Household matters can be so inconvenient."

Mama left with the butler and the duke seated himself again.

This time, next to Adalyn.

She understood what Louisa had meant when her cousin said she was overwhelmed by the sheer size of Camden. He took up a good part of the settee. He was close enough for her to catch the spice of his cologne, as well as feel the warmth of his thigh pressed against hers.

"Why are you really here?" she demanded, not bothering to hide her exasperation when she knew he disapproved of her matchmaking between couples of the *ton*.

His face guileless, he replied, "For the exact reason I told your lovely mother. I am totally lacking in experience as far as Polite Society goes and realize marriage is likely the most important decision I will undertake. I must choose wisely from the eligible women among the *ton*."

"I don't believe you," she said flatly. "You have seemed so opposed to what I'm certain you would deem my interference. Why now?"

Camden grew thoughtful. "I told you of my desire to have several children. From what I gather, that is not necessarily something wives of the *ton* enjoy doing. Providing an heir and possibly a spare seems to be the extent of their duty. I need help in finding a woman who not only will give me children but enjoy doing so."

"So, you want her to be happy in this endeavor? If she is to be happy and your children, as well, it would be wise to proceed as a family and live together. You had told me that you would want to go your separate way from your wife."

"Not necessarily," he said. "I had thought that merely because of the hostile relationship between my parents. While I do not expect to find love as Spence and Tessa have, I believe now that if I am guided to the right woman, I may be able to find a suitable partner who would remain faithful to our vows and wish to live with me and our family."

"You had thought before that your wife would leave you with the children?" she asked, astonished at the idea.

"Yes," he insisted. "My children will always be my priority. I just assumed my wife would do as she pleased once she had them."

"Not many marriages in the *ton* are loving ones," Adalyn admitted. "But there are more than a few where the husbands and wives come to grow fond of one another. They have a mutual respect—even admiration—for one another and live quite happily as a family couple."

The duke nodded thoughtfully. "Then that is what we will seek," he told her, determination filling his handsome face. "I do not think I am interested in the new group of young ladies who will parade themselves on the Marriage Mart. Not that I would rule any of them out but a girl fresh from the schoolroom does not appeal to me. I understand that there will be ladies who did not wed after their come-out Season." He paused and added, "You, my lady, are a perfect example of that."

"I am an exception," she stated stiffly. "I did not wed because I chose not to wed. I have had my share of offers but let it be known I wasn't ready to entertain additional ones."

"But you are now," he pointed out. "Perhaps we might be

able to help one another, Lady Adalyn. You wish to wed this Season. So do I. I don't think it would hurt if eligible bachelors of the *ton* saw a duke escort you to a few events. If I show a bit of interest in you, others may want to throw themselves back into the fray and court you, as well.

"At the same time that you are leading me through society, you can help me in finding the woman who will become the next Duchess of Camden," he concluded.

He was right in thinking she would gain her fair share of attention if in his company. After all, he was a duke and new to society. If the Duke of Camden showed an interest in her, it would be a way to let the eligible bachelors in Polite Society know she was circulating with a purpose, with the intention this time of wedding by Season's end.

"I find it interesting you don't want to wed a girl fresh on the Marriage Mart," she said.

"I want to raise my children. Not to also have to raise a wife at the same time. Just as a duke, a duchess has much influence and responsibility. A more mature woman would suit me better. I am not opposed to even wedding a widow," he mentioned. "I heard that many gentlemen of the *ton* marry later in life, leaving young widows behind."

A thought occurred to her. "You are telling me already you want a mature woman and even possibly a widow. Why don't we compose a list of the attributes you seek in a wife? It would give me a better idea as to which woman would be your ideal match."

"An excellent idea," he said. "When should we start this list?"

"I would say now but Mama and Papa will be here any moment. Perhaps we could take this up again tomorrow if you are free," she suggested.

A pleased look crossed his face. "Shall I call again at two o'clock tomorrow afternoon? Unless you are otherwise engaged."

"I will be available at two o'clock, Your Grace."

"If we are to spend time with each other in this endeavor, we should not be so formal. It is hard for me to think of myself as

Your Grace, much less hear you calling me that constantly."

"Then I will call you Camden," she told him.

He shook his head. "No, I am not happy with that either. I do feel as if we are family. After all, your cousin is wed to a man I consider my brother." He paused. "Would you consider addressing me as Everett?"

Horror filled her. "I cannot! It would be most inappropriate. Why, even couples who have wed rarely use their Christian names with one another. I have never even heard Mama or Papa address one other by their given names."

"Seriously?" He smiled at her, causing her belly to explode with fluttering butterflies. "Then if you must, call me Camden in public. When we are with Spence and Tessa—or when we are working on finding my future duchess—I insist that you call me Everett.

"And I shall call you Addie."

"What? Why on earth would you do such a thing?" It appalled her that he would even suggest it. "My name is Adalyn. I despise any attempt at shortening it to some silly nickname."

The slow smile spreading across his face told her she had made a mistake in revealing that.

"Addie, it is," he proclaimed. "I will take pleasure knowing I am the only one who calls you that."

"You will *not* call me that, Your Grace," she ground out, anger boiling within her.

"Everett. Or Ev if you prefer. It's what the Second Sons call me."

"You don't want to know what I really wish to call you at this moment. I prefer you to leave now, Your Grace," she told him, her temper soaring.

Unfortunately, her parents strolled through the door at that very moment, smiles on their faces, obviously pleased to be entertaining a duke. The way Mama looked from her to Camden let Adalyn know that her mother had high hopes the duke would one day become her son-in-law.

That would be the last thing Adalyn ever wanted.

Camden moved toward her parents, introducing himself to her father and escorting her mother to a seat as the teacart was rolled into the drawing room by two maids.

As Mama poured out for them, she watched the duke raise his cup to his lips, mischief in his once solemn gray eyes.

Adalyn felt as if she were Pandora and somehow had unleashed everything within the Duke of Camden out into the world.

Her world.

And she would have to live with the consequences.

CHAPTER TEN

A DALYN FRETTED ABOUT what to wear, rejecting several of Bridget's choices.

"What is wrong today, my lady?" her maid asked, clearly perplexed since her mistress was usually so easy to please in regard to her wardrobe.

"I am not myself today, Bridget. I do not know what has come over me."

The servant looked at her a long moment and then cheekily asked, "Perhaps a certain duke?"

"Bridget!"

"I don't mean to overstep my bounds, my lady. Well, maybe I do. But we all know a duke came to call upon you yesterday. A duke! We haven't seen the likes of that in the household. At least not as long as I've been here."

She dreaded informing her lady's maid what was in store for today but said, "His Grace will return this afternoon. We have a few matters to discuss."

Bridget whooped. "No wonder you're in a tizzy, my lady. My, but the duke is a handsome one. I don't recall ever seeing such a fetching soul."

"You saw him?"

The maid nodded. "I think just about everyone did. Rainey got to. The two maids who rolled in the teacart. They were aflutter with how he looked. Then when he left, most of the staff—at least the female members—managed to be near a window." She sighed. "That one is all male."

Adalyn silently agreed, thinking of how Everett had kissed her. No, Camden. She must keep her distance from him, both physically and mentally. If she didn't, she would be lost.

Bridget turned back to the wardrobe, pulling out a pale azure day gown. "I think you should wear this, my lady. It'll bring out the beautiful blue in your eyes."

"Whatever you say."

She wasn't going to debate it any further. Let Bridget dress her in any gown. It didn't matter which. The Duke of Camden wasn't coming to look at her. Or even talk with her. He would only be talking about other women. The kind of women he wished to come to know. Adalyn knew they would be nothing like her. She supposed he would want someone as quiet as he was. Dignified. An ethereal beauty who moved with grace and always said the right thing in a situation. That certainly wasn't her. She was known for being outspoken. It had been more than tolerated by the *ton* because she hadn't pursued any gentlemen in marriage so she hadn't been perceived as a threat to any females.

Would that change now that she sought a husband? Would her sometimes outlandish behavior come to haunt her?

Once she was dressed, Bridget began fussing over Adalyn's hair, trying a few different styles.

"Keep it simple," she finally said. "Nothing too fussy."

"Yes, my lady."

She ventured downstairs once she was ready for the day. It was close to noon. She had a tendency to sleep later once she came to town. Yesterday had been an exception since she had awaited word from Louisa and had wanted to be available to go and speak with Uncle Edgar if necessary.

Going to her mother's parlor, she found Mama sitting with Mrs. Rainey. The housekeeper rose, pages in her hand, and Adalyn supposed they had been discussing menus.

Once Mrs. Rainey had left, Adalyn said, "I should tell you that His Grace is coming again today."

Mama's eyes lit up. "Oh, my word. Adalyn, that is marvelous news. Your papa liked His Grace very much and you know Uxbridge isn't the easiest of men to please. They even arranged to meet up at White's sometime so they could play chess against one another."

She went and sat next to her mother. "Mama, we need to talk about His Grace."

"Do you like him?" Mama asked eagerly. "Or do you already love him? To think of my daughter as a duchess."

"That is not going to happen."

Her mother frowned. "Then why is he paying you special attention?"

"He wants me to find him a bride. You heard him say that yesterday, Mama. He is not interested in me."

"But he is, Adalyn. Mothers can sense this kind of thing. Yes, I know His Grace is definitely interested in you. He is only using this matchmaking nonsense as an excuse to spend time with you." She sighed. "You have only met. He would not make his intentions known to you so quickly."

"He thought he wanted Louisa as his duchess."

Mama looked blankly at her a moment. "Louisa? Your cousin?"

"Yes. Remember, Tessa invited the two of us to dinner with the duke so that he could begin to meet a few people in Polite Society. He seemed quite taken with Louisa and indicated he would offer for her."

"But he didn't?" Mama asked, hope in her eyes.

"Louisa is a bit intimidated by his size," Adalyn shared. "The two of them talked about it and they both decided they didn't suit."

"They . . . talked about it?" her mother asked in wonder. "My, that wasn't done in my day, I will tell you that."

"He thought Louisa mature and beautiful. A perfect woman

to be his duchess."

"You would make for a perfect duchess, Adalyn."

Exasperated, she said, "Mama, you love me. Of course, you would think that. I don't want to be a duchess, though. Especially not Camden's duchess."

"Whyever not? He is a lovely man." Mama sighed. "The two of you would have such beautiful children."

"We seem to rub each other the wrong way," she revealed. "It is as if we are oil and water and simply don't mix well together."

"That is absurd. He is a duke, Adalyn," Mama said firmly. "You must learn to do whatever it takes to please him. To make him want you as his duchess."

Wanting wasn't the problem. She still believed the duke desired her. She certainly desired him. But a marriage couldn't be built upon the notion of kisses that ignited her like wildfire. She tried to remember what she didn't like about him—and couldn't remember a single thing.

"Let him come visit you whenever he wishes, Adalyn," her mother recommended. "Eventually, he will share with you what his true intentions are." She looked at her daughter with a critical eye. "It is a good thing you are wearing blue. It suits your coloring well and draws out the color of your eyes. When will His Grace arrive?"

"Two o'clock again."

"I will stay for a little while and then have Bridget come and sit in the corner to chaperone you. Do what you can to encourage his suit, Adalyn."

It was hopeless. Mama was convinced Camden was only interested in her. She would not be able to disavow her of that notion and would stop trying. It would take the duke announcing his betrothal to someone else before her mother would believe he intended someone other than her precious daughter to serve as his duchess.

"Have him stay again for tea," Mama suggested.

"I do not think he will be here as long today."

"Then make certain he stays," Mama said, brokering no argument.

"I cannot tell a duke what to do," she complained.

"No, but you are a force to be reckoned with yourself, Adalyn. Your father and I have always said so."

Adalyn left and decided to stop in to see Louisa. Usually, she would turn to Tessa with a problem of this nature but with Tessa now wed—especially to Camden's closest friend—she worried where her cousin's loyalties might lie. Discussing her ambivalence toward the duke was better done with Louisa.

She summoned Bridget and the two women stepped outside, walking the two houses down to the Goulding townhouse. Jeffers, the butler, admitted them, with Bridget heading back to the kitchens where she usually waited.

"Miss Goulding is in the library, my lady," Jeffers told her. "You may go up if you wish."

"Thank you, Jeffers."

Entering the library, she found Louisa poring over sketches. Her cousin looked up and smiled.

"I am so glad to see you," she told Adalyn. "Come look at these."

Flipping through, Adalyn saw they were sketches for gowns. "Where did these come from? Madame Chevalier?"

"Naturally. I sent word to her that I will need an entire wardrobe for this Season, unlike the few gowns I have had her make up in the past. She has been saving these sketches for me. At least, that is what her note said. I am to see her this afternoon and select fabrics. While I already have the few gowns she has made up for me to start the Season, she will complete these—and more—once I have approved them."

"That was kind of her to keep these sketches with you in mind. Madame Chevalier is not only a talented modiste but a good woman."

Louisa nodded enthusiastically. "Madame wrote that she

knew the day would come when I would be ready to fully enter society. She wanted to be ready when that day came. I particularly like several of these designs."

They went through the stack slowly, talking about the cut of each gown and what colors and materials would best serve the dress.

"Will you come with me this afternoon, Adalyn? I could certainly use your opinion."

"I am afraid I already have another engagement." She hoped Louisa would not press her.

"Is it one of your matchmaking seekers?" her cousin asked.

"It is. In fact, I met with Lord Pierce and Lord Bayless yesterday for that very reason."

Louisa's snorted. "They are both so wild. I do not see how you are friends with them."

"They are not exactly friends. We are friendly, though."

"You should become friends with the Duke of Camden," Louisa suggested.

Adalyn was glad they were not sipping tea for she would have spewed out a mouthful with that comment.

"Why do you say that?"

"I believe him to be a very kind man. He sent a note to me yesterday, asking to come around this morning."

"You have already seen him today?"

"Yes. He felt we needed to clear the air between us. Now that we both know we are not meant to wed, I actually enjoyed sitting and talking with him."

"Just the two of you?" When Louisa nodded, Adalyn added, "You mustn't do so. Servants do talk, whether you believe that or not. You would not want to be tied to the duke against your will."

Louisa flushed guiltily. "Yes. He also mentioned that very thing. I will start having my maid chaperone any visits I receive. Or your maid." She paused. "Papa told me that he will be leaving soon for Vienna. Within a few days. He said I am to go to your parents while he is out of the country. I thought he might wish for me to travel with him to Austria but he said it was important that I stay in London and find what—or rather, who—I was looking for."

"You are welcome to come anytime. Tell Tilly to start packing now. We can also inform Madame Chevalier that your gowns are to be delivered to my house instead of yours. I think you should move in tomorrow."

"No, I would prefer to stay with Papa as long as he is in town. That should be another three days or so. Then I will be happy to live two doors down."

Knowing that Louisa would come to stay so soon, Adalyn didn't have a choice. She would need to tell her cousin about the duke.

"I am also going to look for a wife for Camden," she confided.

Louisa's eyes widened. "Truly? Why would a duke need such help? I think he is the only bachelor of that rank this Season. Every female will be focused on becoming his bride."

"That is why I am to help him. He is a bit overwhelmed by the thought of entering Polite Society and how not only will men fawn over him but that every female will have one purpose—and that is to land a duke for themselves or their daughters. In fact, he is coming today to see me, which is why I cannot accompany you to the dressmaker's. We are going to make a list, much as you and I have done."

"What an excellent idea," Louisa declared. "I really do like him. He is sweet. I don't think once he weds he will spend much time in town. He seems more a type to enjoy country life. Keep that in mind when you manage to steer him toward a lady."

While Adalyn had always enjoyed time spent in the country, she adored being in London. Louisa made a good point. It was another reason she should never consider wedding the Duke of Camden. Not that he wanted to wed her. She certainly didn't want to wed him.

Now, kissing him would be quite another matter.

"I just wanted you to know that he will probably come around often, at least during the early weeks of the Season. He may even escort me to a few events, with Mama and Papa in attendance, of course."

"I see." Her cousin studied her thoughtfully. "What do you make of the duke, Adalyn?"

She worded her response carefully. "I do understand your concerns. He is quite a large, impressive man. He is also a bit different from most gentlemen in society. I believe our making this list will help me to learn more about him. After all, he is Spencer's close friend and I want to see he is taken good care of."

She rose. "I should be getting back home. I don't want to be late for my appointment with him. And you need to leave soon to see Madame. I am so excited you are getting a full wardrobe. I cannot wait to see you in all of those creations."

Louisa stood. "I will tell Tilly to start packing so that when Papa leaves, I can come straight to you."

"I will let Mama and Papa know the plans. You know men—I doubt Uncle Edgar has even mentioned to Papa that you are to come and stay with us while he is abroad."

"You are right about that," Louisa agreed cheerfully. "What would men do without us women?" She laughed.

Adalyn reclaimed Bridget and they returned home. When they arrived, Rainey met her.

"My lady, His Grace is here. I thought you should know."

"Already?" she asked, shocked since the duke wasn't due for another half-hour.

"He is in the library with your parents," the butler informed her.

Once Rainey left, Bridget said, "You should go and freshen up, my lady. You want to look your best for His Grace."

Looking good for him was the least of her concerns. Instead, irritation filled her. Did the man have no idea of proper calling hours? He had called twice on Louisa well before the acceptable hour of calls. And now he was here, far too soon.

"No. I will see him as I am."

As she marched up the stairs, she decided it was time to have it out with the Duke of Camden.

CHAPTER ELEVEN

EVERETT SAT WITH Lord and Lady Uxbridge, enjoying their company immensely. He envied Addie for having such kind, interesting parents. From what Tessa had said, she also had wonderful parents and regretted that Analise would never know them.

The door opened and Addie entered the room. Immediately, he could see her hackles were up. He assumed it was because he had arrived earlier than his appointed time and not found her at home.

He rose as she came toward them, as did her the earl.

"I am surprised to find you here, Your Grace," she said, fire in her eyes.

"I had gone to White's this morning with Spence, my lady," he explained. "We met your father there and he was kind enough to introduce me to several of his friends who were present."

Lord Uxbridge chortled. "Everyone wants to meet a duke. You made a favorable impression on everyone there," he praised.

"Since I was to call upon you this afternoon, Lord Uxbridge suggested after we engaged in a game of chess—where I was soundly beaten—that I should return home with him."

"Come and have a seat, Adalyn," Lady Uxbridge said.

The way the seating was arranged, Everett knew Addie would have to come and sit next to him. She did so, sitting stiffly.

"If you have other things to do before our meeting, Lady Adalyn, I am happy to spend that time in your parents' company," he offered.

She glanced to him. "You are already here, Your Grace. I think we should get about our business."

Lady Uxbridge clucked her tongue. "Please, Adalyn, do not refer to it as *business*. It sounds so pedestrian. You are merely aiding His Grace."

"Whatever we call it, Mama, we do need to address several issues at length."

She rose and Everett followed suit as she said, "I will take His Grace to my sitting room." Looking at him, she added, "I will send for Bridget, my lady's maid. She is used to chaperoning me when I have guests and my parents are unavailable."

"How long will this take, Adalyn?" Lady Uxbridge asked. Then she looked to him. "If you are still here at teatime, Your Grace, we would be happy for you to join us."

He sensed that was the last thing Addie wanted him to do and so he said, "I would enjoy that, my lady. Thank you for your gracious invitation."

Everett watched Addie ring for a servant and Rainey, the butler, appeared.

"Please have Bridget come to my sitting room," she instructed.

"At once, my lady."

"Come along, Your Grace," she said brusquely and motioned for him to follow her.

She took him to a small but sunny room, indicating exactly where he should sit.

Not beside her.

"Before we even talk about the qualities you seek in a wife, we must discuss your manners."

"You find them lacking?" he asked.

She frowned and then bit her lower lip, causing a frisson of desire to ripple through him. He had thought about doing that very thing.

Repeatedly.

"It is not exactly your lack of manners, Your Grace, but rather your lack of knowledge regarding rules of the *ton*."

"Addie, you know you are to call me Everett. Or Ev."

He watched the fire flash in her eyes. "Quit calling me Addie," she demanded. "You know I do not like it."

He grinned. "I know," he admitted. "But I like it for you," he continued. "Adalyn is a beautiful name but very formal. The work we undertake is important to me and I want to feel comfortable in your presence. Surely, you can throw me a bone and allow me to call you Addie. After all, I am a duke. I have heard dukes always get their way."

She bristled, pursing her lips a moment, making him want to kiss her even more than previously.

"All right," she grudgingly said. "You may address me as you wish in private."

He would take that small victory. And be gracious about it.

"Thank you, Addie," he said sincerely.

The door opened and Bridget, her lady's maid, entered, a small book in her hand. She smiled brightly and said, "I'll just sit in the corner, my lady, and read. You won't know I'm here at all."

Bridget retreated to a far corner and immediately opened the book she carried, placing it on her lap and quickly becoming absorbed in it.

"I am glad to see you have a chaperone," Everett said. "I have been concerned about Miss Goulding and her lack of one. She assured me in the future that she would make certain her lady's maid was present if I ever called."

"It won't be a problem for much longer. My uncle will be traveling to Vienna to meet up with Lord Castlereagh and other diplomats since Bonaparte is soon to be formally deposed. It will be a congress of men gathering from across Europe. Uncle Edgar had thought to take Louisa with him. I changed his mind."

"Good thinking on your part, Addie," he praised. "The hours

they would have met would have been long ones, with Miss Goulding left alone, with no companionship."

"Louisa will be coming to stay with us. With the Season at hand, it will be convenient for all. That way, when suitors come to call, Mama or Papa will always be on hand in the drawing room. Even Tessa could serve as our chaperone now that she is a married lady."

"She could? That's interesting."

"It is one of the many rules you have never been exposed to, Everett."

He did like hearing his name come from her lips. He stared at those lips now, tantalizing as they were. Everett blinked, trying to rid himself of the notion that he wanted Addie and no other as his duchess.

Clearing his throat, he asked, "What are a few of the rules I need to know? Please do not barrage me. I already am learning to dance, thanks to Tessa and Abra. I only have room for so much in my head, especially after all I have learned and am learning about being a duke. I have a myriad of responsibilities as a duke and many estates to keep up with. That does not even include my duties I will take up in the House of Lords. So please, keep the rules to a minimum. Only the most important if you would."

"I understand Papa brought you home with him today," she began. "If you plan to see a young lady during the Season, however, you must first arrange to call upon her. The time to do so is to ask her at the previous evening's engagement. I have a feeling you will be quite choosy, so be circumspect in the invitations you seek. Never ask to call if it is not morning hours." She smiled. "Morning hours are held in the afternoon."

"Then why are they called morning hours?"

She shrugged. "Because they always have been. I know it is not much of an explanation. During the Season, females will, what we call, be at home from the hours of one to three. If you asked to call upon them, go between those hours. Those are the appropriate times to visit."

"You are telling me I should not have called on Miss Goulding at eleven in the morning?"

"That is exactly what I am saying. You have called upon her twice before noon. You tell me you want to be nothing like your brother so do not create a small scandal by not adhering to the proper times to visit someone."

"I understand now and will arrange my visits at the proper time in the future," he promised. "When I do arrange to call, is it anytime between one and three?"

"During the Season, yes. You will most likely want to call on more than one young lady in an afternoon so you will keep your visits short. A quarter-hour is perfect. Never longer than half an hour. Though you will be competing with other gentlemen for a lady's attention—and possible affection—you are a duke and will always take precedence over any other suitor."

"Finally, an advantage to holding such a lofty title."

"So be certain you stick to those hours. Today was an exception since Papa invited you home with him but do not try to ingratiate yourself with parents in such an unconventional manner. Once you find a female to your liking, you can curry favor with her parents and the rest of her family in other ways, which we will discuss at a later time."

Her point made, Adalyn changed subjects. "You mentioned Tessa and Abra teaching you how to dance. How is that going?"

Everett shrugged. "I am not the most graceful dancer but I am beginning to understand the steps and am becoming more comfortable with them as I practice them." He paused. "I have yet to learn the steps of the waltz, however. Spence indicated to me it will be the most valuable dance to know and participate in."

"Spencer is correct. It is incredibly hard to hold any type of conversation when dancing a Scotch reel. By the way, has Tessa told you to limit the number of times you ask someone to dance? Once is fine. Twice, and you are showing a good bit of interest in a young lady as far as the *ton* is concerned. Thrice is forbidden. Don't even think of doing that, Everett."

He was pleased that she continued to use his name upon occasion. Ridiculously pleased. He needed to get over that feeling. And he needed to stop looking at her mouth, wanting to discover new things about it and her.

A thought occurred to him. "Perhaps you could help teach me the waltz," he suggested.

A blush spread across her cheeks, making her look even more appealing than usual.

"I will leave that to Tessa. Now, we need to discuss your list."

She rose and went to a small desk and removed paper and pen. Sitting, she opened a bottle of ink and then said, "You are awfully far away. Bring your chair over to me."

Everett did as she asked and they were even further away from Bridget, who had yet to glance up from her book.

He watched Addie write *The Duke of Camden* at the top of the page and shook his head. "No, I don't want my name anywhere on such a list," he insisted. "If for any reason it was discovered by someone, I would not want the contents of the list associated with my name."

"Good thinking, Ev," she said, discarding the page and retrieving a new one.

This time, she did not title it as she looked at him expectantly. "Well?"

He felt awkward and said, "I don't really know what to tell you to write," he admitted. "I have never really thought about this before. Being a second son and knowing I would spend my entire adult life in His Majesty's army, I doubted I would ever wed."

"Your situation has changed and so must you," Addie told him. "Let me help you get started."

He wondered if she did this for everyone she had previously helped find a spouse.

"We should start with physical attributes and then discuss character traits. What type of woman appeals to you, Ev?"

Her. She appealed to him.

"If you are asking if I like a woman who is tall or short, it does not matter to me."

"All right, then what about coloring? Do you prefer a blond or brunette? Or even darker hair? What about eye color?"

He shrugged. "I truly have no preference regarding looks. I think knowing a person and what they are truly made of is more important than any physical characteristic. So I don't believe we need to consider anything regarding looks on this list."

Her nose crinkled, quite appealingly, and she said, "I suppose then that you are going to tell me her family will not matter to you, either."

"What do you mean? I am not marrying her family. I am wedding her."

"Ev, most marriages are made for political or social gain. You, being a duke, should be drawn to and only considering making a match with the women who come from the better if not best families in all of England," she explained. "It would be much more suitable for you to wed the daughter of a fellow duke or a marquess."

"What if I find nothing about them that I like?" he challenged. "What if I am interested in wedding a lowly baron's daughter? Or a woman whose father has no title at all?"

"That won't really do, Ev," she said. "You need to give unattached females at the highest end of the hierarchy your most attention."

"Then why on earth did you not object to my pursuing Miss Goulding? Not only did you not object, you even encouraged my interest in her. *Her* father holds no title, though I am certain he is well thought of in many circles."

She sniffed. "That was quite different. Louisa is my cousin, one whom I think the world of. She is a woman of beauty, maturity, and refinement. I would challenge you to find anyone of Louisa's worth within the eligible ladies in Polite Society. In my opinion, my cousin would have made for the perfect duchess."

She paused, pressing her lips together a moment. "Since the two of you mutually decided that you did not suit—and since you have asked for my help in securing you a bride—I am giving you the best advice possible. A duke should look to the upper echelon of the *ton*. That is what I am recommending to you, Ev."

"And I say hogwash to that." He crossed his arms over his chest. "Get to the important stuff, Addie. I don't care what a woman looks like or who sired her. I won't need to wed a woman with a large dowry because I am obscenely wealthy. I don't need to make a match to improve my social position. I am wedding because I want to do so. Because I desire children."

"I see," she said quietly. "Then tell me—what *is* important to you?"

"Common values, of course. She must value the importance of family above all. My duchess should not only want to give me numerous children but love those children unequivocally. I want her to spend time with them. Play with them. Talk to them."

He watched her scribble on the page and added, "I need a woman with empathy. One who is kind to all, not just her friends. I wish for her to be honest and honorable. She should have a strong sense of duty. She will need to visit the tenants on our estates and truly get to know them and see to their needs. She must never take responsibilities lightly but rather take them to heart. As a duchess, she will be looked up to and become a leader in society. She should use that not to her advantage but for good. My duchess should be dignified. Reserved. Composed. Serene. She must at all times conduct herself in the manner of a duchess."

Everett waited while she caught up to him and finally added, "And she must be faithful. I know I had said before that I thought we would go our separate ways and then mentioned I might not be satisfied with that. I have given the matter more thought and have decided that we both should honor our wedding vows. That we come together as a couple and family and remain that way. For the rest of our lives."

She stopped writing and gazed up at him, her blue eyes intense. "Are you seeking love, Ev?" she asked softly.

"No," he said.

But he knew he lied.

Because looking at Addie, Everett knew he had already found it.

CHAPTER TWELVE

T ONIGHT WAS THE opening night of the Season.

Adalyn watched as Bridget styled her hair. The week leading up to the Season had gone quickly. Uncle Edgar had left the country for Vienna with a group of English diplomats and Louisa had moved into the Uxbridge household. She was across the hall from Adalyn getting ready now and the cousins had already spent many days and nights in conversation.

Adalyn had also taken tea with several leading members of the *ton*, gaining as much information as she could about the new group of young ladies who would make their come-out this Season. She had decided to limit her matchmaking abilities to the three bachelors she had previously promised to help, in part because she wanted to also concentrate on Louisa and herself making the best possible match. With both of them wishing to find a husband, that was where her focus would be.

It was a shame that Ev and Louisa had decided they would not suit. Adalyn believed her cousin to possess all the qualities which would have made her an excellent duchess. On the other hand, it was probably for the best because it would have torn at her heart to see Ev happy with Louisa.

She no longer could think of him as Camden or His Grace. He was Everett—or actually, Ev—to her. She had not seen him since he had come to call and they had composed his list. It had surprised her that he did not truly care for beauty or the size of a woman's dowry. She had never met a man who didn't want one if not both of those things, even if they themselves had adequate wealth.

At least her dowry was ample. She still, unlike Louisa, did not want to wed someone in dire need of that money. She understood what Louisa meant because Adalyn had seen men inherit titles, only to find themselves stripped of riches by a father who had lost the family fortune. She believed that tendency to gamble possibly ran in a family and wanted to avoid it at all costs.

"Looking forward to tonight, my lady?" Bridget asked as she stepped back to admire her handiwork.

"I am. Probably more than my first Season."

"It's because you are ready to settle down with a husband finally," the maid told her. "You're looking at everything with different eyes this year."

The lady's maid studied her carefully. "I hope you find what you are looking for, my lady."

"I hope so, too, Bridget."

Adalyn rose from her dressing table and went across the hall, where Tilly was fastening a locket around Louisa's neck.

"Thank you, Tilly," Louisa said and rose to face Adalyn. "Oh, you look beautiful."

"I was about to compliment you for the very same thing, Louisa. Madame Chevalier has outdone herself. Are you excited about tonight?"

Her cousin nodded. "It is still hard for me to imagine going to so many different events this time around."

"You will receive many invitations," Adalyn assured her. "Once others know that Uncle Edgar has left for the congress and that you are staying with us, they will be sent here."

"You said you have subtly put out the word that we both aim to wed?"

"I have. I took tea with the right people this past week. Not only did I learn much about the girls making their debuts, but I also made certain that others were aware you and I are going into this Season with the goal of finding our husbands."

"I am relying on you, Adalyn, to steer me away from the rogues and rakes."

She chuckled. "It will be hard to avoid all of them," she shared. "We will have to dance with a few of them, else we would hardly dance at all. I do know, however, which ones to tell you to avoid and not grow serious about."

"I am reassured by that," Louisa said with conviction. "Shall we go downstairs?"

Adalyn slipped her arm through her cousin's and led her downstairs to the foyer. Papa awaited them and complimented both on their new gowns. Mama arrived and they went to the waiting carriage. It took three-quarters of an hour to travel but a few blocks and the coach came to a halt. The carriage door opened and a footman aided them from the vehicle.

Adalyn looked about, seeing the swell of people moving toward Lord and Lady Pauling's townhouse. They joined the crush and entered, spying Tessa. Naturally, she was with Spencer and it did not surprise Adalyn that Ev accompanied them.

He looked perfectly splendid in his formal evening wear, his coal black hair gleaming. She saw hesitancy in his eyes as he looked warily about.

Then their gazes met and he seemed to stand a bit taller.

There were only two couples separating them in the receiving line and Tessa encouraged both to move ahead of them so they could all stand together.

"I am so happy to see you both," Tessa declared.

She and Louisa greeted Spencer and Ev, Adalyn careful to address him formally since others were nearby.

"Is it appropriate to compliment both of you ladies on your attire?" Ev asked.

"It is," she assured him. "Women of all ages enjoy hearing compliments on our gowns."

Tessa said, "I want both of you to dance with Everett this

evening. I have discussed it with him and think that one of you should partner with him for the opening number and the other take the supper dance. Are you agreeable?"

Louisa said, "I am happy to do so. Do you have a preference, Your Grace?"

"I will leave that up to you, Miss Goulding," Ev said.

Adalyn was torn. If she danced the supper dance with Ev, they would be able to spend supper together. She knew, though, that Lord Pauling always insisted the first number to be a waltz. To be in Ev's arms, dancing so close, would be a dream come true.

Spencer settled the matter for them by saying, "Why don't we all have supper together? Ev is comfortable in all of our company." Then he added, "Dance the first number with Adalyn and the supper dance with Louisa." Looking to Adalyn, Spencer added, "Ask your supper partner if he would not mind supping with our group."

"I can do that," she assured him, knowing now she would dance the first dance—a waltz—not only with a duke, but with Ev.

Eventually, they made it to where Lord and Lady Pauling received them and then their group entered the ballroom, where a footman handed them their dance cards. The women took turns attaching the programmes to each other's wrists and then encouraged Ev to sign both in the agreed spots.

Tessa said, "As we discussed before, both of you dancing with a duke will only enhance your chances of being noticed early on. Everett is new to the *ton* and others will be curious about him and the choices he makes tonight. Spencer and I will take him around now and introduce him to a few people."

Adalyn said, "I have four young ladies that I would like His Grace to dance with this evening." She revealed the four names, two making their come-out this season, one having done so last Season, and the final one a widow.

"Commit those names to memory, Your Grace," she instructed. Looking to Tessa, she said, "Be sure he signs each of their programmes."

The trio moved away and Adalyn looked to Louisa. "Brace yourself," she said, "because I see a hoard of young men making their way toward us."

Quickly, she whispered two names to Louisa that she thought might suit her cousin and then greeted the group of bachelors arriving in front of them. Soon, both cousins' dance cards were filled. The entire time, however, Adalyn's gaze followed Ev as he circulated about the ballroom, meeting women and signing their programmes. She tried to tamp down the twinge of jealousy that rippled through her. She was determined to put aside her growing feelings for this man.

After this first waltz.

Ev made his way toward her as the musicians began tuning their instruments. Her heart sped up as he did so.

He reached her side and smiled. "My face already hurts from smiling so much," he confessed.

"Smiling and the Season go hand-in-hand," she told him, chuckling. "Are you ready to dance?"

He hesitated and then said, "I hope so. My greatest fear is that I will trample upon your toes during our waltz. I have still had trouble mastering its steps. The country dances and reels came much more easily to me."

Surprise filled her. "There are very few steps in the waltz, Ev," she said, catching herself and looking about quickly. "I mean, Your Grace."

He shrugged. "Spence told me that I will need to feel the music. Tessa has hummed to me as we have practiced but even she said the orchestra playing will make a huge difference."

The room grew silent and she saw the musicians taking up their instruments in a ready position. Couples began moving toward the center of the dance floor.

"This is it," she said. "Come along, Your Grace. We will tackle this together and get you off to a good start."

She felt the gaze of many as she took his arm and he led her onto the ballroom floor. They faced one another and he slipped her right hand into his left, causing goosebumps to appear on her arms. Then his palm pressed against her back, flooding her with warmth. The music began and he swept her away.

She could tell he was an inexperienced dancer by his hesitant moves and so she did not try to engage him in conversation. Gradually, though, she saw he began to feel the beat of the music and they began gliding across the floor as one.

Wonder broke out on his face as he said, "I am actually doing it, aren't I?"

"You are, Ev," she said softly, rewarding him with a smile.

That was all they said during the entire dance. It was enough.

When the last strains of the waltz sounded, the dancing ceased. Ev held her a moment longer before releasing her. He smiled, a radiant one that tugged at her heart.

"Lead me off the floor now, Your Grace," she prodded and he did so, returning her to the same spot he had claimed her. Louisa's partner had done the same and she saw her cousin's cheeks flushed with color.

Ev took her hand and bowed to her, kissing her fingers. As he released her hand, Adalyn wanted to cry out for him to never let her go.

"I will see you at supper, my lady," he said and moved away.

Adalyn's next partner claimed her for the upcoming, lively reel. She determined not to watch Ev tonight anymore and instead focus on the gentlemen she had agreed to dance with. She did occasionally glance about in order to find Louisa, who constantly wore a smile and seemed to be enjoying herself immensely.

The supper dance arrived and Lord Rosewell approached her. She found him most handsome and quite witty but knew how he had no intentions of settling down anytime soon. His own father, the previous earl, had not wed until he was close to sixty and was fortunate to have produced an heir before he died two years later.

The son seemed to be following closely in his father's footsteps, which meant Lord Rosewell wouldn't think of wedding for almost three decades. If ever here was a rake, his name was Rosewell.

"Lady Adalyn, might I say how lovely you look this evening," the earl said smoothly.

"Thank you, my lord," she replied distractedly, knowing he was always full of false compliments. She glanced over his shoulder, wondering where her next partner was since couples were already moving onto the dance floor.

"If you are looking for your supper partner, he won't be coming," Lord Rosewell said.

That got her attention.

"Why would you say that?"

He grinned, his eyes twinkling with mischief. "Because I convinced him to allow me to partner with you instead."

Before Adalyn could object, he placed her hand on his forearm and escorted her through the crowd until they stood in the center of the room. She would have objected but now too many couples surrounded them. She would have to see the dance through.

Unfortunately, it was the second waltz of the evening.

Lord Rosewell took her into his arms as the music commenced. He danced divinely, as only a rake could, so at least she would enjoy herself for the next few minutes.

Then Adalyn remembered she was supposed to ask her supper partner to dine with her family. Disappointment filled her. For some reason, she didn't want Ev to think she was interested in this man.

At least he didn't bother with conversation as they moved about the ballroom. He seemed content to merely stare into her eyes as they danced. That made her want to look anywhere but at him.

When the music ended, he possessively took her hand in his and proclaimed, "It was worth it."

"What was?" she asked, curious as to the statement.

"I forgave your dance partner a small debt he owed me in order to claim this spot on your programme." He gave her a wolfish smile. "Now, I have you all to myself at supper."

She frowned. "I had already made arrangements to sup with my family, my lord." Then keeping to her good manners, she added, "Naturally, I would extend that invitation to you."

"Your family?"

"Yes, my two cousins. Lady Middlefield and Miss Goulding. We are as close as sisters and enjoy one another's company immensely."

As the swell of people moved toward the doors, Lord Rosewell said, "I would be delighted to dine with them. I have met Lord Middlefield but would like the opportunity to get to know him better. And Miss Goulding is quite the beauty. I certainly wish to spend time with her, as well."

Adalyn needed to keep this rogue far from Louisa. She doubted Spencer would like Lord Rosewell.

And neither would Ev.

They headed toward the room designated for the midnight buffet and she spied Tessa and Spencer.

Lord Rosewell must also have seen them for he steered her in their direction. They arrived and she introduced him to Tessa since the two had never met. Spencer stared coldly into Lord Rosewell's eyes as he shook his hand.

Then Louisa arrived with Ev, who looked relaxed as if he had been enjoying himself. The moment he saw Lord Rosewell, his features grew hard.

She indicated her partner. "Your Grace, may I introduce—"

"We've met," Ev said succinctly.

"Yes, His Grace and I enjoyed a brief conversation at White's last week," Lord Rosewell revealed. "And you must be Miss Goulding." He took Louisa's hand.

"Come and sit," Tessa said and everyone took a place at their table meant for six.

"Shall we go to the buffet, my lord?" Adalyn asked, hoping to draw her partner away from the table, where Spencer and Ev looked openly hostile.

"It is far too crowded to do so, my lady," Lord Rosewell told her and then turned to speak with Louisa, who looked puzzled.

"I have never minded a crowd," Spencer said, rising. "I will be back with everything you like, love," he told Tessa and strode off.

Ev also rose. "Why don't you accompany me to the buffet table, Lady Adalyn? It is my first time at a midnight supper. You might have some interesting suggestions for me."

"I would be delighted to help you, Your Grace."

He pulled out her chair and she rose, feeling perturbed that Lord Rosewell was totally ignoring her. The earl glanced up and smiled lazily at her and said, "If you would get a sweet or two for me, that will be enough." He turned back to Louisa.

Adalyn let Ev lead her away. The moment they were out of earshot, he turned angrily to her.

"What are you doing with a man like that?"

CHAPTER THIRTEEN

"Do not take that tone with me, Your Grace," Adalyn told Ev.

"Why are you even dancing with that man in the first place?" he demanded.

"Not that it is any of your business, but I did not allow Lord Rosewell to sign my programme."

She watched Ev's brow crease.

"Then why did you dance with him?" His concern was obvious and it touched her.

"He took the place of my expected partner," she said succinctly, not wanting to explain what the earl had told her about the debt owed him and the favor he had negotiated.

They reached the buffet table and he handed her a plate before taking two, one for himself and one for Louisa. She placed a few of her favorite foods on hers, thinking to add a couple of sweets for Lord Rosewell. Though Adalyn had a sweet tooth, she would abstain from sweets tonight and give those she selected to the earl.

They did not speak as they went through the buffet line, only to begin their conversation again once they crossed the room, with others not around them.

"Addie," Ev said quietly, "I am asking you to stay away from Lord Rosewell. I met him the other day at White's and while I know very little about him, he did something that made a poor impression upon me."

"And you aren't going to share that with me?" she asked.

His face hardened. "No, I am not."

Adalyn saw something in his eyes that made her wonder exactly what Lord Rosewell had said or done to upset Ev so.

Before they reached their table, she said, "It was awkward to learn that Lord Rosewell took the place of the man on my dance card. I could not turn him away without causing a scene. I want to assure you, though, that you do not have to warn me about his reputation. It is black indeed and I will have nothing to do with him in the future."

Ev's features relaxed and he gave her a crooked smile. "Good."

They reached the table and Lord Rosewell rose and seated her. Adalyn saw concern on both Louisa's and Tessa's faces and gave them a reassuring smile.

Ev placed Louisa's plate in front of her and then put his own on the table as he took a seat opposite Adalyn. Spencer had also returned and brought food for both Tessa and him.

Adalyn could feel the tension at the table, obvious to everyone. Lord Rosewell seemed amused by it. It angered her that he was ruining not only her evening but that of her friends.

"What did you bring me, Lady Adalyn?" the earl asked her.

She pushed her plate so that it sat in front of him and said, "I do not have an appetite this evening, my lord. You may have everything I brought back."

"Tsk-tsk," he said, popping an olive into his mouth and smiling.

Finally, conversation began at the table, with Lord Rosewell inserting a comment every now and then, not bothering to hide his smile when it was ignored.

When supper was ending around them, he helped her rise and said, "Allow me to escort you to the ballroom, my lady."

"That will not be necessary, my lord," she told him. "I plan to visit the retiring room with my cousins."

He cocked an eyebrow and said, "Speaking of visiting, might I call upon you tomorrow afternoon?"

Adalyn stared hard at him a moment and then replied, "You may not."

She turned to go but he caught her elbow and pulled her back, making her incredibly uncomfortable.

Gazing into her eyes, he asked, "What is wrong, my lady? I have heard you are on the hunt for a husband this Season. Do you not think I am marriage material?"

She shrugged off his arm and said, "No. Not at all."

He looked taken aback for a moment and then laughed heartily. "You are correct," he agreed. "I have never thought myself being a man who would make for a good husband. Actually, any kind of husband at all. But I do know I will have to pass on my title someday and will need to wed."

He studied her for a long moment and said, "Are you certain you would not be interested in being the Countess of Rosewell?"

"I have no interest in being your countess, Lord Rosewell," she said firmly, putting the issue to rest. "If you will excuse me."

She moved away from him and joined Tessa and Louisa, who had waited for her a short distance away. The three women linked arms and exited the supper room. Once they were alone, Louisa said, "He scared me."

"He does more than scare women," Tessa observed. "He has a dreadful reputation, Adalyn. Why on earth did you agree to dance with him?"

"He took the place of my supper partner." She explained briefly how Lord Rosewell had used a card debt to claim her for the supper dance.

Louisa shivered. "Please, Adalyn, do not have anything more to do with him."

"I have no intention of doing so, Cousin," she replied.

They entered the retiring room, which was packed with women conversing. Adalyn spied two of the young ladies she had asked Ev to dance with this evening and wondered what they thought of him. They were both making their come-outs this year and although he had said he didn't think he was interested in women this young, she had heard good things about both of them and thought he should at least meet them and see for himself.

Making her way toward the pair, she smiled brightly. "Good evening, Lady Agatha. Lady Bertha."

They both stared at her in awe. She knew of her reputation as being a leader of the *ton* and could understand why these two girls making their come-out might be taken aback by her approaching them. However, she needed to learn a bit about them in person, especially if one of them was meant to be Ev's bride.

Even if the thought brought her hurt.

"How are you enjoying your first ball?" she inquired.

Both girls smiled and Lady Agatha said, "It is everything I dreamed of."

"The same for me," Lady Bertha said. "I have danced with a duke, a marquess, and two earls."

"Why, that is wonderful," Adalyn said, thinking up close both of them appeared to be quite pretty. "It seems as if you are getting off on the right foot in Polite Society." She paused and then said, "I would like to invite you both to tea tomorrow afternoon."

This would be the best way to speak with them at length and evaluate their potential as a future duchess.

Lady Agatha brightened. "I would be delighted to come, my lady." She turned to her companion, and Lady Bertha nodded enthusiastically.

"You will certainly be entertaining callers tomorrow afternoon but I am happy you will make the time to come and see me. Four o'clock?" she asked.

The pair agreed to the time and Adalyn left them, giggling among themselves.

She rejoined Tessa and Louisa and they returned to the ballroom. She decided she might as well invite the other prospective brides for the same afternoon tea and excused herself, seeking out Lady Minceton and Miss Peterson, extending an invitation to both. They seemed thrilled at being invited and Adalyn thought tomorrow afternoon's teatime would prove to be quite interesting.

The remainder of the ball went quickly and as she climbed into the carriage with Louisa and her parents to return home, Adalyn hoped that among tomorrow's callers, there might be a gentleman who would become her husband.

⇥⤜⇤

ADALYN SMILED AS the last of their callers left the drawing room, which was full of fragrant bouquets. Her mother left with them, saying she was exhausted and would return in an hour's time when their guests for tea would arrive.

Turning to Louisa, she asked, "Well?"

Her cousin looked a bit lost. "I don't know. If I am to be perfectly honest, I feel so overwhelmed. Having never had callers before—at least gentlemen callers who might serve as a suitor—I found it hard to keep up with everyone. And so many were here for you, Adalyn. Not me."

"I did have my fair share but I think several of your bachelors are worth taking a second look at."

She led Louisa to a settee and they sat discussing their prospects for several minutes.

"This was just the first day," Adalyn reminded. "We have probably another fifty to sixty balls we will attend, not to mention all the other social events of the Season."

"How do women decide whom they will wed?" Louisa asked and sighed. "So many gentlemen. And even though I spoke with many briefly last night and several called upon me this afternoon,

I still don't feel as if I truly know anything about any of them. Our conversations had no substance."

"There is no rush," she assured Louisa. "Many women do not wed after their first Season because of that very thing. In a way, this is almost like a new come-out for you."

"I don't think I could go through this over and over. I truly want to find a husband this time around, with no delays."

She took Louisa's hand. "Your heart will tell you what you should do. What if you do find a husband? Will you wait for Uncle Edgar to return?"

"No. We discussed that very thing before he left. Papa said he would be in Vienna for many months if not a year or more. Those present will truly remake the map of Europe. It is important work. While I would love for Papa to see me wed, I also do not want to wait so long. He has given me permission to choose a husband of my liking since I am of age. I believe, though, that he discussed this with your father, who will act as my agent, along with our solicitor, regarding the marriage settlements."

"Do you want Papa to have final approval?" Adalyn asked.

"No. My father said he trusted my judgment and I could wed or remain unattached. It would be up to me."

"That is good to know." She stood. "We should go and freshen up before our guests arrive for tea. Mama is probably sneaking in a short nap so she will be refreshed for both tea and this evening's soiree."

They went to their bedchambers and Adalyn returned first to the drawing room, thinking through everything she knew about their four guests. Mama and then Louisa joined her.

"Your father is taking tea in his study," Mama informed them. "He said it is bad enough having too many men clog up his drawing room during the Season but that seven ladies would be infinitely worse."

Rainey appeared and announced the four visitors and their guests streamed in. Adalyn introduced everyone to her mother and Louisa and they sat as servants pushed in two teacarts. Mama poured out for their guests from one pot while she did the same for the rest of them.

Their conversation centered on last night's ball, which Adalyn knew was happening in drawing rooms across the city. Her mother took the lead, which Adalyn had expected. Mama had a genuine curiosity about others and was so sweet-natured that no one thought her questions imposing or too personal. Mama asked many of the things Adalyn herself would have.

She had an excellent memory and was able to keep the four women and their responses separate. As the hour progressed, she eliminated Lady Agatha from consideration. The blond was vapid and had little conversation. Lady Bertha was only slightly better but Adalyn kept her as a candidate. The petite brunette had a tendency to giggle, which would never do in a duchess. However-er, Adalyn decided it was due to the girl's tender age. If she learned to control her emotions better, she might have a chance with Ev.

Adalyn much preferred the other two women. Miss Peterson comported herself well. She had lively blue eyes and light brown hair and was said to be quite choosy, which is why she supposed-ly had not wed after her first Season. Based upon her conversation, Adalyn thought Miss Peterson had a little bit of a bluestocking in her because she was well informed in many areas.

Her choice for Ev, though, would be Lady Minceton. The widow, who looked to be three or four years past twenty, displayed more maturity than most women. She was dark-haired and curvaceous and spoke fondly of her two-year-old daughter, the only child from her union with the much older Lord Minceton. Adalyn would need to speak with Ev soon and determine what he had thought of each of these women before seeking any new candidates out for him.

Tea was almost over when her father made an appearance. What surprised her was that Ev accompanied him.

"Oh, sorry to interrupt," Papa said, not looking a bit sorry.

"Are His Grace and I too late for tea?"

"Not at all," Mama said, taking charge of the situation. "Do come in, Your Grace. Have you met our guests?"

Ev went to each of their visitors, greeting them by name, before he came to say hello to Louisa and Adalyn. Adalyn gave him a questioning look, which he proceeded to ignore. Then he sat next to Mama and they began talking like old friends.

Lady Agatha and Lady Bertha giggled into their handkerchiefs. Miss Peterson looked on with curiosity. And Lady Minceton didn't look at Ev at all, rather focusing her attention on Adalyn's father.

"It is good to see you again, my lord," she said pleasantly.

"I could say the same, Lady Minceton. I was sorry to hear of your husband's passing."

"He did enjoy playing chess with you," the widow said, dabbing the corner of her eye with a handkerchief.

The clock chimed a few minutes later and their guests all rose, looking to Adalyn. They thanked her for the invitation and her parents said they would see their guests out.

Louisa rose, as well, and as the others left said, "It is good to see you again, Everett. Will you be at tonight's soiree?"

"I will. Though I haven't the foggiest idea what a soiree is. Mr. Johnson, my secretary who keeps track of these things, told me he had accepted the invitation for me."

"I am glad you will be there. It will be good to see a friendly face and actually remember the name attached to it. Excuse me," Louisa said, leaving Adalyn alone with Ev.

He came and sat next to her. "I see you called together what you termed my best prospects. Were you reviewing their backgrounds and conduct and evaluating whether or not they would make for a good Duchess of Camden?"

"I was. I would like for you to also share your opinions about them. You did dance with all of them last night, I'm assuming."

"I did. For all the good that did." He scowled. "A ball is not the place to conduct a decent conversation. Tessa had warned me of that. The more lively dances only let you exchange snippets with your partner. I suppose having one of them accompany me into supper would have been better instead of escorting Louisa but I much preferred her company to any of theirs."

"Oh, have you changed your mind about Louisa?"

He shook his head. "No. We are not meant to wed."

Adalyn waited but he said no more. "Then tell me what you thought of the four," she ventured. "Before I give you my opinion."

Ev snorted. "The two young ones are insipid. I could have a better conversation with that wall over there than either of them."

"They are both quite pretty," she pointed out.

"Pretty to look at is one thing. Having a woman I can actually talk with is something else." He paused. "Miss Peterson seemed nice. A bit on the thin side."

"I thought you didn't care about looks," she reminded.

"Well, I need a woman who won't blow away," he said. "She seemed to be able to converse well but, then again, we didn't get much time to talk."

"What about Lady Minceton?"

"She is nice," he admitted. "Attractive. Poised. If it were a horse race, I'd say the two young misses were out of the running, Miss Peterson was the dark horse, and Lady Minceton was in the lead. But it's early, Adalyn. You can't expect me to know my mind after only a day."

He glanced about. "And you can't expect me to know the rules if you haven't gone over them with me. I had no idea I was to send flower arrangements."

"Oh, dear," she fretted. "I am sorry I overlooked that. It is just something I assumed everyone knows."

He snorted. "I discovered that when I went to call upon Lady Bertha. I made the rounds of all four of them this afternoon. Two lived next door to each other. One around the corner. The other across the street. So I was able to get all four calls in. Unfortunately, they must all think me rude for not having sent flowers to them. What is Polite Society's unwritten rule regarding that?"

Adalyn sighed. "If you asked to call upon a lady, your bouquet should arrive before you do. Preferably by noon."

"What if I have called upon them before?"

"You should send something each time you call."

"The florists must make a tidy bundle this time of year," he commented.

"They do earn most of their living during the months of the Season."

Ev raked a hand through his thick hair. "Because I was embarrassed by my faux pas, I only stayed five or ten minutes at each place. That certainly wasn't enough time to learn anything about them, especially with chaperones hovering about."

"That is fine," she assured him. "One, calls need last no longer than fifteen or so minutes. We discussed that before. And two, you are a duke, so you will be forgiven for not having sent them flowers. Especially if you begin to pay special attention to any of them." She gazed at him, trying to keep from looking at his sensual lips. "Have you decided if you will single any of them out?" she asked lightly.

His eyes seemed to fall to her mouth, causing goosebumps to spring up along her arms.

"Do I have to single any of them out?" he asked huskily.

She swallowed, trying to maintain her composure. "If you want to find a bride, you should. Of course, I am still learning about some of the new girls making their come-outs and may have more suggestions for you. And I have a few thoughts about others who are more mature and might appeal to you."

"You appeal to me."

Adalyn felt her cheeks immediately heat and glanced away, no quick retort coming to mind.

Ev took her chin and lifted it until their eyes locked. They stared wordlessly at one another. Her heart beat so fast and hard that she was afraid it might burst from her chest.

Then he lowered his mouth to hers.

CHAPTER FOURTEEN

EVERETT HAD TOLD himself he wouldn't kiss Addie again. Even promised her he wouldn't do so.

And yet here he was, his lips next to hers, where they had wanted to be ever since the last time he had kissed her.

Rationally, he knew Addie wasn't duchess material. She wasn't calm and unapproachable and dignified. While his mind recognized this, his body—and heart—only wanted her. Her warmth. Her fire. Her delectable body in his bed.

His hands grasped her shoulders, afraid she might flee, as he nibbled on her plump, lower lip. She shuddered, her hands going to his waistcoat, clutching it.

She wasn't going anywhere, after all.

Everett ran his tongue along her lips and then the seam of her mouth, teasing it open. She tasted like a lemon cake that she must have eaten at tea. His tongue swept along hers, stroking it lovingly. His hands glided up and down her arms slowly, entranced by her vanilla scent. Need rose within him and he devoured her mouth greedily, hearing the little noises she made, soft whimpers.

He needed her closer and maneuvered her into his lap, the full swell of her breasts tantalizing him. He broke the kiss and trailed his tongue down her throat until he reached one and swept his tongue along the curve where it peeked from her gown.

A long sigh escaped from her. Her hands pushed into his hair, her fingers kneading his scalp as she held him close. Everett's fingers brushed along her neck, moving lower, until they slipped inside her bodice and freed one of her breasts. He slid his tongue across the pink bud, hearing her gasp.

His hands kneaded her breasts as he laved and sucked at her nipple. Addie squirmed and sighed and wriggled her bottom, causing him to grow hard.

He couldn't keep this up. They had been left alone accidentally and someone might enter at any moment. A servant. One of her parents. Her cousin returning.

Still, he wanted more time. More of her.

More . . .

Raking his teeth across her nipple, she gripped his hair, pushing against him. He wanted to touch her core. Bring her a bit of pleasure. But he couldn't. He wouldn't.

He eased her breast back into place and kissed his way up to her beautiful mouth, pausing for one last kiss. Then he broke it and slid her back onto the settee as he stood.

Looking at her brought a myriad of emotions, none of which he wanted to analyze in this moment.

"I broke my promise to you. By kissing you."

She still looked dazed but asked, "Then why did you?"

"I don't know," he lied.

He did know. He'd kissed her because he'd wanted to. No woman had ever affected him the way Addie did.

"I think you do," she said, standing and smoothing her gown. "I suppose it's a good thing you did."

"How so?" he asked suspiciously.

"Tessa has advised both Louisa and me to kiss a few men before we decide on a husband. I suppose it is to give us something to compare to. I have been kissed a few times—but never like this." Her face reddened as she obviously reflected upon what had just occurred between them. "I know now that kissing will be an integral part of marriage. And that I better like the kisses of the man I wed."

She moved away from him. "Thank you, Ev, for helping me to experience what a true kiss should be. And that," she swallowed, "a kiss isn't always on the lips."

"Addie, I—"

"No. I refuse to hear another apology from you. I don't blame you for anything. If anything, I thank you for enlightening me." She clasped her hands in front of her. "As of now, I would suggest that you get to know Lady Minceton and Miss Peterson a little better. Do not bother calling on Lady Bertha or Lady Agatha again. They are too immature for you. Call upon the first two again. Be sure you send flowers this time. Make certain you dance the supper dance with both of them at a ball in the near future. That way, you can spend more time in their company."

She moved toward the door and he followed, feeling bereft.

"Addie, I am sorry for kissing you. I know that . . . complicates matters between us."

Her gaze met his. "Do you intend to make me your duchess?" she boldly asked.

"No," he said reluctantly, knowing they were all wrong for one another.

For a moment, Everett saw the hurt in her eyes. It was gone in a blink.

And he wished he could take back his remark, knowing it had cut her to the quick.

"You need a woman with a cool, steady hand as your duchess. One who is quiet and dignified. One who will manage your many households with ease and have a bit of an air of mystery about her within Polite Society. That is not me. I am lively and outgoing. Not nearly proper or sober enough to be a duchess."

But it was her vivaciousness which drew him to her like a moth to a flame. She was so different from him.

"You will make for a wonderful wife, Addie," he told her. "You are bright and beautiful. Spirited and effervescent. You will be a true asset to your husband."

"I hope so. Just not you, Ev," she said wistfully. Then she stood taller. "I will continue to advise you regarding a bride but insist we are always in the company of others when this takes place." Addie paused. "We really cannot be alone together again. I hope you understand that. I want to remain your friend if that is possible."

He didn't want to be merely friends with her. He wanted to be her lover. Her everything. Somehow, though she seemed wrong for the role of duchess, she was right.

For him.

Everett was never supposed to be a duke. No one would have cast him in that role before he assumed the title through a fluke. Why couldn't Addie be a duchess?

His duchess . . .

"Go home, Ev," she urged. "Look at the list we composed together. Review the qualities you see on it. I am certain we will find a woman who fits your requirements."

He didn't need a bloody list anymore. But he felt Addie distancing herself from him.

"I didn't mean to hurt you."

She looked taken aback. "You didn't. I have discovered that we only truly hurt ourselves."

With that, she opened the door and quickly hurried out.

When they reached the staircase, she paused and asked, "Can you see yourself out?"

He nodded, afraid to speak.

"Then I will see you at tonight's soiree."

She moved away from him and headed up the staircase while he descended to the bottom floor. When he reached the foyer, a footman saw him out.

Everett walked home slowly, contemplating what had occurred. Just because he was staid and earnest, he had thought that is the match he should make. That he should find a woman who was as serious about life as he was. Instead, he was drawn to a woman with a zest for life, one a bit irreverent and outspoken.

One he was attracted to, both in body and mind.

Was it too late to tell her he had changed his mind and that his list was at least partly wrong? That he was mistaken when he thought he needed someone entirely different from her as his duchess?

Everett didn't know if Addie would believe him if he did so.

He realized he might want her but her wanting him was another story. Yes, she responded to his kiss but he was dull. Boring. Retiring. A woman who sparkled as Addie did needed a man who matched her brilliance. Her future husband needed to be as joyous and full of life as she was. If he pursued her, she would feel obligated to him. Knowing the importance Polite Society placed upon titles, even Addie's parents would most likely pressure her to marry him if he offered for her.

No, it wouldn't be right. Tying Addie to him would be like keeping a butterfly from emerging from its cocoon in all its beauty and glory. She should be admired and allowed to radiate that special light that came from within her. He could never be the man she could truly be happy with.

Much as it would hurt, Everett would need to let go of the idea of making Lady Adalyn Goulding his duchess. She deserved better than him. Even though they shared a mutual attraction, it would be for the best. Determination filled him. He needed to decide upon a bride quickly.

That way, Addie would have the freedom to make the choice right for her.

ADALYN WAS SILENT as Bridget chattered away, preparing her for this evening's soiree hosted by Lord and Lady Fowling.

It stung that Ev had come out and told her she had no chance of becoming his duchess. Not that she ever thought she could or even should.

But she had fantasized about it all the same.

At least Ev had been completely honest with her. Given her no false hopes. He didn't try to lead her on. She must accept that what he was looking for in a wife and what she was were as far apart as the Atlantic and Pacific Oceans. She never should have put him on the spot and asked if he intended to make her his duchess. He had never given her that impression and it was wrong of her to even mention it. She hoped she hadn't mucked things up between them beyond repair.

What she had to come to terms with was that a physical attraction existed between them. They had acted upon it a couple of times. She must make certain they never did again. It was already going to be hard enough to even think about kissing a man other than Ev, much less agreeing to wed him.

"There you go, my lady. You are all set to go," Bridget declared.

Adalyn barely glanced into the mirror before she murmured a quiet thank you. Dismissing the maid, she crossed to Louisa's bedchamber, making sure she smiled broadly as she entered the room. No one could know how down she felt. She would give no hint of her mood.

"As always, you do Madame Chevalier's creation justice," she said lightly.

"Do you think so?" Louisa asked, glancing back at her image in the mirror. "It's a rather pretty gown."

"And all the prettier because of the pretty girl who wears it."

Her cousin snorted. "I don't think I would call me a girl, Adalyn. I am three and twenty. Some would say I am already on the shelf."

"Never," Adalyn said, kissing Louisa's cheek.

They arrived at the soiree, which was a much more intimate event than last night's opening ball. Only about eighty guests were expected.

Including Ev.

Going through the receiving line, she greeted Lord and Lady

Fowling and their daughter, Lady Gwenda, who had made her come-out last year. Adalyn didn't care for any member of this family. It was a toss-up who was a bigger gossip, the earl or his countess. Lady Gwenda certainly followed in her parents' footsteps, not only being prone to gossip but having a rather wide mean streak. Avoiding their company would be at the top of Adalyn's list this evening.

Her parents went to join friends and she and Louisa took a turn about the drawing room. Immediately, Ev stood out in a group which included Lady Minceton. A mixture of sadness and jealousy overwhelmed Adalyn as she thought how the pair complemented one another. She could easily see Ev offering for Lady Minceton soon. The young widow would be a good catch, even if she came with a child.

Louisa said, "Your two viscounts are motioning us over."

Sure enough, Lord Bayless and Lord Pierce waved and they joined the pair.

"Can we talk about last night before anyone joins us?" Lord Pierce asked, proceeding to tell Adalyn about the women he had danced with and those he preferred over others.

Lord Bayless did the same, mentioning two ladies in particular that Adalyn had thought would suit him.

"But what is your opinion?" he asked.

Her opinion had changed. Knowing Bayless—and most like Pierce—would be unfaithful to their spouses, she wasn't certain she should meddle anymore, knowing these viscounts' future wives would be in for heartache.

Before she could reply, however, Lady Gwenda and Lord Talflynn joined their circle. The viscount had supposedly been looking for a bride for a good three years now and had even offered for Adalyn. She had turned him down, knowing Lord Talflynn was not only a terrible rake but that he was also petty and small-minded. The way Lady Gwenda clung possessively to his arm, Adalyn thought Talflynn might finally be ready to settle down. The fact that Lady Gwenda's dowry was rumored to be one of the largest among the unattached ladies of the *ton* could be influencing the viscount's decision.

Another couple joined them, as did Ev and Lady Minceton, which didn't stop Lord Bayless at all once everyone had greeted the newcomers.

"So, what do you think, Lady Adalyn?" Lord Bayless inquired. "About my prospects?"

"Your prospects?" Lady Gwenda said, her curiosity obvious.

Lord Talflynn laughed and patted her hand. "I believe we interrupted a conversation about matchmaking, my lady."

"Matchmaking?" Lady Gwenda looked from her to Lord Bayless. "Is Lady Adalyn supplying brides for bachelors now?" she asked and laughed a bit too loud.

"I have helped bring together a few couples during previous Seasons," Adalyn replied.

"Lady Adalyn is being far too modest," Lord Pierce said. "She has had more than her fair share of successes. She is hunting for brides for both Bayless and me. We need to get our heirs, you know."

Lady Gwenda sniffed and gave Adalyn a withering look. "Perhaps you should turn your attentions to yourself—and your poor cousin—since neither of you have ever wed, Lady Adalyn. Both of you are getting rather long in the tooth, wouldn't you say?"

She saw Ev about to speak, knowing he wanted to come to her rescue, but Adalyn had dealt with spiteful women ever since she had made her come-out.

Keeping her composure, she said, "Having had the good fortune of being out for some time, I do know many of the eligible bachelors in Polite Society, Lady Gwenda. I know that will help me make an informed choice in my husband. My cousin will also benefit from my knowledge."

"At least you are still fairly pretty," Lady Gwenda noted. "Your large dowry will also help you land a husband. If you truly seek one this Season."

Lord Talflynn chuckled. "You had better hurry, Lady Adalyn. The bets are all on for this Season."

His comment perplexed her. "What do you mean by that remark, my lord?"

The viscount looked uncomfortable and glanced away without answering her question. Adalyn looked about their circle and saw Lord Pierce and Lord Bayless suddenly interested in looking about the drawing room, as well.

Lady Gwenda smiled smugly, though, and asked, "Oh, you have not heard about the betting book at White's? You have been in it for *ages*. So many gentlemen have lost money they wagered on you since you have never wed. I have heard the betting has gone crazy this year since it is public knowledge that you finally do plan to wed."

Adalyn felt her cheeks burn in humiliation. She had heard of the White's betting book but only that it involved silly bets.

Not ones involving a lady's reputation.

"If you will excuse me," she said, leaving the circle and the drawing room itself, rushing down the stairs and stopping, unsure where to go. She only knew she needed to be alone and collect her thoughts before butting heads with Lady Gwenda again, which was a certainty.

She spied a passing footman and called out to him. "Where is your garden?"

"This way, my lady," he said, leading her to a set of French doors.

"Thank you."

She entered the garden and because it was only dimly lit, she paused at a bench just a few steps into it. Sitting, she breathed deeply, trying to quell the emotions rumbling within her. Wondering how long she had been a part of the betting book filled her mind. Was she a laughingstock that others gossiped about behind her back? She had never thought so. Then again, Lady Gwenda was the child of malicious gossips so it shouldn't surprise her at what the woman had revealed.

"Is something troubling you, Lady Adalyn?"

She looked up and saw Lord Rosewell standing before her.

"Go away," she told him.

He didn't leave. Instead, he took a seat on the bench.

"I wish to be alone, my lord."

He clucked his tongue. "You look as if you need some company."

"Not yours," she muttered loudly enough for him to hear and he chuckled. "I don't need your company or anyone's right now."

"It seems you have tangled with Lady Gwenda," he noted. "I heard the end of her conversation. About the wager regarding you."

"I never knew of it," she said hotly, her face flaming at the mention of the book.

He brushed the back of his hand along her cheek. "Why don't we make a few souls who have wagered on you happy? Wed me, Adalyn."

She bristled at him using her name so informally. "I told you, Lord Rosewell, I am not interested in becoming your countess."

His hands suddenly squeezed her shoulders. "You should be. I am considered quite the catch. Handsome. Wealthy."

"And I told you that you aren't marriage material. At least not for me."

His fingers tightened and she winced. "Wed me to quiet the gossips, Adalyn. Let me get an heir off you." He smiled. "Then we can each do as we please. You can take as many lovers as you choose while I do the same."

She only wanted Ev and knew that could never come to pass. She wondered if she was truly meant to wed at all.

"Thank you for your offer, my lord, but I do not want a marriage with you."

Now, he gripped her painfully and she gasped. "But I want one with you."

His mouth slammed down on hers and Adalyn pushed hard against his chest, trying to break the kiss. Lord Rosewell tried to force her lips open as she struggled to escape.

Suddenly, the earl was gone.

She looked up to see Ev had arrived and pulled Lord Rosewell off her. Ev slammed his fist into her attacker's face and blood gushed from his nose. Ev angrily pushed the earl away and he fell to the ground.

With hate flashing in his eyes, Lord Rosewell said, "You will be sorry, Camden." He pushed himself to his feet and pulled out a handkerchief to brush the blood from his face. "As it is, you may congratulate me."

Glancing to Adalyn, the earl smiled triumphantly and revealed, "I now have my fiancée."

"What?" she gasped.

"Why, dear girl, we have been caught in an embrace by the Duke of Camden, one of the most powerful men in Polite Society. He will be the first to acknowledge that you are ruined. Naturally, being a gentleman, I will wed you quickly. It's the right thing to do."

Ev crossed his arms. "Since I am the only one who witnessed this—and will never say anything about the incident—Lady Adalyn's reputation is still intact." He paused and then spoke again, his tone deadly. "I suggest you leave the soiree, Rosewell. I wouldn't want the ladies present to see your pretty nose all out of joint. Perhaps it will give you some character now. Perfection is so bland."

"I do not need your confirmation of this kiss, Camden," Rosewell said tersely. "All I have to do is make mention of it within my circle of friends—and let them know I *want* word of our tryst to become public. If anyone asks, I will freely admit that Lady Adalyn and I were carried away by passion and kissed. That we are now betrothed and planning our wedding." He smiled smugly. "There isn't a thing you can do about it, Your Grace. I have won the prize I sought."

Tears sprang to Adalyn's eyes, knowing the earl would do exactly as he said. She would be trapped in not merely a loveless marriage but one that started in mistrust and hatred. The future she had once looked forward to would now be like a death sentence.

Except it would go on until either Rosewell or she was dead and buried.

Then Ev's hands shot out, latching on to the earl's lapels, jerking Rosewell close until their noses practically touched.

"You are never to mention this incident," Ev growled, his eyes narrowing, his tone deadly. "I will not see Lady Adalyn's life ruined by you forcing her to wed you."

The duke paused and she saw how he barely restrained his rage.

"I am a duke," he continued. "A *duke*. A man you should never tangle with. I have the power. The position. The wealth. The friends. Everything it would take to break you. If you dare to ruin Lady Adalyn, Rosewell, then I will destroy you ten times over. I will see that you lose everything. Your estates. Your fortune. Your name. I won't stop until I see you in rags, begging for a hard crust of bread."

Lord Rosewell's jaw fell open. No words came out. Adalyn saw the fear in them, knowing the earl realized this duke would do exactly as he promised.

Ev released Rosewell, shoving him back.

"My apologies, Your Grace. I will keep silent."

Ev glared at the earl. "You should be apologizing to Lady Adalyn."

Rosewell turned to her, a defeated man. "My lady, I offer my sincere apology to you. I beg that you accept it."

"As long as you never speak to me—or His Grace—ever again, then I will accept it," she said dismissively.

"Thank you, my lady. Your Grace." Lord Rosewell made a quick exit. Relief swept through her, knowing she would not be shackled to the wicked earl.

"Thank you, Ev," she said quietly. "If anyone but you had seen us together, I would have had to marry him. You have saved me from a miserable existence."

She leaned up and brushed a quick kiss along his cheek to thank him.

But Ev caught her elbows and turned so that her mouth touched his.

And the world exploded in fire.

CHAPTER FIFTEEN

EVERETT SLIPPED HIS arms about Addie as he devoured her mouth. He had thought to offer her comfort, knowing how hurt she must be at learning of the betting book at White's and the wagers placed upon her. She was a confident, proud woman but he had seen her hurt and humiliation as that awful Lady Gwenda gleefully spoke about the bet so casually.

He also knew Addie had meant to give him a brief kiss, thanking him for protecting her and her reputation from the nasty Lord Rosewell. He hadn't liked the man from their very first meeting and now would claim him as a sworn enemy for trying to force Addie's hand and make her his wife.

As he kissed this woman, Everett tried to convey the depth of his feelings for her. He knew it was love. He had been an idiot not to tell her before. He had hurt her but that would stop. Here. Now. He needed to show her how precious she was to him.

And ask her to be his wife.

He broke the kiss to do that very thing, his breathing hard from their encounter. Addie's dazed face was so very beautiful that he almost resumed kissing her again. But first, the proposal. Everett didn't know exactly how to start.

That hesitation cost him dearly.

She jerked away and took a step back to put distance between them. She was panting.

"Ev, this is foolish," she declared. "I know there is some odd attraction between us but we must douse the flame. We cannot be seen like this. It would be the same situation as I was in with Lord Rosewell. If someone stumbled upon us, I would be ruined."

She shook her head. "You would do the honorable thing and wed me since you are a gentleman but we both know I am not the woman you want for your duchess."

Before he could reject her claim, Addie rushed away. He knew following her could lead to danger and gossip, things she was trying to avoid. As it was, she had already been gone from the soiree for too long. With both Rosewell and him also absent, gossip might already be occurring.

He took his time in returning to the house, entering and climbing the stairs, trying to think of an excuse as to why he had absented himself at the same time Addie had. Then he saw Lord Uxbridge coming down the corridor and stopped to chat with him for several minutes. Everett asked the earl's advice on a financial matter, which pleased Uxbridge to no end. Then they began discussing the younger Uxbridge brother's work for the War Office and how Sir Edgar had left England recently with a contingent of others in order to attend the upcoming congress in Vienna.

The pair returned to the drawing room, taking glasses of port to sip on as they continued their conversation. A few other gentlemen drifted toward them and Everett held court for over an hour, deliberately sharing war stories and keeping the men's attention.

Finally, he said, "We don't want the ladies to think we have abandoned them."

The group broke up, going several different ways. Everett had located Addie the moment he returned to the drawing room and had kept a watchful eye on her until now. Intentionally, he gave her a wide berth, talking with as many other guests as he could, even for a time politely listening to Lord Talflynn go on and on as Lady Gwenda hung upon his every word.

Finally, guests began moving toward the door. He was grateful the evening had come to an end. He thanked Lord and Lady Fowling for inviting him and returned to his carriage.

On the way home, Everett decided on a bold scheme. If ruining Addie is what it would take to be able to wed her, by God he would do it.

>>>><<<<

THE NEXT DAY, Everett rose, allowing Roper to tend to him. The valet had learned to work in silence, only asking the occasional question of Everett. Once dressed, he went downstairs for breakfast and then went to his study, where he summoned Mr. Johnson, his secretary.

"What does my social calendar look like for the next few days?" he asked.

"There is a garden party this afternoon, Your Grace, followed by a ball this evening."

"You have responded to both in the affirmative?"

"I have, Your Grace. Do you wish to change your plans?"

"I do. Send my regrets to the garden party but I will attend the ball this evening."

"Of course, Your Grace."

Once Johnson had left, he rang for Bailey and had the butler summon his carriage for a trip to White's.

Inside, Everett was greeted by the affable Mr. Orr.

"Good morning, Your Grace. It is good to see you again. Might you wish for the newspapers? Coffee?"

He wanted neither but decided if he was to draw the proper amount of attention, he needed to stay instead of scribbling in the betting book and leaving.

"I wish for both, Mr. Orr. Thank you."

Everett told the host where he could be found and moved to

the room, greeting the few he knew by name. He made himself comfortable and, almost immediately, a servant brought him several of the daily newspapers, while another brought a tray with coffee. His preferences had obviously been noted because the brewed beverage included just the right amount of sugar. He made certain to stay for an hour, perusing the newspapers and speaking to those who passed.

Then the two young viscounts, Pierce and Bayless, appeared and asked if they could sit with him.

"Certainly, gentlemen," he said graciously.

Coffee was brought to both men and then Everett asked the servant delivering it, "Would you please bring me the betting book?"

"At once, Your Grace."

His companions' eyes widened and Bayless asked, "Are you going to place a bet, Your Grace?" Then with a sly smile, he added, "Or looking to see the ones placed on Lady Adalyn?"

Everett did his best to stare down the young pup until he cringed and looked away. He returned to his newspaper, not focusing enough to read a word but pretending to do so all the same.

The servant returned with the betting book and placed it on the table. "Is there anything else you might need, Your Grace?"

"Not at the moment. Thank you."

Everett made a great show of opening the book and looking at several pages until he stopped at the one reserved for Adalyn. It was actually more than one. Several new wagers had been placed since it seemed apparent she was intending to wed this Season.

He signaled the same servant and asked him to bring a quill and ink so that he might place a bet of his own.

"What are you going to place a wager on, Your Grace?" asked a subdued Pierce.

Everett smiled enigmatically.

When the servant returned with the requested items, Everett thanked him and then dipped the quill into the ink. He scribbled his wager into the book as the servant and now Mr. Orr himself stood nearby.

Placing the famous betting book on the table before him, he said, "Allow the ink to dry," as he rose and sauntered away, knowing at least half those present in White's were watching his every move.

Then he heard Bayless loudly proclaim, "Camden has bet that Lady Adalyn will be engaged by the end of today!"

As Everett passed others, they started asking if he had knowledge of something. He merely shrugged, hoping he looked mysterious, and heard the movement behind him. As he reached the doorway to the room, he glanced over his shoulder and saw the mad scramble to the betting book, knowing wagers would now be flying left and right.

Returning home, he dashed off a note to Lord Uxbridge, asking if he might accompany the Uxbridge family to tonight's ball and escort Lady Adalyn inside. He even offered to retrieve them in his carriage, knowing the earl wouldn't be able to resist arriving at a ball with a duke. Everett had a footman deliver the note and within an hour he had received a reply. Uxbridge wrote that he and Lady Uxbridge would be delighted to be in the duke's company and he would inform his daughter of the plan.

Everett smiled.

At the appropriate time, he went to his coach and instructed his driver to first stop at the Uxbridge townhouse before proceeding to Lord Starfeld's residence, where tonight's ball would take place. He climbed from the carriage and went to the door, greeting Lord and Lady Uxbridge as Adalyn and Louisa looked on.

"I am delighted you could accompany me this evening," he told the married couple.

"Anything for you, Your Grace," Lady Uxbridge said with a smile before glancing at her daughter. "Uxbridge says you wish to escort our daughter into the ball."

"With your permission, my lady," he said gallantly.

"Come along, girls," Uxbridge called out and then took his wife to the carriage.

Everett offered his arms to the two cousins and they followed. He handed up Louisa first and then gave Addie his hand.

She frowned. "Why are you doing this? No one saw me with Lord Rosewell."

"We had talked about me escorting you to a few events in order to draw attention to you if you recall. You agreed to me doing so."

"I do remember." Reluctance filled her face.

"I know it is difficult to be in my company, Addie. But you aren't to be embarrassed anymore over the betting book at White's. I forbid it."

She chuckled. "Because a duke says it, then I suppose I must fall in line."

She stepped into the carriage and he followed.

They spoke of the garden party that afternoon, telling him about it since he had missed attending it.

"I had business that needed my attention," he offered as an excuse.

As they exited the carriage and moved toward the Starfeld townhouse, he made certain Addie was on his arm and that Louisa was led in by her uncle and aunt.

"We will dance the opening number and the supper dance," he informed her. "That should draw sufficient attention and see that your programme quickly fills. Though I know it does at every ball."

She shrugged. "I enjoy dancing and try to dance every number."

Addie would do more than dance to an orchestra this evening.

She would dance to his tune.

The opening number was a spirited country dance. By the time it finished and he escorted her to the sidelines, he saw the color in her cheeks and the sparkle was back in her eyes. He knew those eyes would be full of anger later this evening, anger directed at him. Still, it would be worth it. They would have a lifetime to make up.

"I will see you in a few hours," Everett told her.

He danced a few times, knowing she would be watching. Deliberately, he did not sign Lady Minceton or Miss Peterson's dance cards, not wanting to lead either woman on. They were both quite nice and if not for his love for Addie, he might have found happiness with one of them.

When the supper dance arrived, he was thrilled to learn it was a waltz. He was growing in confidence with the dance and enjoyed the minutes he was allowed to hold Addie close. She seemed to understand his wish for silence and they simply enjoyed the dance.

When he led her into supper, he took her to a table for two and seated her.

"We are drawing more attention than we should by sitting apart from others," she said hesitantly.

"You don't wish to be seen with me?"

"No, Ev. It is not that. Sitting alone together, though, will cause talk. I do not wish for it to hinder your efforts with other women. How are your pursuits going?"

He motioned for a servant and asked for him to go through the buffet for them. The footman readily agreed. Now, he truly had Addie to himself, far from the other guests.

"As I have told you, I have not committed to any of them. They are still strangers to me."

"I noticed you did not dance with Lady Minceton."

"Nor Miss Peterson," he added.

"Why?" she asked.

"Can we talk about something else?" he pleaded.

She studied him. "I have found a few others who might suit you if you have decided against Lady Minceton or Miss Peterson. Perhaps you could come see me tomorrow and we might discuss them."

Wanting to appease her—for now—he agreed.

Finally, they talked of other things. Addie really knew quite a bit about current events. Everett didn't think she gave herself enough credit.

She seemed to be picking at her food and so he asked, "Would you care to take a brief stroll on the balcony before supper ends?" He tugged at his cravat. "It is rather warm in here."

Always one to please others, something he had counted on, she said, "Of course."

A few other couples were also leaving and Ev followed them, leading Addie back to the ballroom and exiting through the French doors onto the terrace. He had made certain as they left that he caught Lady Gwenda's eye and nodded graciously to her and Lord Talflynn, her supper partner. He had learned the woman to be a gossip and had witnessed firsthand at last night's soiree how she tried to cut Addie to the quick. Though he felt moderately guilty for what he was about to do, he was counting on Lady Gwenda's innate curiosity to help see things through.

Only one other couple was outside and they looked guilty as Everett and Addie passed them. They quickly said hello and then ducked back inside the ballroom.

He strolled with her the length of the terrace and paused at the end, looking up at the bright moon.

She glanced up in the sky. "It's lovely, isn't it?"

"Not as lovely as you," he replied.

Everett captured her waist in his hands and her mouth with his. She froze a moment and then gave in to the kiss, sighing. He kissed her deeply, becoming lost in her taste and scent. She was wrong. It wasn't some attraction between them that would fade over time. His need for her engulfed him, like a living, breathing thing. He poured himself into the kiss, wanting his actions to show her what he had been too timid to speak of last night.

Then he heard a loud gasp, causing the fog his brain had been in to clear.

Everett broke the kiss and looked to see they had an audience of four. As he suspected, Lady Gwenda and Lord Talflynn were present. Accompanying them were her parents, Lord and Lady Fowling. He had witnessed Lord Fowling spreading gossip at White's and recalled Fowling was one of the first to reach the betting book after Everett had placed his own wager earlier today.

He sensed the tension in Addie and relaxed his grip on her waist but still kept his hands on it. With an apologetic smile, he said, "Please forgive me. I allowed my exuberance to overcome me. Lady Adalyn has just agreed to be my duchess. We are newly betrothed."

"Oh!" Lady Fowling said as her husband looked on with interest. "Well, I suppose we are the first to offer you felicitations."

"Yes, Your Grace," Lord Fowling said. "Our very best to you and Lady Adalyn."

Lady Gwenda looked put out and merely nodded, while Lord Talflynn said, "It seems you actually did find a husband after all, Lady Adalyn. You even looked stunned to have done so."

Everett didn't like the viscount's snide tone.

"If you will give us a moment so we may compose ourselves, we will see you inside the ballroom," he suggested.

The four understood his dismissal and left.

"Why did you tell them that?" Addie hissed when they were out of earshot. "This is all wrong."

"I thought it better to say than having you face being ruined."

"But it will force you to wed me," she said, tears brimming in her eyes. Then she shook her head, determination settling over her. "I cannot allow you to do this to yourself, Ev."

"It's already been done," he said firmly. "I cannot take it back. Even if I wanted to. Come, we should return to the ballroom."

He released her waist reluctantly, wishing he could stay and kiss her some more but knowing he had already pushed the boundary of good manners.

"Let us go find your parents."

CHAPTER SIXTEEN

MISERY FLOODED ADALYN as Ev escorted her from the terrace to the ballroom. She made certain not to show it, however. When they came through the door, she had a smile on her face.

Even if she had no plans to become the Duchess of Camden.

Adalyn knew she was not the woman Ev envisioned as his wife. She knew because of what was on his list. Not to mention he had specifically told her he would not make her his duchess.

She planned to keep to that.

As she saw Spencer and Tessa approaching them, she knew word had already begun to spread, thanks to the gossiping Fowlings and their mean-spirited daughter. Lord Talflynn, too. She had turned him down before and now he was gleeful in making known the awkward situation she had found herself in.

It didn't matter. She had no plans to wed Ev. He was too much a gentleman to ever beg off their supposed betrothal. She, however, was enough of a lady to make sure he would not be bound to her for the next several decades. Of course, breaking their engagement would leave her reputation in tatters. It was ironic that if a man severed an engagement, his former fiancée suffered society's wrath. If she ended the betrothal, she was ostracized. Women couldn't seem to be treated fairly no matter what the situation. But she would not see through a marriage with Ev. Though she did love him, she would not tie him to her because she couldn't bear to see how unhappy he would become.

When the moment was right, she would break it off with him. She might have to wait a bit or else it would reflect poorly upon Louisa. A woman's actions, especially a broken engagement, caused gossip to run rampant about her and her entire family. She couldn't risk Louisa's chances at happiness. She thought Ev and she could be engaged throughout the Season. By the end, hopefully Louisa would have found a husband. While others were away from London, Adalyn would break her own engagement and ensure Louisa had her wedding. Next Season, some gossip would abound once it was made known that she and Ev had not followed through with their plans. By then, Louisa would be safely wed.

And Adalyn would deal with being excluded from most of Polite Society.

"Is it true?" Tessa asked, reaching them. "Are you betrothed?" Hope filled her eyes.

"Yes," Ev said. "We are. Addie was right in front of me all this time and I was wise enough to finally realize it."

"Addie?" Tessa said, frowning at the nickname.

Spencer offered Ev his hand and shook it, then threw an arm about him. "You sly fox. Sitting in the henhouse, you plucked a bride. I knew it was nonsense, all this having Adalyn find you a bride. You were perfectly capable of doing so yourself."

"Addie?" Tessa repeated.

Ev smiled. "It is my name for her. Mine alone—so don't steal it from me, Tessa." He glanced to her. "We should go find your parents. Hopefully, our good news hasn't reached them yet and we can share it in person."

"Excuse us," she said stiffly, allowing Ev to lead her from the ballroom.

They came across her parents and Louisa. Mama beamed at her. Louisa smiled shyly. Papa looked pleased.

"I see I am welcoming a son into the family," Papa said. "So, you are betrothed."

"Only if you and Lady Uxbridge give us your permission, my lord," Ev said. "It seems I am doing things a bit backward and should have sought your permission first."

Papa smiled. "I cannot think of a finer son-in-law. But Adalyn knows her own mind. She is of age. You do not need our permission as long as you have hers." He looked to her and she gave him a weak smile.

"Are you all right, Adalyn?" Mama asked. "You look a bit pale. I am sure this was quite a surprise to you but it certainly isn't to Uxbridge or me. Why, I told him after the first time His Grace came to tea with us that I simply knew the two of you were made for each other."

Dread filled Adalyn, hearing those words. She had known her mother had hopes of an engagement with the duke. She wanted to shout at everyone to stop talking and tell them all the marriage would never take place. She kept quiet, though. For Louisa's sake.

Louisa took her hand. "I am so happy for you, Adalyn." She looked up to Ev. "And to you also, Your Grace. Now, I have two brothers, in you and Spencer."

"Everett," he corrected. "We are going to be family."

"Everett," Louisa repeated, smiling at him.

After that, they were flooded with good wishes by the entire *ton*. Adalyn hoped her dance partners forgave her because she didn't dance one number the rest of the night, being busy receiving congratulations from everyone. Lord and Lady Starfeld seemed the most pleased by the announcement.

"To think that the first betrothal of the Season occurred at our ball," Lady Starfeld said in awe. "And a duke's proposal, no less. Why, our ball will be the talk of the *ton* for weeks to come."

The final number ended and they joined the crush of those leaving the ball. Every eye remained on them and Adalyn smiled until her cheeks ached.

They arrived at Ev's carriage and he handed her up, with the others joining her.

"We must talk about the wedding tomorrow," Mama said. "I would venture Tessa will want to hold the wedding breakfast. You will need to tell her all your favorite foods, Your Grace. And Uxbridge, you must go with His Grace and see about booking St. George's for the wedding." Mama looked at Adalyn. "Do you have a date in mind, dear?"

"I was thinking—"

"A quick wedding," Ev said, speaking over her. "I would prefer purchasing a special license but if Addie wants the banns read, I suppose I can wait the three weeks for us to be wed."

He took her gloved hand and raised it to his lips, kissing her fingers tenderly.

"But we need time to prepare, Camden," Mama insisted and then laughed. "Oh, what am I saying? To be young and in love. Of course, you want to wed soon. But I do hope it will be at St. George's. I have always envisioned Adalyn wedding there."

Ev held her gaze as well as her hand and asked, "If the chapel is available, how about a week from today?"

Adalyn felt as if she had lost all control of the situation.

It seemed he took her silence for consent and looked back at her parents. "A week it is, then. Lord Uxbridge, would you accompany me to St. George's after breakfast tomorrow? We can confirm the date and then call at Doctors' Commons and purchase the special license."

"A sound plan, Camden," Papa said.

Ev continued holding her hand the entire way home, with neither Mama nor Papa scolding him for doing so. She turned her head and stared out the window, too numb to say anything.

The carriage pulled up at their townhouse and Ev finally released her hand, climbing down first and helping the others before aiding her. He took her by the waist and swung her to the ground, his hands lingering.

"I hope you are happy, Addie." He bent and brushed a quick kiss against her lips.

What was she to do? She could ruin her life and his by going through with the marriage. Or ruin Louisa's because of the scandal that would follow once she broke her betrothal.

"Are you certain you would not prefer a longer engagement?" she asked hesitantly.

"That is the last thing I want," he said. "We want to be wed quickly and put any gossip behind us. I do not trust Lady Gwenda nor Lord Talflynn, much less Lord and Lady Fowling."

Ev was right. If they did not wed soon, who knew what those four might circulate through the *ton*.

She took a deep breath knowing the die had been cast.

"Next week at St. George's will be fine," she said primly.

Her fiancé escorted her to the door. "After your father and I accomplish our errands, I will stop by to see you. If I may."

He looked so boyish and eager that, for a moment, Adalyn forgot how this marriage would ruin both of their lives.

"Of course, you may call."

He gave her a crooked grin. "It might be before noon," he warned.

"I am sure Mama and I can overlook that," she said, smiling weakly at his attempt at humor. "You are taking this quite well, being forced into marriage with me."

Ev's gaze was intense. "No one has forced me to do anything."

Of course, he would say that. Above all, Ev was a gentleman.

"Goodnight," she said crisply and turned away before he felt the need to bestow an obligatory kiss.

"Goodnight, Addie," he called out as she entered the foyer.

Louisa waited for her and linked an arm with Adalyn as they mounted the stairs.

"So, Everett chose you." Louisa's eyes glimmered with tears. "I am so happy at this outcome. I think you will be perfect together."

She didn't reply, the knot in her throat growing.

They reached their rooms and her cousin told her goodnight.

Adalyn opened the door to her bedchamber and found Bridget waiting for her.

"Please undress me quickly," she said. "I feel a headache coming on."

"Yes, my lady."

The maid had Adalyn prepared for bed in no time. She watched Bridget leave and then climbed beneath the bedclothes, blowing out the candle.

Only then did the tears come.

***

EVERETT CALLED UPON Lord Uxbridge the next morning during breakfast, disappointed that Addie wasn't at the meal.

"Cheer up, Camden," the earl said. "I can tell by that unhappy look on your face that you were hoping for a glimpse of your new fiancée. Adalyn is like her mother. They rarely rise before noon during the Season and always take their breakfast in their bedchamber before they dress for the day."

He disliked hearing that. While he was attending balls and parties because it was expected, he longed to return to Cliffside and escape the social crush. It was hard for him to picture Addie outside of London. She sparkled at every event. Guilt ran deep through him, knowing he had trapped her into marriage.

What if the physical attraction between them wasn't enough? What if they were doomed to be exactly as his parents were, growing to loathe one another? His parents rarely attended the same events. They sometimes spent months apart. Following the same pattern was the last thing Everett wanted to do.

Yet he had known before he manipulated Addie into marriage that they were two very different people. That he wasn't good enough for her. Selfishly, he had pushed those feelings aside, thinking if he loved her enough for the both of them she would come around.

What if she never did?

Lord Uxbridge rose. "We should be off to St. George's."

"Is it far?" Everett asked.

"You most likely have passed it, Your Grace, though not the street itself. The church is in the middle of Mayfair off Conduit Street. People say it is in Hanover Square but it is not Hanover Square proper. It is on George's Street, which is rather quiet."

"My carriage is outside if you wish to take it, my lord."

Uxbridge brightened. "I would be delighted to travel in your ducal carriage."

They boarded the vehicle and were at the church within minutes, meeting with a curate who gave them a brief tour of the church since Everett had never visited before.

"Everyone in Polite Society attends this parish church," the curate assured him. "I know our vicar will be happy to marry you and Lady Adalyn. She and her parents have attended St. George's for years."

"We are looking at next Thursday," Lord Uxbridge said. "Or any day after that which is open."

The curate smiled. "We are happy to accommodate His Grace and Lady Adalyn next Thursday, my lord. It is so early in the Season that the rash of weddings have yet to begin." He turned to Everett. "Halfway through the Season, the weddings begin in earnest. Sometimes we host two or even three a day," the curate declared. "You will be our first society match this Season. Do you have a time in mind?"

Everett looked to his soon to be father-in-law for help and the earl said, "Anything before noon and my wife and daughter would have my head on a platter. Shall we say two o'clock?"

"I shall mark two o'clock on our schedule, my lord."

They left and Everett told his driver their next stop was Doctors' Commons.

"Where is that?" the coachman asked, reminding Everett that Mervyn had never requested to be driven there. His brother, rake that he was, might not have wed for years if he had lived.

"South of St. Paul's Cathedral. On Knightrider Street," Uxbridge responded.

He was glad he had asked the earl to come along this morning, especially when they arrived at Doctors' Commons. Navigating the bureaucracy within the place proved frustrating, as well as time-consuming.

Finally, after moving from one office to another and a wait close to two hours, they were admitted to the authorized representative of the Archbishop of Canterbury. Everett had thought to obtain a special license he would have to speak with the archbishop himself but learned that wasn't the case.

After being asked a few questions, the representative established that the Duke of Camden and Lady Adalyn Goulding were eligible to wed and placed both their names on the special license. He was told that the license allowed them to wed in any location at any time, without the banns having to be called. He then paid a clerk a hefty sum for this privilege and the license was presented to Everett.

In his carriage, talk turned to the marriage settlements.

"I know you are wedding rather quickly, Camden, but we must see the contracts signed before the ceremony takes place. Have you notified your solicitor of your upcoming marriage?"

He hadn't thought to do so and merely said, "No, my lord. What is involved?"

"You and I, along with our solicitors, will need to meet together as soon as possible to arrange this. When we return home, I can send footmen to each of our solicitors. Are you free tomorrow? The sooner we start, the better. Although I doubt there will be any problems, sometimes these things can take time."

"Yes, tomorrow is fine, my lord. Whenever it is convenient for you. Is there anything I need to know going into this? Having been in the army, I never thought to wed and am unaware of my role in these contract negotiations."

"I see." Uxbridge paused a moment. "The marriage settlements are sometimes referred to as marriage articles. They will establish the financial agreements regarding your marriage to Adalyn. They include what will happen to her dowry, which I will tell you is quite substantial."

He chuckled. "I assure you, my lord, that I am not marrying Addie for her dowry."

Uxbridge smiled. "I know. They will also dictate the terms of her pin money and establish her income in the event she becomes a widow. Your heir, naturally, will inherit your title and all entailed properties, but a properly executed marriage settlement will provide for the other children that result from your union. That will include the amount to be set aside for your future daughters' dowries."

Baffled, he said, "But we do not know how many daughters we will have."

"The amount still needs to be stipulated in the settlements," Uxbridge insisted. "The more girls you have, the arranged sum will need to be divided. Not evenly, though. That is left to your discretion. However, you may add to the dowries during your lifetime, Your Grace, if you so choose though that is not a requirement."

"Have no fear, Lord Uxbridge. Your granddaughters will be well taken care of."

The earl smiled. "Having only one daughter, I am especially partial to girls. It is good to hear you say this, Camden."

"Might I ask what pin money is? You mentioned it earlier."

"Ah, that is the money Adalyn is able to spend without having to answer to you. Some wives use their pin money to purchase their annual wardrobes."

The thought of Addie having to pay for her own clothes appalled him. "Once again, my lord, I will assure you that I will pay for everything Addie needs or wants."

"Still, a provision for pin money will be written into the settlements," the earl insisted. "Adalyn should not have to come to you for money to buy a book or parasol."

Everett nodded. "So, this pin money gives her a bit of independence."

"Exactly."

They arrived at the Uxbridge townhouse and Rainey, the butler, met them. Lord Uxbridge instructed him to send footmen to both his and Everett's solicitors, asking each man to call tomorrow morning at eleven o'clock in order to begin hammering out the marriage contracts. Everett didn't think any hammering would be necessary. Whatever Addie's father wanted in the contracts, he would make certain it appeared.

The two men went upstairs to the drawing room. It was much later than Everett had thought it would be since the wait at Doctors' Common had been so long.

Entering the room, he saw Addie sitting with two gentlemen, talking animatedly. A surge of jealousy rushed through him at the sight. She glanced in his direction and he hoped he might receive one of those special, secret smiles that he saw Tessa bestow upon Spencer. Instead, her smile faltered and she quickly returned her focus to her guests.

As he made his way toward her, he saw her cousin seated beside her and realized the two gentlemen must be callers for Louisa. Both women rose and the two men did the same.

"Ah, Your Grace," Addie said formally. "How nice to see you."

She smiled at him—but the smile did not reach her eyes.

CHAPTER SEVENTEEN

"LET ME INTRODUCE you," Addie continued, naming the two guests, who greeted Everett and then thanked both women for allowing them to call this afternoon.

Rainey hovered at the door and helped guide the visitors from the drawing room. Everett turned to Addie.

"Louisa had five callers this afternoon," she told him.

He glanced to Louisa. "That is good to hear. I hope you enjoyed their company."

"Your Grace," called Lady Uxbridge. "Do come over here. The teacart will arrive soon."

He accompanied the cousins to where Lord and Lady Uxbridge sat. Addie took a seat on a settee and he joined her, getting a whiff of vanilla, which made Everett wish they could share a few minutes alone so that he might explore that further.

"I have asked Tessa and Middlefield to tea," the countess revealed. "There are wedding plans that must be made. Uxbridge told me you were able to arrange for the wedding to occur next Thursday at St. George's."

"Yes, my lady. Two o'clock." He turned to Addie. "If that suits you."

She nodded.

"It took a good while to purchase a special license," Uxbridge said. "They don't make it easy on these young fellows. We went from office to office and had an excruciating wait."

"You did get it, though?" Lady Uxbridge asked, worry creasing her brow.

"We did," her husband confirmed.

"Lord and Lady Middlefield," Rainey announced and Spence and Tessa came through the doorway, Spence holding Analise in the crook of one arm.

"Hello, everyone," Tessa said as she came forward and greeted the group.

Spence smoothed his daughter's hair, which was sticking up a bit, and thrust Analise toward him, saying, "Why don't you hold her, Ev?"

Suddenly, Everett found a baby in his arms and found himself terrified.

"What if I drop her?" he asked worriedly, glancing from Analise to Spence and back at the baby again.

"Did you drop your rifle when you charged into battle and bullets were flying about you?" Spence asked. "You won't drop her. Just be sure to support her head and neck. Her neck is getting stronger every day," he said, pride evident on his face.

Everett gazed at the baby he held. A flood of warmth rushed through him. Analise looked back at him as if puzzled by this new person who held her.

"How are you, Analise?" Everett asked softly. "It is your Uncle Ev. The man who tries his best—next to your mother—to keep your father in line."

Tessa laughed. "It is a two-person job," she agreed.

The teacart arrived and cups of tea were passed around. He had Addie set his on the table, knowing he didn't have the skills to balance a saucer with a teacup and manage a baby at the same time.

As the conversation progressed, he barely listened, all his focus on Analise. This time next year he might actually be holding his and Addie's daughter or son. The thought caused his throat to grow thick with emotion.

Then Everett longed to see his betrothed with a child in her arms. Turning, he said, "Would you like to hold her now?"

Addie's eyes lit up as she glanced down at the baby, who had fallen asleep. "Yes. Please."

She placed her saucer on the table and he transferred Analise into her arms. For a moment, he just gazed at the pair. A tranquility settled over him, a feeling deep and peaceful, one he had never known. Addie looked so right with a babe in her arms. He hoped that she would want many children. It was just one of the many things they needed to discuss with one another.

Privately.

Everett needed to address the list they had composed together. How he had thought he wanted one kind of woman and had completely changed his mind—because of her. He felt unsettled, not having told Addie that he loved her. She had come across so cold when he first arrived. He would make things right between them, given the time to do so.

Tessa asked him about what he wanted served at the wedding breakfast so he assumed that she and Spence had volunteered to hold it at their townhouse.

He shrugged. "I really don't care, Tessa. Having been in the army several years, anything your cook makes will be an improvement. I swear, sometimes I thought we were eating boiled shoe leather that they pretended was meat."

Addie placed a hand on his arm. "I am sorry to hear that. But you must have a few favorite dishes you enjoy that can be served."

"What do you want?" he asked.

"Cake," she said succinctly. "I have a fierce sweet tooth. I truly do not care what is served as long as there is plenty of cake."

He burst out laughing and the others joined in.

Wiping his eyes, he told Tessa, "Make certain there are three kinds of cake for my bride. I want her to have her choice—and her fill." He looked to Addie and said, "Chocolate, for one. Shall we say raspberry for another? And what about lemon?"

She nodded her approval. "I will be sampling some of all."

They talked about how it would be only family at the wedding ceremony and the women discussed the types of flowers to use in decorating the church. He paid particular attention to what Addie wanted and learned that daffodils were her favorite blooms.

Talk moved to which gown she would wear and he asked Spence what he was supposed to show up wearing since he had no idea, having never attended a wedding before he went to his own.

"We will go to your tailor tomorrow," his friend said. "I can help you there."

"I am meeting Lord Uxbridge here tomorrow morning, along with our solicitors, so that we can arrange for the marriage settlements," Everett shared. "Can we see the tailor late tomorrow afternoon?"

"I'll send a note around tomorrow morning, telling him what is needed and that we will see him late afternoon," Spence said.

By now, Addie was handing Analise to Louisa, who had begged for a turn to hold the babe.

Louisa settled Analise against her and asked, "What of a honeymoon? Will you embark upon one after the Season ends?"

He hadn't thought of a honeymoon at all and glanced to Addie. "Is there somewhere in particular you would care for us to go?"

"What is your primary ducal estate?" she asked.

"Cliffside. In Kent."

Addie turned to Louisa. "We will go to Cliffside the day after our wedding."

Louisa frowned. "You won't finish out the Season? I had hopes that you would continue to steer me through it."

"No, I think that going to Kent is what we will do," Addie said firmly. "I need to get to know about Ev's country seat and learn about his tenants."

"But you have always loved the Season," Tessa said. "Surely, you can stay for it. Or if not for all of it, for another month or two."

"No, I feel we should be at Cliffside," Addie insisted.

He wondered why she was so adamant about leaving and wondered if she did not want to attend Season events with him in tow. Everett knew he lacked the polish and wit so many of her other friends had and hoped she was not ashamed of him.

"What if I do find a husband?" Louisa asked.

"Kent is not that far," Addie said. "Ev and I will be happy to return to London for your wedding. In fact, we should plan on it because I know one of your suitors will offer for you."

Louisa frowned. "I don't know about that."

"Don't be so gloomy," Addie admonished. "Tessa will be here to guide you. Mama, too."

Analise began to stir and started whimpering, causing Spence to rise and say, "It is time for her feeding. We should be leaving."

Tessa rose and took the baby from Louisa, kissing Analise's brow and shushing her. Everett hoped that he would now have an opportunity to speak to Addie.

Instead, Addie told him she would see him at tonight's ball and quickly left the room.

Everett would have to make the time to see her somehow. Though Addie was still an unmarried female, surely the rules of Polite Society could be relaxed somewhat since they were engaged. He felt it imperative that he tell her he loved her before they wed.

EVERETT STOOD BESIDE Spence in St. George's, his eyes focused on the door that Addie would come through in just moments.

In a few minutes, they would become husband and wife.

He hoped she had seen the flowers he had sent to her this morning. In the rush of getting ready for the wedding, they might have been overlooked. At least he had gotten her a wedding present. One he hoped she would like. He would give it to her tonight.

Before they made love.

A moment of regret filled him. He had not been able to spend a single minute alone with his fiancée in the week leading up to today's ceremony. So many things had to be done. He had met twice with the solicitors, ironing out the generous details of their marriage settlements. Twice, he'd visited his tailor for fittings of the suit of clothes he now wore. As for Addie, she was forever busy with her modiste or the florist or talking with Tessa's cook about the wedding breakfast. In a way, he had felt left out of everything.

Spence had picked up on his mood and assured Everett that a wedding day was all about the bride. The focus should be on her. But it was only one day, Spence reminded him. The rest of their days would be for them together.

Everett only hoped Addie wanted to spend those days with him.

He still experienced twinges of guilt and regret for pushing her into this marriage. He had wanted her so much, though, that he had manipulated her into it. All honor had seemed to fly out the window. He had deliberately ruined her so he could have her to himself. Not Lord Rosewell. Not any other man of the *ton*. Everett wanted Addie as his wife.

He hoped they were not making a mistake.

The doors opened and Tessa and Louisa walked down the aisle together, arm in arm. Addie had proclaimed she could not pick one over the other and insisted they both stand with her as she spoke her vows. The pair reached the altar. Louisa gave him a sweet smile, while Tessa winked at him.

Then Addie appeared in the doorway on her father's arm. She took his breath away. His heart pounded fiercely as Lord Uxbridge escorted her down the aisle to him.

She wore a gown of the palest blue, which complemented her

honey-blond hair and clear, blue eyes. Bridget had arranged her hair high atop her head, with a few wisps escaping to frame her face. As Addie moved toward him, his throat squeezed tight with emotion.

Lord Uxbridge halted and kissed his daughter's cheek, his eyes brimming with tears.

"I love you dearly, Adalyn," he said softly and kissed her cheek again. Looking to Everett, he said, "I entrust her to you now, Your Grace."

He nodded in acceptance and reached for Addie's hand. Even through her glove, he could feel how chilled it was as he slid it through the crook of his arm. Fear kept him from looking into her eyes. If he did, he was afraid he might see her doubt.

And that would crush him.

The vicar began the ceremony. Everett only caught phrases here and there.

". . . *join together this man and this woman in holy matrimony . . .*"

". . . *ordained for the procreation of children . . .*"

". . . *one ought to have of the other, both in prosperity and adversity . . .*"

He blinked, trying to concentrate on the words being said.

"Wilt thou have this woman to thy wedded wife, to live together after God's ordinance in the holy estate of matrimony? Wilt thou love her, comfort her, honor and keep her in sickness and in health; and, forsaking all others, keep thee only unto her so long as ye both shall live?"

Everett swallowed hard, forcing the lump down. "I will."

He heard Addie promise the same as he had.

Then the clergyman had them join their right hands and, for the first time, Everett looked directly into Addie's eyes. He saw uncertainty in them and wondered if he should stop the ceremony. Then she blinked and her self-assurance seemed to return. She squeezed his hand, seeming to give him consent to continue.

Everett followed the instructions, claiming the ring from Spence and handing it over. The vicar placed it upon the book he held and said a prayer before returning it to Everett. He slipped the glove from Addie's left hand and placed the wedding band upon her finger before repeating words which bound him to her forever.

"With this ring I thee wed, with my body I thee worship, and with all my worldly goods I thee endow: In the name of the Father, and of the Son, and of the Holy Ghost. Amen."

More prayers occurred, with them kneeling side by side, and then they were declared man and wife.

He gazed into the eyes of the woman he loved. The opinionated, spoiled, determined, mischievous woman who held his heart. Lowering his lips to hers, he gave her a brief, tender kiss.

The rest passed in a blur. The signing of the register. The congratulations from family and friends. For a moment, he wished Owen, Win, and Percy could have been here to share this with him but he knew the Second Sons were with him in spirit. They would certainly be surprised when he wrote to them, informing them he had wed as Spence had.

He escorted his bride outside, where his carriage awaited them, along with the other vehicles which would convey them to Spence's townhouse a few blocks away. The day was cool but sunny, which he thought a good omen as he handed Addie into the coach and followed behind. Sitting beside her, he entwined his fingers through hers.

"We are wed," he said.

"We are."

He didn't know what else to say. Usually so comfortable around her, he grew suddenly shy. They continued holding hands but neither spoke for the next few minutes.

When they arrived at Spence's, he climbed from the carriage and helped her down the stairs, escorting her inside, where a large group of guests awaited. About half were friends of her parents and the other half were friends of Addie's. For a minute, loneliness set in, knowing he only had Spence and Tessa here for him.

Joyous greetings occurred and he and Addie were seated at a table in the center of the ballroom, with dozens of other small tables surrounding them. Several courses appeared, one after another, while he and Addie circulated among their guests between them. It surprised him that she wasn't more vibrant and enthusiastic. Instead, she was quieter, subdued, her bearing almost regal.

Then three enormous cakes were rolled out and he finally saw his bride with a smile. This one seemed genuine, the first of the day, and he tried to relax as servants cut each one and distributed them.

His duchess took a bite from each slice and told him, "You were right to have three cakes. I could not have decided between flavors. I like having some of each."

He nodded, at a loss for words.

"Thank you for the daffodils," she said shyly.

He glanced up from his plate. "You received them?"

"I did. It was very thoughtful of you, Ev."

"I heard you mention they were your favorites. I didn't know if you would see them or not."

"Mama made certain I did. We both agreed it was a sweet gesture."

"I am glad you liked them."

Once they finished their cakes, Addie suggested they make the final rounds before they departed. They moved separately about the room and eventually met in the middle.

Spence approached and said, "Your carriage is waiting, Your Graces. And Her Grace's trunks were already transported to your townhouse."

Addie looked perplexed a moment and Everett realized she was being addressed as a duchess for the first time.

"Then Her Grace and I will now depart," he said as Tessa stepped up. "Thank you for everything today, Tessa." Everett kissed her cheek and Addie embraced her cousin.

Spence announced that the newlyweds were leaving and the

guests followed them outside to the carriage, waving goodbye as it rolled away from the curb.

They were finally alone. It was quiet. He turned to Addie, ready to tell her he loved her.

"It was a lovely ceremony, don't you think so?" she asked brightly. "And Tessa's cook did a marvelous job preparing the wedding breakfast."

She kept up a constant chatter until they arrived at his townhouse, where Bailey and Mrs. Bailey greeted them and led them inside. The entire staff was lined up to greet their new duchess.

Everett allowed Mrs. Bailey to guide them through the line as she introduced every servant to Addie, who took time to speak with each one. He was perplexed how she seemed to keep her distance even while she spoke with every member of the staff.

Once the introductions were complete, Mrs. Bailey said, "Her Grace's trunks have been taken upstairs and her maid is waiting for her there. I also sent up a small meal to your sitting room, Your Grace."

"Thank you, Mrs. Bailey," he replied and then looked to Addie. "Would you care to go upstairs?"

"Yes."

He took her to what had been his mother's rooms and wondered how to address what was to occur next. Addie seemed to sense his hesitancy and placed a hand on his sleeve.

"Give me an hour and then you may come to me, Ev."

One hour.

And then their marriage would truly begin.

CHAPTER EIGHTEEN

ANXIETY FILLED ADALYN as Bridget removed the wedding gown and dressed her in some filmy night rail that Tessa had pressed upon her as a gift. Her cousin had insisted it was something a husband would enjoy seeing his new wife wear. She glanced down and saw she could see through it.

And if she could, Ev certainly could.

She wished she knew what lay ahead. Mama had been no help in addressing the matter. Adalyn realized she should have pulled Tessa aside to learn what was expected.

"Sit at your new dressing table, Your Grace," Bridget instructed.

"Why?"

"You have a lot of pins in your hair."

"You are removing them?" she asked.

"Yes. A simple braid will do."

Adalyn's heart pounded against her ribs, tension rippling through her. She disguised her agitation, though, as she had all day.

By thinking as a duchess should.

No duchess would worry about any matter, especially a coupling with her husband. She would be stoic and hope that the act would result in getting an heir. At least that's what Adalyn hoped would occur. She had heard vague talk among the women of the *ton.* How once you were with child, your husband left you alone.

She definitely needed Ev to leave her alone.

Even if she craved his touch.

The marriage was complete. There would be no going back. Adalyn had done her best all day to act as a duchess would. She tamped down her natural exuberance. Instead of rushing to hug guests at their wedding breakfast with enthusiasm, she had smiled graciously and allowed them to take her hand. She kept her voice modulated and strove to practice perfect posture.

Bridget finished unpinning the elaborate hairstyle and brushed her mistress' hair before braiding it. Then she held up a dressing gown and Adalyn gratefully slipped into it, belting it tightly. Uneasiness filled her.

"I'll leave you now, Your Grace," the maid said. "Ring if you need anything else." She grinned saucily. "I doubt you will, though."

After Bridget departed, Adalyn paced the room, restlessly awaiting Ev.

Her husband . . .

She didn't want to think of him as a duke. She didn't want to look ahead to the ways she would disappoint him. The list was foremost in her mind. She fit a few of the things he had wished for in his duchess—and would do her best to try and fulfill the other ones. Leaving town for Kent was one thing she could do. Ev had wanted a wife who would take her responsibilities seriously, including those regarding the tenants at his estates. He would appreciate leaving London since he wasn't comfortable at *ton* events and would relax once they returned to the country. She would show him that she could do her best to be a good duchess, though she feared it would take her years to grow into the role.

A soft knock sounded, coming from a different door than the one she had entered. His rooms and hers most likely connected for convenience. She thought of what Tessa had said about the night rail and quickly untied it, placing it across a chair.

"Come," she called out, butterflies filling her belly.

Ev stepped in, wearing a banyan of midnight blue and dark trousers. No shirt or cravat lay beneath the banyan and she could see his smooth throat and a bit of chest hair peeking out. Her mouth grew dry.

He closed the door behind him and came to her, admiration in his eyes.

"You look lovely, Addie. Like an angel wrapped in a gossamer of silk."

She swallowed. She wanted to say something but no words formed in her mind.

"Are you apprehensive?" he asked.

"Yes," she whispered.

Ev placed his large hands on her shoulders and warmth rushed through her. She caught the spice of his cologne.

"Do you know anything about what is to come?"

"No. Well-bred English misses aren't supposed to know about things such as that."

He frowned. "So, your mother didn't share anything with you."

She bit her lip. "Mama told me that all I had to do was lie still and that you would take care of the rest. That men . . . knew what to do."

Ev swore softly under his breath. "I do have experience in these matters."

For a moment, a pang of jealousy erupted. Knowing what they were about to do, he had already done with other women.

"But lovemaking requires two partners, Addie," he continued. "You lying there simply won't do."

"What . . . what am I supposed to do?" she asked, uncertainty filling her.

"Be an active participant. If I kiss you, kiss me back. If I touch you, touch me."

"T-touch you where?"

He smiled. "Wherever you like. And I will do the same." He

paused. "As we get to know each other's body, you must tell me which touches please you."

Adalyn could think of a few places she wanted him to touch and felt the hot blush stain her cheeks.

"I see you already have a few ideas of where I can touch you. Have you ever touched yourself?"

She frowned. "Of course. How could a person not touch herself?"

The back of his hand stroked her cheek. "I mean have you ever touched yourself for pleasure?"

"I . . . I don't know what you mean," she stammered.

He cradled her face in his hands. "Then you haven't."

"How would you know?" she demanded.

Ev smiled gently. "I just do. And I plan to find those places which will bring you the most pleasure, Addie. That is my job as a husband. Everything I do, I do for you."

His words brought a warm rush through her. Even though she wasn't the woman he had wanted, he still would be good to her.

His thumbs stroked her cheeks. "We should begin. I will warn you that it is a slow process. We won't learn everything this first time."

"We won't?" she squeaked.

"No. It will take hours of exploration." He kissed her softly. "Of kissing. Of touching. Of joining our bodies together as one."

"To make a baby," she said quickly.

"Oh, I hope we will make plenty of them. But we will make love to one another not just to conceive a child. We will do so because we are man and wife. We will do so because we want to experience the special closeness that occurs between a wedded couple."

"I see," she said, trying to understand and yet totally failing to do so because she had no idea what was involved. Kissing, yes. And touching. She supposed how the pads of his thumbs brushed her cheeks was one way to touch.

"Then let's get this over with," she said, wanting the process to begin.

Ev chuckled softly. "You make it sound as if it some arduous task."

"It isn't?"

"No, not at all. Especially if . . ." His voice trailed off and his mouth took hers.

Adalyn didn't have time to think about what he would have said because his kiss was too demanding. Her hands wound about his neck and she pushed her body against him. His tongue slid inside her mouth, stroking hers, causing heat to fill her. Her breasts began to ache. The place between her legs pounded steadily. His hands moved up and down her back and then slipped to her bottom, squeezing it. A frisson of what she guessed must be desire rippled through her.

His assault on her mouth did not let up and Adalyn found herself clinging to him. Her heart beat rapidly as she pressed against him and felt his own pounding out of control.

She made his heart race. She did. No one else.

Smiling, she began kissing him with a fierceness she hadn't known she possessed. She heard his growl and his arms banded about her, making her his prisoner. They kissed endlessly, causing the throbbing between her legs to demand attention.

His attention.

Ev released his hold on her body but not her mouth, kissing her as his fingers slid under the straps of her night rail. He eased them from her shoulders. He broke the kiss, his mouth hot as he trailed kisses along her throat and down to her bare shoulder. His tongue glided along it, causing her to shudder.

Before she knew what was happening, he had lowered the night rail to her waist and was kissing one breast. Heat enveloped her as his mouth closed on her nipple, sucking and laving it.

"Oh!" she cried, pressing his head to her breast.

One hand cupped her bottom as the other kneaded the breast he wasn't kissing. She found she liked all the places he was touching. Very much.

He worshiped the first breast and then moved to the other, bringing a deep yearning within her. For what, she was uncertain but she knew Ev would take care of her.

He pushed her night rail down her hips, his hands trailing along the bare skin. As it fell to the ground, he stroked her hips, moving slowly up and down along their curves. Now totally naked, she thought she should be embarrassed. Instead, curiosity filled her as to what came next.

Ready to be the active participant he might want, Adalyn slid a hand inside his banyan, feeling the hard, muscled chest beneath, covered by a matting of soft hair. Her fingers smoothed it and then found one of his nipples. If she had enjoyed what he did to her, she thought he might feel the same.

Unbelting his banyan, she pushed it aside and pressed her lips against his chest, kissing the hot skin. His fingers thrust into her hair as she allowed her teeth to graze the nipple. He tensed and moaned as she brushed her teeth against it and then licked. His skin was salty and on fire. Utterly divine.

He shrugged from the banyan and suddenly scooped her up, carrying her to the bed Bridget had thoughtfully turned back. Placing her down gently, his eyes roamed over her.

"Perfection," he said.

Adalyn stared at his broad shoulders and chest, noting the hair moved down in a line that disappeared into his trousers.

She wanted to see where it went.

"Would you remove your trousers?" she asked, afraid she sounded too bold and far too unduchesslike—but desperate to know more of him.

Ev grinned. "With pleasure."

He unbuttoned them and pushed them past his hips, stepping from them and tossing them aside. He stood utterly still then and allowed her to drink her fill.

The man was imposing. In every way. And something stood at attention, jutting from his body. She blushed, knowing it was his manhood. Then panic filled her.

He was going to try and put that inside her.

He must have seen her consternation because he sat on the edge of the bed and brushed his hand against her hair.

"I know it seems large but once you are ready, you will accept it."

"I don't see how," she replied, not really knowing where he was going to put it, only having overheard servants talking about how a man put something inside a woman in order to make a baby.

"It is my job to make certain you can take me in." He paused and she saw the worry in his eyes. "It will hurt you the first time, Addie. I cannot lie to you about that. But don't let that color the experience. Once I have broken through your maidenhead, it will never pain you again."

Apprehension filled her. She wasn't good at all with pain. Even when she accidentally stuck her finger with a needle when sewing caused tears to come.

"I don't think we should do this," she voiced.

"And I think we should," he countered.

"But what if I don't want to," she said stubbornly.

He grinned. "Then let me change your mind. I promise I won't do anything you don't want me to do."

That gave her some comfort.

"I do enjoy your kisses," she admitted. "And the places you have kissed me."

Now, his smile grew positively devilish. "Oh, there are more places to kiss you, Your Grace. And I plan to show you."

He certainly did.

Adalyn found herself panting. With exertion. With want. With need. All because of this man's fiery kiss.

Then he ran a finger along the seam of her sex and she came undone.

The throbbing there dominated her every thought.

"Do you like that, Addie?" Ev asked.

Before she responded, he pushed a finger inside her. She gasped.

"It is just another place to touch you."

Her cheeks grew hot, thinking of him touching her so intimately. The blush continued as he began stroking her deeply and she moaned. Her hips moved, meeting his stroke. Ev kissed her deeply now, his tongue mimicking what his finger did. Then a second finger joined the first and she thought she might lose her mind. Pressure began building and she thought she might explode at any moment.

Ev broke the kiss and said, "Let it come, Addie. Let it wash over you. Drown yourself in the pleasure."

She whimpered and raised her hips and then a blinding warmth spread through her as she squealed. A dam within her burst, flooding her with unimaginable pleasure. She laughed and Ev joined in as she danced with the tidal wave consuming her body. It finally ended, exhausting her, and Ev kissed her deeply as he moved so that he crouched just above her.

Before she knew what he would do, he pressed his cock against her and pushed hard. She shrieked, her nails clawing his back. He didn't move again. The pain quickly receded.

"I am sorry I had to do that," he apologized. "It's done."

A feeling similar to the one before began building within her and she moved against him. It felt good. Right. He withdrew a bit and pushed into her again. Adalyn tensed but found no pain. Just friction—which felt awfully good.

"Shall I continue?" he asked, his voice low and husky as his lips grazed her ear.

"Yes."

He did, moving in and out, each thrust going deeper and bringing with it the most marvelous feeling. Soon, she clung to him as they danced a dance more intimate than any waltz, building to a crescendo that caused her to call out his name as the same feelings of bliss encompassed her. At the same time, Ev shouted hoarsely and then collapsed atop her, driving her into the mattress.

Adalyn held tight to him, not wanting this moment to ever end.

He rolled slightly and she found herself on her side, gazing into his stormy gray eyes.

"How do you like lovemaking, Your Grace?" he asked playfully.

"It did involve a lot of touching. And kissing. I see what you meant about finding places on one another." She tweaked his nipple and he growled.

"You are a fast learner."

"When can we do it again?" she asked eagerly, forgetting that a duchess would never ask such a question.

Ev chuckled. "Not for a while. It takes a man a while to recover. And this was your first time, so you will be sore."

He slipped from her arms and left the bed. Going to the pitcher, he poured water into the basin and dipped a cloth into it before wringing it out. Bringing both to the bed, she pulled the sheet up to cover her.

"Let me clean you. It is just a bit of blood. Nothing to concern yourself with. It won't happen again now that I've breached your maidenhead."

"It didn't hurt as bad as I thought it would," she admitted.

And then she realized how very unlike a duchess her behavior had been. With a frosty tone, she told her new husband, "I would prefer to attend to myself."

She watched him stiffen. Reluctantly, he set the basin down and brushed a lock of hair from her brow before pressing a kiss upon it. She winced as he did so, disappointed in her wanton behavior.

"I will see you in the morning," he told her.

Ev left without a backward glance as Adalyn's heart ripped in two.

CHAPTER NINETEEN

E VERETT AWOKE, HIS thoughts immediately turning to Addie. *Last night had been magical . . .*

If he had ever worried that he and Addie did not suit physically, making love with her changed that thought. He wished he could go back to her even now and lose himself in her body.

He had intended to stay the night with her but her attitude after had been off-putting. The warm woman he had made love to suddenly went cold. That was why he had left her and returned to his own bed. He knew couples of the *ton* kept to their own bedchambers. Spence and Tessa were rare exceptions. Something Spence had said once let Everett know the two shared a bed.

He had hoped it would be the same with Addie. Now, he doubted it. She seemed to want her privacy and to keep her distance from him.

Once again, he hoped they would not become his parents.

He rang for Roper and the valet appeared soon after, helping Everett shave and dress for the day. He had not thought to retrieve the clothes he had shed in his wife's bedchamber last night and supposed Bridget would return those to Roper.

"Is there anything else you require this morning, Your Grace?" the valet asked.

"No, thank you, Roper. Merely be ready to depart for Cliffside once Her Grace has breakfasted. That may be in a few hours. Make certain all my and Her Grace's things are in the carriage."

"Of course, Your Grace."

Leaving his rooms, Everett made his way downstairs to the breakfast room, where it surprised him to find his wife already sitting there, sipping on a cup of tea.

"Good morning, Your Grace," she said. "I have waited for you before I ordered breakfast."

As he seated himself, he said, "I had the impression you always breakfasted in your room."

"That is something I do during the Season," she agreed. "However, it will be different in the country. Do you know what you wish to eat?"

"Anything is fine," he told her.

Addie called Bailey over and instructed the butler as to what they would both have. The servant left and Everett asked, "Are you ready to depart for Cliffside?"

"Yes, Bridget has everything in hand. We only opened one of my trunks last night. How long will it take to reach your estate?" she inquired.

"It is fifty-four miles. We will have to stop once to change the horses out but if we leave shortly after we eat, we can arrive a little after one this afternoon, I would think."

She asked him a few questions about Cliffside, which he happily answered, having lived at the estate since last autumn until his recent journey to London for the Season.

Their breakfast arrived and they ate in silence.

Once they finished, Addie told him she would be ready to leave within a quarter-hour and left the room. Everett went to his study and signed a few papers before summoning his secretary. He told Johnson to send regrets for the invitations that had already been accepted—but only for the next week. He thought after a week in the country that Addie might change her mind and wish to return to town to be with Louisa and attend the remainder of the Season. If that was the case, he was happy to accommodate her.

Soon, Bailey arrived and told him the carriage was waiting. As he stepped outside, he actually saw two carriages standing there. Addie arrived moments later and he asked about it.

"The second carriage is for Roper and Bridget and our luggage," she informed him.

He hadn't known that was the practice of the *ton* since he and Roper had ridden together to London. Everett realized he still had much to learn about Polite Society. He was grateful he would have Addie by his side to help him through everything.

He assisted her into the carriage and sat beside her. Everett wanted to take her hand and yet something held him back. He wanted to tell her he loved her. Yet the words wouldn't come.

Hours later, they arrived at Cliffside and were greeted by Arthur, his butler, and Mrs. Arthur, the housekeeper. Everett had sent word ahead that he would be arriving with his duchess so that the house would be prepared for Addie. As before, the entire staff was lined up and Arthur took Addie through this line. Once more, it struck him how reserved she behaved and he supposed she was conscious of keeping a polite distance when in the presence of servants.

Mrs. Arthur took Addie in hand and took her upstairs to show her the duchess' bedchamber and sitting room, while Everett met with Mr. Painter, his steward.

The men discussed estate matters and what had occurred during Everett's absence. Eventually, Arthur arrived and told Everett tea was waiting for him in the library. He ventured there and found his wife. Addie poured out for him, adding just the right amount of milk and sugar to his cup. He liked that she noticed details such as that and knew it would be an asset to her in the coming years.

"How do you find the house?" he asked.

"Mrs. Arthur was kind enough to take me on a thorough tour of it. I must say, it is the largest country house I have ever visited."

"You aren't a visitor here, Addie," he said. "It is your home now."

She stiffened. "I am aware of that." A veil seemed to drop over her.

For the next half-hour, they discussed the house itself and she suggested a few changes she wished to make.

"Only if you are agreeable to them," she insisted.

"The household is your domain. Make whatever changes you wish in order to see you are comfortable here."

"I also want to see to your comfort, too, Ev," she said quietly. "The Duke of Camden should enjoy his home."

He looked at her and felt a wide gulf between them, not understanding why it was there or how he could breach it.

She ended the awkward silence between them by saying, "Will we be keeping country hours now that we are at Cliffside?"

"We will keep whatever hours you wish."

"You don't know what country hours are, do you?"

"No," he admitted. "But I am a former army man and used to taking orders." He smiled sheepishly at her. "I suppose as far as Polite Society goes, I look upon you as my commanding officer. I hope to learn as much as I can from you—even what country hours are."

She quickly explained to him that it meant adjusting both meal and teatimes so that both occurred earlier in the day.

"Usually, when living in the country, people go to bed earlier. Thus, the changes."

He thought about her in bed and desire flickered within him. Since they were alone, he asked, "Are you very sore today?"

A blush tinged her cheeks and she said, "A little bit. Nothing to concern yourself with," she assured him. "If you wish to come to me tonight, I am agreeable."

It seemed so impersonal, so detached, arranging for him to visit her for sex. Everett hoped he could somehow melt the ice she seemed to be encased in.

"Yes, that would be agreeable. If it is with you."

"I said it was," she said abruptly. "You may come to my bed anytime you wish, Ev. I know what my duty is as your wife. That is to provide you with an heir to the dukedom."

"I'd hoped that you would enjoy me coming to visit you."

Her pink cheeks deepened to red now. "Yes, I quite enjoyed . . . what . . . we did last night."

"You don't have to be shy discussing it with me, Addie. I told you that it will take time for us to learn one another's body and what pleases us."

"I am uncomfortable discussing this with you," she said briskly. "You can do what you did last night. It was perfectly adequate."

She rose. "I will see you at dinner."

Everett watched his wife leave the room, totally confused by her behavior. It seemed she had been one woman before marriage and was quite a different one after. He knew last night had been an eye-opening experience for her but hoped she truly had enjoyed it. He struggled with finding a way to find the old Addie. The one he loved. This new one seemed so foreign to him.

He returned to his study and brooded until he was summoned to dinner. Their conversation seemed stilted, most likely due to the presence of the two footmen in the dining room. He knew she would not agree to dismissing them and didn't even bother to ask.

When the meal finally ended, he escorted her to the library, where they both sat and read silently. At least he sat. Reading seemed to be impossible. So he stared at the page and turned it every now and then, not wanting her to know how upset he truly was.

The clock chimed eight. She rose. He did the same.

"I am going to my bedchamber now," she told him. "Please give me a quarter-hour before you arrive. Then we should be finished by nine o'clock."

Addie did not wait for him and left the library quickly without another word. Confusion filled him as he made his way to his own bedchamber and found Roper waiting for him. He removed his coat, waistcoat, cravat, and shirt, tossing his banyan on. He had Roper remove the Wellingtons since it was an arduous process. Barefooted, he paced the room for another few minutes before he decided to leave his trousers behind, as well. By now, his body was on fire, eager to join with hers and he made his way to his wife's room.

He knocked on her door and heard her call out for him to enter. He did so, disappointed that tonight she wore a dressing gown over the deliciously sheer night rail.

He closed the distance between them and lightly clasped her waist as he bent and touched his lips to hers.

As always, there was electricity when they kissed and all the fears that had built up since he had left her last night now fell away.

Everett enfolded Addie in his arms, her vanilla scent surrounding him. He kissed her hungrily, longing to find the woman he loved within her. She responded to his kiss, her tongue warring with his, her hands clutching his shoulders, kneading them. He broke the kiss and buried his face against the slender column of her throat, inhaling her sweetness. He playfully nipped at her throat, causing a whimper, and he soothed the place with his tongue. Finding where her pulse beat wildly, he licked at it and nipped again.

Addie's arms went about his neck, holding him tightly. His fingers worked at the belt of her dressing gown, untying the knot and ridding her of the garment. He caught her wrists and lifted her arms away, the better to see her body's silhouette beneath the silk, its enticing curves calling out to him.

Reaching for the hem of the flimsy night rail, he pulled it up and over her head, tossing it aside. He took her hand and led her to the bed, backing her against the mattress and easing her down. Her legs hung from the bed and he kissed his way from her throat down to her core.

"Ev," she said, uncertainty in her voice. "What are you doing?"

He dropped to his knees. "Learning more about you."

Capturing her knees, he pushed them apart, feeling her stiffen.

"Ev," she warned again.

He glanced up, his gaze pinning hers. "Trust me, Addie."

She swallowed, her sky-blue eyes filled with doubt. "All right," she said shakily. "But you'll stop if I ask?"

"Yes. But you won't want me to," he said confidently.

He skimmed his fingers along her inner thighs, trying to soothe the tension from her. Then he pulled on her legs slightly, bringing her body to the very edge of the bed for better access. He ran his tongue along the seam of her sex and she gasped.

"Ev! For goodness' sake! What was that?"

He didn't reply. Instead, he repeated the gesture—and then plunged his tongue inside her.

A strangled cry emerged from her. He ignored it and began to feast upon her, using his tongue and teeth to pleasure her. Her little cries and whimpers told him all he needed to know and he continued making love to her. Then her body shuddered violently, her hands fisting in his hair, and the storm moved through her as she jerked and sighed.

When she stilled, he tore the banyan off and hovered over her a moment before thrusting inside her. Addie cried out, her back arching. He moved in and out, increasing and then slowing the pace before speeding up again. She kept calling his name, begging him to move faster and he finally did.

They both climaxed at the same time, shouting their pleasure, before he nuzzled her neck, his body against hers. She smelled divine. She tasted divine.

And she was his. All his.

Everett pushed himself up and pulled out, lifting her onto the pillows and then slipping beside her. He encased her in his arms and held her to him, smoothing her hair and kissing her gently, not wanting to leave her tonight.

Slowly, he sensed her withdrawing from him and he broke the kiss. For a moment, Everett thought he saw regret in her eyes and then a steely resolve replaced it. She moved away from him and climbed from the bed, retrieving the filmy night rail he had removed from her. She brought it over her head and then stood, arms crossed, waiting expectantly. He realized she expected him to leave.

He left the bed, claiming his banyan and shrugging into it. He walked to the door and turned, pausing to drink her in, regret filling him that she wished him gone.

"Thank you," she said primly. "Goodnight, Ev."

Her dismissive tone let him know he was no longer welcome. Everett left his wife's chamber and returned to his cold, empty bed.

CHAPTER TWENTY

A DALYN DIDN'T KNOW what she was going to do.

She was desperately in love with her husband—though he had never mentioned a word of love to her. She knew he wouldn't because she wasn't the woman he had intended to wed. During each day, she tried her best to be the perfect duchess. She managed the household with ease. Ev had taken her to meet many of his tenants. She comported herself as a duchess should when meeting them. Regally. A bit haughty, which wasn't in her nature in the least, but she emulated the few duchesses she did know in the *ton*, hoping Ev would be pleased that she could be polite and detached in the company of others.

It was difficult, though. She tried to show concern for his tenants and yet keep her distance from them. A few of them mentioned how they had never seen a duchess, which led her to believe that Ev's mother had never gone out on the estate to talk with any of the farmers or their families. She supposed that was why he had been emphatic in wanting his duchess to take her responsibilities seriously.

Because his mother never had.

He had briefly shared that his parents were a typical couple of the *ton*. A woman who wed and provided an heir and a spare. Two parents who spent little time with their children—and no time at all with one another.

Adalyn didn't want that.

But she didn't know how to please her new husband.

In the light of day, they were courteous and formal with one another. At night, though, his visits to her bedchamber unlocked a sensual world of passion and desire. Though she tried her best to behave with decorum, Ev had unleashed something within her.

Something only he could satisfy.

Sometimes, she longed to have him stay after he had made love to her but the expectation had been established. He came. He pushed her to the heights of passion. Then he left. She would remain awake for hours afterward, weeping into her pillow, torn by wanting to be the duchess he expected and knowing she never could. Knowing she loved him desperately and that he had been trapped into marrying her.

Her behavior embarrassed her. She should behave more like a duchess and not a wanton. But Ev's every caress—his every kiss—seemed to liberate her. Make her want more of him.

Ringing for Bridget, she tamped down her frustration and put on a smile for her maid.

Bridget's brow creased. "You are looking very tired, Your Grace. Perhaps you might want to go back to bed and try and get some more rest."

Adalyn glanced into the mirror and saw the dark circles under her eyes. "No, I am fine. His Grace expects me at breakfast so that is where I need to be."

Bridget snorted. "His Grace is putting that fatigue on your face. If he's going to keep you up half the night, he shouldn't expect you up and about so early."

She felt the heated flush coat her cheeks. "That is none of your business," she said dismissively.

Her maid's mouth set in a taut line. No words were exchanged until Adalyn was dressed for the day.

She went downstairs to the beautiful breakfast room, which faced east and got strong morning light. Ev was already present, sipping on coffee. He rose as she entered and frowned as a footman seated her.

"You look exhausted."

"I have not been sleeping well," she said and took a sip of the fortifying tea another footman brought to her.

"I am sorry to hear that." He studied her a moment. "I think you should go back to town."

"Back to town?" she echoed.

"Yes. You seem to thrive there. I hate that I have taken you away from the society you crave. I believe once back in London, you will feel much better."

"Where . . . will you be?" she asked, since he had stated she should go back to town.

"I have business to attend to here. I will join you at a later date. You can have Bridget pack your things today and leave first thing tomorrow morning."

Her throat swelled with emotion. She determined not to cry in front of the staff.

Ev was dismissing her. He was already tired of her. Sending her from his sight. They had only been wed a week—and she was a miserable failure as his duchess.

It took everything she had to swallow a few bites of toast before she excused herself and returned to her room. Rejection filled her and the tears she had held back flowed freely. Adalyn allowed herself to feel sorry for her situation for a few minutes and then she dried her cheeks. She might be wretchedly unhappy, married to a man who didn't want her, but she couldn't spend the rest of her life feeling glum. She was the Duchess of Camden. She had duties to perform. She did not want to disappoint her duke.

Today, she had planned to take baskets of food to several of the tenants, ones who had small children and needed a bit of help. She would follow through with that instead of locking herself away in her room and crying pointless tears. She was a duchess. She would use her position for good, as she was meant to do.

Bathing her face in cool water, she hoped it wouldn't be

obvious she had been crying. She rang for Bridget and informed her that they would be returning to town first thing in the morning.

"Pack what I will need for the remainder of the Season," she instructed. "Some of my clothing can be left here at Cliffside."

"Yes, Your Grace," Bridget said, eyeing her with concern and then glancing away.

"I will be out and about on the estate today so if you have any questions, I can answer them once I return."

"Yes, Your Grace."

Adalyn left her bedchamber, her heart still heavy but her step lighter. She had a purpose to fulfill today. She would do her best to see the task through. It would help her get to know some of the tenants' wives better. And with Ev not around to watch her every move, perhaps she could let her guard down and speak to them in a more friendly fashion.

She went to the kitchens and spoke briefly with Cook, who already had the baskets assembled. A cart was brought from the stables and footmen loaded the baskets into the vehicle's bed. Porth, one of the grooms, would drive her from cottage to cottage, where she would spend a few minutes with the women and any of their children.

Porth helped her into the cart and they set off.

"How long have you worked for His Grace?" she asked the groom.

He looked taken aback that she would attempt to converse with him.

"I grew up at Cliffside, Your Grace. My father was a groom and is now the head groom."

"You must be very proud of him. That is a position of huge responsibility, especially on an estate as large as Cliffside. Do you hope to follow in his footsteps?"

The tips of the groom's ears turned pink. "That would be nice, Your Grace. But he's in good health. He should be working for years to come."

As they drove, she found out he had two other brothers who also worked in the stables and a sister who was a parlor maid, albeit in Ev's London townhouse. Adalyn felt good to hear Porth's story and know about his family and background. She hoped that someday she could say the same about all their servants and tenants.

They spent the remainder of the day delivering their baskets of food, with Adalyn visiting for several minutes to a half-hour with the wives. When it came time for the last stop, Porth helped her down and retrieved the final basket.

"Let me deliver this one to Mrs. Haggert," she said. "You can return to the stables."

"But how will you get back, Your Grace?"

"I will walk."

Porth looked at her as if she had gone mad.

"I enjoy walking. Go along, Porth. We started at the cottage which was the greatest distance from Cliffside and came closer to the main house with each delivery. I won't have far to go."

"If you are sure," he said, uncertainty lingering in his eyes and obvious in his voice.

"I am. Now, go."

Adalyn watched him drive away and then took the basket to the door. She knocked and the door was answered by Mrs. Haggert, who was heavy with child. A young girl of about four years of age clung to her skirts.

"Good afternoon, Mrs. Haggert. I have brought you some things."

The woman's eyes grew large. "Oh, my goodness. Well, if that isn't kind of you, Your Grace. Please, come in."

Adalyn entered the cottage and placed the basket on the table. Then she knelt and looked at the little girl. "What is your name?" she asked.

"Sarah," the child mumbled and then buried her face in her mother's skirts.

"Come have a seat, Mrs. Haggert. I would like to get to know you and Sarah better."

The woman waddled to a chair and waited for Adalyn to seat herself before she did the same.

As with the others she had visited today, it took a few minutes before the conversation began flowing freely. Once it did, though, Adalyn was pleased. Even young Sarah began talking, eventually coming and standing next to Adalyn. She scooped the girl into her lap.

"There, that's nice, isn't it?" she asked.

Sarah nodded.

"Are you excited about having a new sister or brother?"

"I want a girl," Sarah said emphatically.

"Boys are nice, too," Adalyn told her as she looked to the mother. "Do you have a preference?"

"I am hoping for a boy, Your Grace. I think that would please Mr. Haggert. Oh!" She grasped her burgeoning belly and cried out, "It's too soon!"

Adalyn slipped Sarah from her lap and stood. "Is it the baby?" she asked anxiously and glanced down, seeing water trickling onto the floor.

"Yes. But it's not due for another two or three weeks. That's what the midwife said."

She went to the mother and clasped her hand. "Babies tend to come when they want to. Not when we wish them to."

"But Sarah came right on time," Mrs. Haggert said, fear in her voice. "What if . . . something is wrong?"

"The midwife will take care of it," she said firmly. "Let me get you settled and then I will go for her."

She helped Mrs. Haggert rise just as a swoosh sounded, leaving water everywhere. Adalyn swallowed her own fear, not knowing the first thing about how babies came. She hadn't known water was involved at all.

Helping Mrs. Haggert over to the bed on the far side of the room, she removed the woman's boots and clothing, placing a night gown over her head before settling her into the bed. All the while, Mrs. Haggert was moaning and panting.

"It's coming. Oh, this is too soon," she told Adalyn. "There isn't time for the midwife. What will I do?"

Adalyn took the woman's hand. "It is what *we* will do," she emphasized. "You have done this before. I have not. Tell me what I must do. Quickly, Mrs. Haggert," she said as the woman curled up and then screamed.

Little Sarah also let out a piercing scream, echoing that of her mother. Knowing the girl was frightened, she knelt and wrapped her arms about Sarah.

"Your mama is going to have her baby now," she said as calmly as she could. "It requires privacy. It is a pretty day. Do you think you could go and play outside?"

Sarah nodded, her thumb jammed into her mouth. Taking her hand, Adalyn led her to where she saw a doll lying on a pallet.

"Is this your baby doll?" she asked.

The girl nodded.

"Let's take her outside then. You can practice caring for her just like you will help your mother care for your new sibling."

She led Sarah from the cottage and looked about to see if she could see anyone nearby. Another cottage was about a quarter of a mile in the distance. She wondered if she should go there now and summon help. Then another earth-shattering scream pierced the air.

"Stay outside and play until I come and get you, Sarah. All right?"

The girl nodded and sat upon the ground, cuddling her doll.

Quickly, Adalyn returned inside and saw Mrs. Haggert trying to rise from the bed.

"Where are you going?"

"The chair," the woman panted. "The midwife said sitting up makes things go more quickly. That it . . . eases the babe out better."

"I see you have a neighbor. Should I go to her? Have her send for the midwife?"

Mrs. Haggert hissed through gritted teeth. "I don't think there's time, Your Grace."

"Then I will send Sarah and stay with you. I will be right back."

Adalyn left the cottage and knelt before Sarah. She lightly took the girl's shoulders and said, "Your mama may need some help getting the baby out. Would you like to help her?"

Sarah nodded. "What do I do?"

Pointing to the cottage, she said, "Do you know who lives there?"

"Mrs. Parker."

"Have you been there before with your mother?"

The girl nodded.

"I need you to go to Mrs. Parker's. Tell her your mama's baby is coming."

"Why?"

"She can help. Or she will send for help. And you can stay there and play until your little brother or sister comes."

"I want a sister."

Adalyn smiled. "I know you do. But you will love the baby, no matter if it is a girl or boy."

She rose and took Sarah's hand. "Go there now. What are you going to tell Mrs. Parker? Practice on me."

"That Mama is having her baby."

She smoothed the girl's hair. "That's very good, Sarah. That will be so much help. Go now and do this for your mama."

She helped Sarah to her feet and watched the girl walk a few paces before she turned around. Nodding encouragingly at the girl, Sarah continued on her way and Adalyn returned inside.

By now, Mrs. Haggert was perched at the edge of one of the chairs, which she had pulled out from under the table.

Though fear raced through her veins, Adalyn asked, "What do I need to do?"

Soon, she had gathered the items Mrs. Haggert asked for, trying to focus on them and not the anguished cries from the mother-to-be.

Adalyn moved two chairs from the table and placed them against the wall at Mrs. Haggert's instruction. She helped the woman stand and move her chair directly in front of the other two. Then she retrieved several clean cloths, a blanket, and a knife, all things the woman had requested and placed them in one of the chairs. Mrs. Haggert sat again, bracing her feet against each of the chairs. Adalyn stepped over the panting woman's leg until she was centered between the chairs and the woman's legs.

Hiking up Mrs. Haggert's night gown, she saw the baby's head emerging, its crown visible.

"I can see your baby's crown," she said, smiling reassuringly as Mrs. Haggert gritted her teeth.

Another wail came from the woman and Adalyn said, "Push, Mrs. Haggert. Push harder. Your baby wants out as much as you want it out."

Several minutes later, Adalyn's hands hovered as the baby was expelled. She took hold of the infant, seeing a cord attached to it and remembered how she was to cut it. She wrapped the silent babe in one of the larger cloths and took a smaller one to wipe about its face.

"The nose," Mrs. Haggert said frantically. "Clean the nose. It needs to breathe."

"He, Mrs. Haggert. You have a son."

Adalyn wiped around the nose and face but the babe's eyes remained closed. No sound came from him. Panic filled her—but she determined to see this through. Cutting the cord, she dropped the knife and turned the infant facedown over her knee. Gently, she tapped on his back with two fingers. When nothing happened, she poked him harder between his shoulder blades.

A wail sounded, loud and hearty. Relief swept through her as she turned the babe over again and saw his large eyes now open as he shouted to let the world know he had arrived.

Half an hour later, the babe was cleaned and resting in his mother's arms when the cottage door flew open. Two women rushed in. A tired, messy Adalyn glanced up.

"Are you Mrs. Parker?" she asked.

"I am, Your Grace," the woman said, her eyes wide. "And this is the midwife."

"This is James," she told the pair. "Named after his father."

The midwife clucked her tongue as she looked on. "Ah, a fine boy for you, Mrs. Haggert. Let me see to you." She glanced at Adalyn. "The afterbirth?"

"It is still coming out," she said, brushing a loose strand of hair from her face.

"I can see to things now, Your Grace," the midwife said.

"Very well." Adalyn stood. "Congratulations again to you, Mrs. Haggert."

The new mother smiled. "It is thanks to you, Your Grace, that James is alive. I couldn't have done it without you."

"I am going to London in the morning and will be gone for a while but I will come to visit you and James upon my return."

Mrs. Parker walked outside with her and said, "Thank you, Your Grace."

"Thank you for listening to Sarah. Is she still at your cottage?"

The woman nodded. "She is. With my two. They're five and seven."

"I hated to send her alone but I was loath to leave Mrs. Haggert with things happening so quickly."

"You did the right thing, Your Grace," Mrs. Parker said. "We won't forget it. None of us."

"I am just glad that Mrs. Haggert and little James seem to be doing well."

Adalyn said goodbye and slowly walked back to Cliffside. She entered the house through the kitchens.

Cook spied her and immediately came to her. "Whatever happened to you, Your Grace? Are you all right?"

She glanced down and saw the blood smeared on the front of her wrinkled gown. "I am fine, Cook, but in need of a hot bath and cup of tea. I helped deliver Mrs. Haggert's babe."

Mrs. Arthur was summoned and helped get Adalyn up the stairs. Bridget stripped off the bloody gown as Adalyn briefly told the two servants what had occurred.

"I don't feel like going to dinner after my bath," she said. "Mrs. Arthur, would you please have a tray sent to my room and tell my husband I will be eating here instead?"

"Of course, Your Grace," the housekeeper assured her.

Bridget washed her hair and bathed her gently and dressed Adalyn in her night clothes and dressing gown. The maid combed through the wet hair and left it down in order for it to dry. The tray arrived and Adalyn picked at it, so tired she only ate a few bites. Knowing, though, that Ev would visit her as he did every night, she fought to stay awake as she sat in the chair by the window.

When she awoke, she found herself in bed. Darkness surrounded her. She didn't remember Ev coming but he must have. Sleepily, she burrowed her face into the pillow and closed her eyes.

CHAPTER TWENTY-ONE

EVERETT ACCOMPANIED HIS steward to a neighboring farm in order to inspect a group of sheep. Mr. Painter had suggested they start raising livestock as well as crops and this farmer had an excess within his flock that he was willing to part with for the right price. Painter had grown up on a farm and so Everett allowed him to haggle with the farmer over the cost of the livestock, taking pride when he surmised his steward had made a good deal.

Satisfied, the two men rode back to Cliffside, stopping to inspect crops in the fields and look at a fence which would soon need repair. Painter thought it could wait until after the harvest was collected but Everett was not fond of procrastination.

"We'll do it ourselves," he told his steward.

They rode to retrieve the necessary tools and then both men stripped off their coats and rolled up their shirtsleeves and spent an hour of hard labor seeing the fence mended. The work left Everett feeling happy.

Until he remembered he was sending Addie back to London tomorrow.

All day, the cloud of her leaving had hovered over him, finally dispelled as he pounded away at the fence. Now that the job had been completed, his guilt returned.

He was not the man for her. She had to be disappointed in

him. He hadn't the wit or effervescence she needed in a husband. His selfishness had backed her into a corner, giving her no choice but to accept him or be ruined. He longed to confess his sin against her to her but feared even the fragile bond they had forged—through lovemaking—would be forever broken.

He had missed teatime since the fence had taken longer to repair than he expected and he was soaked with sweat because of his labors. Calling for a bath before dinner, he soaked in the hot water, thinking of things to talk to Addie about before she left.

And fantasizing that she would tell him she truly didn't want to leave him behind.

After dressing for dinner, he arrived and found she wasn't in the dining room. A footman seated him and Arthur stepped forward with a decanted bottle of wine.

"Your Grace, Her Grace is feeling tired and will not be coming to dinner this evening. Mrs. Arthur had Cook send a tray up to her."

The butler poured the wine into Everett's glass and stepped aside.

With an ache in his heart, knowing Addie was avoiding him even before she left for town, he sipped the wine. The various courses arrived and he ate a bite or two before pushing it aside and indicating for the next one to come out. He skipped port after his meal, never really liking the taste of it, and retreated to his study where he brooded for two hours.

Finally, he went upstairs and Roper helped him from his clothes and into his banyan. Everett dismissed the valet and sat on the edge of his bed, debating whether or not to go to Addie. If she hadn't wanted to eat with him, she surely wouldn't want him in her bed. Yet the lure of her curves caused him to rise and go to her. She had said she would never turn him away. He needed her tonight. This last night. Especially since he had no idea when he might see her again.

He had no business that kept him in Kent. He had merely used that as an excuse. If he stayed here five days or five weeks, it probably wouldn't matter to her.

Going to her door, he knocked softly.

No reply.

Perhaps she hadn't heard him. Everett knocked again, harder this time. Still, no response. Worried about her now, he turned the doorknob and pushed the door open. His eyes went directly to the bed, which was empty. Then they swept the room and he saw her.

Asleep in a chair.

Moving to her, he saw a tray of food on the table beside her, barely touched. He wondered then if she truly had been tired since she hadn't eaten much of anything. For a moment, he merely gazed down at her as her chest moved slightly up and down, the curve of her breasts enticing him.

"Addie?" he called softly.

She did not stir.

At least he believed she hadn't been avoiding him. She truly looked exhausted. Even in sleep, he saw the shadows under her eyes and the frown on her brow.

Slipping his arms underneath her, he carried her to the bed and gently placed her upon it. Her hair, not in its usual braid, fanned out on the pillow. He ran his fingers through the silky waves, inhaling the vanilla that clung to her. Her lips parted and she seemed almost ready to say something in her sleep. He waited.

"Ev," she breathed softly and then turned her face into the pillow.

That one word gave him hope. Hope that whatever was so wrong between them might eventually work its way out. That the knot they had entangled themselves in would be untangled.

That they might find their way back to one another.

Everett took the bedclothes and pulled them over her. He sat on the bed beside her, watching her sleep for a good hour. She lay there looking beautiful and vulnerable.

He rose and pressed a kiss to her brow.

"I love you, Addie," he softly said.

Fighting the urge to slip into the bed beside her and hold her the entire night, he retreated to his own room. Sleep took its time coming.

He awoke, his eyes feeling gritty. A soft whine echoed in his head, telling him his lack of sleep would make for a difficult day.

After he rang for Roper, he mentally prepared himself for when he would tell Addie goodbye. He put on what he termed his army face, a look of stoicism he had acquired that he used when he addressed his men.

Roper prepared him for the day and Everett went downstairs to the breakfast room. He had only been there a few moments when Addie appeared, looking fresh and achingly lovely.

"Good morning," he said brusquely and then added, "Are you packed?"

She took her seat and said, "Yes. Bridget handled everything. We are departing after breakfast."

"That's good to hear."

They ate in silence. But even silence was full of noise to him. He tried to think of something to say to her. Nothing came.

He finished eating and said, "Have Arthur tell me when you are ready to leave and I will see you off."

She nodded and took a sip of her tea.

Once again, he sat in his study, pondering the marriage he had made and how unhappy he had made the woman he loved. Everett had no idea how to fix things. If only Addie were a fence, he would know what to do in order to mend her and their relationship.

A knock sounded and Arthur appeared in the doorway. "Her Grace is about to depart."

"Thank you."

He went outside where the carriage awaited, noting only one stood there. Several trunks were atop it but not all of the ones she possessed. That small fact gave him hope that she was leaving part of her wardrobe behind. That she had plans to return to

Cliffside.

To him.

Addie stepped from the house with Bridget, who went straight to the carriage and was handed up by a footman. Four footmen accompanied the driver. Everett had requested two extra ones accompany Addie for her safety.

She came toward him, her eyes clear, her gaze steady. Her beautiful mouth was set in a tight line.

"I hope you will have an uneventful trip," he told her.

"When are you coming to town, Ev?"

"I am not certain," he said evasively. "It depends upon how long my business takes."

"Don't . . . don't be long," she said, glancing away toward the carriage and then back at him.

He brushed his lips against her cheek in a perfunctory kiss, fighting the urge to gather her in his arms and give her a true kiss. If he did, though, he might never let her go.

Taking her hand, he led her to the carriage and handed her up.

"Give my best to your parents and cousins," he said.

Sadness filled her eyes. "I will. Goodbye, Ev."

"Goodbye, Adalyn."

He closed the door and stepped back, then motioned the driver, who flicked his wrists. The horses started up and Everett watched the carriage rumble down the drive.

Needing to escape, he strode toward the stables and called for his horse. He didn't care where he rode. He only needed to go.

EVERETT BURIED HIMSELF in work about the estate and three days later, he had never been more miserable in his life. He missed Addie dreadfully but would refrain from dashing back to her in London. Perhaps time apart might help her see things more clearly and give him a better chance at winning his wife's heart.

Today would be a huge one at Cliffside. The herd of sheep he had purchased from the neighboring farmer would be delivered this morning and Everett and Mr. Painter would be supervising not only the delivery but discussing how to divide labor on the estate. Several of the farmers had expressed interest in tending to the flock, some permanently, while others would continue to farm and care for the herd part of the time.

Everett met up with his steward after breakfast and watched as the sheep were driven onto Cliffside land. Since they had been discussing this purchase previously, sheep pens had been built, which saved them time and had allowed the sale to go through more quickly than usual. Next month would begin shearing season and that is why Everett wanted to decide today which farmers would work with the sheep permanently and which ones would be utilized to help in the shearing process.

His steward presented him with a list of names and Everett skimmed it, trying to picture as many of the faces as he could based upon the names he read. Painter had assembled the small group interested in caring for the sheep full-time and Everett spoke with each one individually.

The last farmer that came through, a Mr. Haggert, seemed quite enthusiastic about the idea.

"My father raised sheep," Haggert told Everett, "and I thought that would be the last thing I wanted to do. Don't get me wrong, Your Grace, I have enjoyed my time on your land but I actually have missed being around sheep. They're sweet creatures."

"Tell me a little about your experience on your father's station," Everett encouraged.

Haggert did so and from all the man said, Everett knew this would be the man he would choose to place in charge of the herd. They had a lengthy discussion regarding the shearing process and Everett asked Haggert's ideas on how to organize the process, impressed by everything the farmer said.

Painter had joined them and Everett caught his steward's eye. Painter nodded his approval and Everett turned back to Mr. Haggert and said, "If you are serious about leaving farming, I would be happy to place you in charge of the livestock I have just purchased."

He thrust out his hand and Haggert took it, pumping it enthusiastically.

"I would be happy to take on this responsibility, Your Grace."

Everett turned the discussion over to his steward, who discussed a salary with Haggert, which would allow him a small percentage of the profits from the wool that would be sheared. The man agreed to their terms.

"I cannot wait to share this news with my wife, Your Grace." Haggert smiled and added, "Please give our best to Her Grace if you would. My missus knows our babe is alive, thanks to Her Grace."

He stared at the man. "What do you mean, Haggert?"

The farmer smiled broadly and said, "I suppose Her Grace did not take any credit when she should have."

Confused, Everett asked, "Credit for what?"

"Why, Her Grace delivered our son four days ago."

His words stunned Everett. That would have been the day before Addie left Cliffside. The day she had been too tired to come to dinner.

"I will certainly pass along your words to Her Grace," he said, recovering his composure. "In the meantime, might I call at your cottage and convey my best wishes to your wife and see your new son?"

Haggert nodded. "Oh, Mrs. Haggert would be delighted for you to do so, Your Grace."

"Then why don't we go there together?" he asked. "We can also share your good news about transferring from farmer to shepherd."

He turned to his steward. "Once Mr. Haggert has given his news to his wife, he can return here and begin his supervisory duties regarding the sheep."

"Very well, Your Grace," said Painter. "In the meantime, do you know which of the other men you would like to work with the sheep?"

"I suppose I should discuss that with Mr. Haggert now."

Haggert said, "I have a couple of men in mind, Your Grace. I know you also spoke to them and a few others."

They quickly decided without argument which men would be included in managing the sheep though it would take more once shearing began in June.

"I will leave those details up to you, Mr. Haggert. You can work closely with Mr. Painter regarding any of these issues and he will report to me directly."

The pair left the steward in charge and he went to tell the other waiting men who would be handling the sheep now and in the future.

Haggert obviously didn't have a horse and Everett did not want to ride his while the man walked alongside him. He collected his reins and then Haggert said, "If you don't mind, Your Grace, I would rather remain here with Mr. Painter and the others. I want to set the proper tone among the men and see this operation through from its beginning. You are still welcome to visit my wife if you wish."

"Thank you, Haggert. I will do so. However, I will save your good news and allow you to share with your wife what your future at Cliffside holds."

Haggert bobbed his head up and down several times, saying, "Thank you, Your Grace. You are most generous." He gave directions to his cottage and then returned to the men.

Everett mounted his horse and rode directly to the Haggerts' cottage. He knocked on the door and a woman of about thirty answered.

"Mrs. Haggert?" he asked.

"No, Your Grace, it is Mrs. Parker. I live in the cottage just to the south of here. I have come today to help Mrs. Haggert a bit with her newborn."

"I have come to see the new babe," he stated.

She moved aside and said, "Do come in."

He stepped inside the one room. To the right was a table and chairs and a fireplace. A pot of stew bubbled, the delicious smells filling the room. He looked to his left and saw a woman in bed, holding a newborn in her arms. Everett went toward her and also saw a small girl who sat at the foot of the bed, playing with a doll.

As he approached, the woman beamed at him. "Your Grace. How nice of you to come. I suppose Her Grace told you about how she delivered young James here."

Everett smiled at the woman. "My wife is very humble and I only learned about her role from your husband this afternoon."

Mrs. Parker joined them and said, "Oh, Her Grace was wonderful! She sent wee Sarah here to me and I fetched the midwife. By the time we arrived, Mrs. Haggert had already given birth."

Mrs. Haggert nodded in confirmation. "Her Grace had stopped by to deliver a basket of food to us when my labor pains began. Though it took nearly a day for my Sarah to make her appearance in the world, I knew second babies take far less time. Her Grace was so friendly and had such a calming effect upon me. Though she had never delivered a child, I told her what had occurred the first time, and she took charge with ease. By the time Mrs. Parker and the midwife arrived, Her Grace already had the babe cleaned up. It was touch and go for a moment before my James began to breathe but Her Grace kept her head and encouraged him to do so. I will be forever in debt to her."

A warmth spread through Everett. This was the compassionate Addie he knew and loved. He wasn't sure why she had disappeared after they wed but now, more than ever, he was eager to be with her again. He decided he would leave for London at once.

"I am leaving for town immediately," he told the two women. "I will most certainly convey your gratitude to Her Grace and let her know that James is thriving."

The baby awoke and frowned a moment then let out a lusty cry.

"He's hungry, Your Grace," the new mother explained.

"Then I will leave you so that you might feed him. When Her Grace and I return to Cliffside, we will stop in and call upon you and Mr. Haggert."

Everett took his leave and mounted his horse, riding it at breakneck speed back to the stables. He let Porth, his head groom, know he would be leaving for London in the next half-hour and to notify his coachman and have the carriage readied.

Racing back to the house, he found Roper in the kitchens sipping a cup of tea.

"We are leaving for London as soon as you can pack for me. The quicker, the better."

The valet rose and said, "I can have you ready in half an hour, Your Grace."

"See to it," Everett said.

He went to his study and dashed off a quick note to Painter, telling the steward that he was returning to London and wasn't sure when he would be back at Cliffside. He asked for a weekly report to be sent regarding both the crops and the sheep.

He rang for a footman and handed the note to the servant, asking him to place it on the steward's desk. He tidied up his desk, making sure he was leaving nothing undone.

Then he went upstairs and claimed the wedding gift he had yet to give to Addie, handing the box to Roper and asking that it be packed with his clothes.

Roper opened the trunk and said, "Then this is the last of it, Your Grace. We are ready to leave."

Within five minutes, Everett was sitting in his carriage, eager to reach London.

And finally tell Addie that he loved her.

CHAPTER TWENTY-TWO

ADALYN.
　　Ev had called her *Adalyn*.

Three days had passed since her husband had put her inside a carriage bound for London and this was the only thing she could think about. One word which had cut her to the bone.

And told her exactly how he felt about her.

She had tried her best to be the wife he wanted and had thought she was doing a decent job of things. But it seemed her husband no longer wanted anything to do with her. He couldn't stand to be in the same household. He had sent her away. True, London wasn't that far from Kent but she might as well have journeyed to China. The wide gulf between her and Ev seemed impossible to close.

She wondered if her forwardness in the bedroom had been to blame in her banishment. Or if he merely found her lacking in everything a duchess should be. Perhaps he even sent her back to town in order for her to observe other duchesses in Polite Society and learn how to imitate them. She had no idea how to repair their relationship and had spent her time locked inside this townhouse, brooding or weeping.

Attending a *ton* event hadn't even crossed her mind. If she did go, others would immediately ask her about her duke. Where he was. When he would return to town. How their marriage fared.

Adalyn didn't trust herself to hear these questions without bursting into tears, which was why she knew she couldn't go out in public. She hadn't even sent a note to her parents or cousins to let them know she was back in town.

Curling her feet underneath her, she propped her elbow on the arm of the settee and gazed out the window, trying to think of ways to please Ev.

A knock sounded at the door and Bailey appeared.

"Lady Middlefield has come to call, my lady. Are you home to her?"

Tessa was one of the most intelligent people Adalyn knew. Perhaps she could share with her cousin a bit of her distress and see if Tessa had an answer.

"Yes, please escort her to me," she replied, standing and smoothing her wrinkled gown, thinking it was too late to go and change.

Bailey arrived with Tessa in tow and she did her best to give her cousin a smile. Once the door closed, though, her smile faded.

Tessa came closer and embraced her. "Why did you not let us know that you and Everett were back in town?"

Adalyn burst into tears.

Tessa hugged her fiercely as Adalyn sobbed for several minutes. Then the sobs subsided, with a hiccough or two.

"Come and sit," Tessa said soothingly. "Tell me what is wrong."

She took a deep breath. "Ev sent me away."

Tessa's brow furrowed. "You fought?"

"No. Not exactly."

"Then tell me why you are here and he is at Cliffside. Leave nothing out."

A single tear trickled down Adalyn's cheek and she wiped it away. "It all goes back to the list."

"The list?" Tessa asked, looking puzzled for a moment. "Your list as to what you wished for in a husband?"

"No, not my list. *Ev's* list. You see, when I agreed to help him find his duchess, I thought about how Louisa and I had created our own lists. I suggested to Ev that he do the same so that he could see what he was truly searching for in a bride."

Adalyn bit her lip. "And I possess very few qualities on his list, Tessa. He wished for a woman who would conduct herself as a duchess at all times. He wanted a woman who was dignified and reserved. Serene." She shook her head. "I am nothing like the ideal woman he wished to wed."

Tears began streaming down her face again. "You see, Ev was forced to marry me so I wouldn't be ruined."

"What?" her cousin asked.

"It's true. I don't exactly know how it happened but we were kissing at the Starfelds' ball and of all people, Lady Gwenda, her parents, and Lord Talflynn came upon us. You know what gossips Lord and Lady Fowling are and their daughter is absolutely vicious when it comes to spreading rumors."

"Yes, that is how Spencer and I heard you were betrothed. Lord and Lady Fowling were circulating the news throughout the ballroom."

Adalyn's throat tightened. "When we realized others were present, Ev was a gentleman. He told them he was kissing me because he had gotten carried away by my acceptance of his proposal. You see, he never intended to wed me, Tessa. He only did what he did to keep me from being ruined. And now he is stuck with a woman who is nothing like the duchess he wished for. I fit very little of what was on his list."

Tessa snorted. "First, let me say that Everett didn't seem to be forced into anything, Adalyn. I clearly recall him saying you were right in front of him and he finally realized you were the one for him."

"That is because he is so honorable," she said, sniffling.

"You didn't let me finish," Tessa admonished. "Second—and most important—Everett didn't need a list. I see how he looks at you, Adalyn. He loves you."

She shook her head. "No, he doesn't. He has never said those words to me. And he called me Adalyn when he sent me back to London. He never calls me that."

A wave of fresh tears came and she wiped them away angrily.

"It is all the worse because I do love him. Desperately. And I feel terrible that he only wed me to save my reputation from being forever tarnished. I let things go in that moment but I planned to insist upon a long engagement. That way, I could have ended it once the Season wrapped up. By then, I was hoping Louisa would be betrothed and she could wed before the scandal of my broken engagement became public knowledge."

Tessa shook her head sadly. "If you had ended your engagement, you know how Polite Society would have viewed you."

Adalyn nodded. "I know. But it would have kept Ev from being tied to a woman who was never fit to be a duchess."

"Why would you say that? You have good breeding, beauty, intelligence. Everything a duchess usually embodies."

"But I am not the calm, reserved, solemn woman Ev wants," she explained. "And now he has sent me away, only a week into our marriage. Because I couldn't behave like a duchess with him. Especially when we were alone."

"What do you mean?" Tessa asked sharply.

Her face flamed. "You know. When we were . . . together."

"In the bedroom?"

"Yes," she whispered.

"You are saying you did not behave as a proper duchess in the bedroom," Tessa said. "And might I ask how a duchess should respond to her husband?"

"Mama said I should lie there and let my husband do what he knew how to do."

Tessa burst out laughing. "And that is what has you so upset?" She took Adalyn's hands in hers. "Did you merely lie still?

"No. Quite the opposite, which I am sure appalled him. I was quite unladylike."

Tessa squeezed Adalyn's hands. "No, no, no. Your mother is all wrong. Especially because I know in my heart that Everett loves you. If you responded to his kiss—his touch—then that is perfectly normal. Very few *ton* marriages are ones where a couple likes each other, much less loves one another. Spencer and I are fortunate to have that kind of marriage. Let me tell you, my sweet friend, that my husband may be a lion in our bedchamber—but I am a tigress."

She felt her face flush. "What?"

"I am just as active in lovemaking as Spencer is. Sometimes, even more so. Spencer has taught me that whatever we do in our marriage bed is perfectly fine, as long as it pleases the two of us. He encourages me to do anything but lie there. If you have been a true partner to Everett in your bed, that is what he wants. Not some staid, unfeeling woman who refuses to participate in the act of love."

Adalyn thought back on the times Ev and she had coupled. How he had encouraged her to participate as much as he had. How his body responded to what she did. The noises he made. The pleasure they shared.

"Then . . . if Ev didn't mind me acting so unduchesslike in our bed, then why did he send me away?"

Tessa's brow creased. "I am not certain, Adalyn. I will have to think upon that. In the meantime, you cannot stay locked away here forever. It will do you good to get out tonight. There is a ball at Lord and Lady Martindale's. Spencer and I will call for you in our carriage. I won't take no for an answer."

Though she couldn't imagine being out in public and dancing with other men besides Ev, Adalyn agreed to go.

And hoped she wouldn't regret her choice.

⇥⇥⇥⟨⟨⟨

ADALYN DISMISSED BRIDGET, who had been very quiet as she helped her mistress dress for tonight's ball. Adalyn would never share her marital woes with a servant but she knew the maid had picked up on her unhappiness ever since they had left for London.

She glanced into the mirror, seeing the sad face reflected, and determined not to let her emotions show once she left this room. When asked about Ev this evening, she would smile brilliantly and say he was attending to business but would return to the social whirl soon—and then quickly change the topic.

Knowing it was almost time for Tessa and Spencer to arrive, she left her bedchamber and decided to wait in the sitting room on the ground floor that was designated as the duchess' place to take quiet time to herself or to entertain a small group of visitors, as she had received Tessa there this afternoon.

When she turned the corner, however, she paused on the landing.

Ev paced in the foyer, his hands behind his back.

Her heart slammed against her ribs and a small gasp came out, causing him to glance up quickly. Their gazes met.

She had no idea what he was thinking.

"Good evening," he said as she somehow managed to put one foot in front of the other and descend the remaining stairs.

"Good evening," she answered, noting he was dressed in his evening clothes. "Are you planning upon attending Lord and Lady Martindale's ball tonight?"

"Only if you are going," he replied cryptically.

"When did you arrive in town?" she asked, her mouth as dry as cotton batting.

"An hour ago. Would you mind if I accompany you to the ball? Bailey says you have not been out since your arrival."

She wouldn't mind at all. She would be thrilled to be on his arm. But she needed to know why he had ordered her to London while he stayed behind.

And the thought of asking him—and learning the truth—terrified her.

"I decided to take a little time to myself," she told him, surprised her voice sounded even and calm. "Tessa came by this afternoon, though, and encouraged me to attend this evening's affair. She and Spencer will be here soon in their carriage."

"Would you come to my study before they arrive?" he asked, his voice sounding strained.

"Of course."

Adalyn followed him the short distance from the foyer to his study. Guilt rippled through her as they entered and she glanced at the chair behind his desk. She had sat in it yesterday, wanting to be close to him. She thought she could smell the faint tang of his cologne as she did and had cried for an hour.

Ev closed the door and went to the desk, retrieving a black velvet box, square in shape.

"I had meant to give this to you earlier. It is a wedding present."

She tensed. "You did not have to give me anything, Ev. We married rather quickly. And I have nothing for you."

"I wanted you to have this." He handed her the box, looking apprehensive as he did so.

Adalyn swallowed and opened the lid. Inside against the black velvet lay a stunning sapphire necklace and bracelet.

"They are magnificent," she whispered.

"I am glad you are wearing blue tonight. Would you . . . that is, might you wish to wear them?"

"Yes, I would."

Ev took the box from her and set it on the desk. Stripping off his gloves, he removed the bracelet and opened the clasp, then placed the bracelet against her wrist and fastened it. The stones glittered brightly.

Gazing at it, she said, "I have never owned anything so lovely. You were already quite generous in the marriage contracts, Ev. You did not need to give me something so grand."

His gaze pinned her. "No. I wanted you to have them. They are not a part of the estate. I bought them because I wanted you to have something all to yourself. And because I thought they would bring out the blue in your eyes."

His words pulled at her heart.

He reached for the necklace and Adalyn turned so her back was to him. He lifted the necklace over her head and she inhaled the spice of his cologne. His hands rested gently against her bare shoulders as he fastened the clasp, his hot fingers brushing her nape, causing her to shiver.

For a moment, she thought she sensed him bending toward her and she longed for his lips to caress her neck. The moment passed, though, and she turned to face him.

"As the Duke of Camden, naturally, I have access to the family jewels. We should go through the entire collection tomorrow and see if there are any which might please you. After all, the Duchess of Camden should always be bejeweled at *ton* events."

Adalyn stiffened at the mention of her being the Duchess of Camden. All her insecurities rose again, thinking by wearing the various Camden jewels, many would be looking at her—and finding her inadequate—just as Ev did.

"If you wish," she said, straightening her spine and raising her chin a notch, trying to look the part of Ev's duchess.

Without waiting, she went to the door and opened it, continuing to the foyer. There, Bailey was opening the door.

The butler turned and announced, "The Earl of Middlefield's carriage has arrived."

"Thank you, Bailey," Ev said from behind her.

He offered Adalyn his arm and they went out to their friends.

As her husband assisted her into the coach, she realized he hadn't once called her Addie. He hadn't called her anything at all.

CHAPTER TWENTY-THREE

F OR THE LIFE of him, Ev couldn't understand why Addie blew hot then cold.

She had looked so achingly beautiful as she came down the stairs and it was hard for him to imagine that this magnificent woman was his wife. When he presented her with the sapphire necklace and bracelet, she had seemed genuinely moved by his gift. As he placed it around her neck, he had longed to kiss her but refrained from doing so, still feeling as though he walked on eggshells around her.

Then she suddenly changed again, a veil dropping over her. He couldn't understand what he had done wrong or why she had withdrawn so quickly from him.

They walked outside and a footman lowered the stairs, allowing Everett to hand Addie into the carriage. He followed her and was greeted effusively by Spence and Tessa.

"It is good to see you back in town, old friend," Spence told him.

Tessa gave him a sweet smile. "It is always good to see you, Everett. How was Cliffside? Adalyn said that you had business there which kept you from returning to town with her."

He saw the questioning look in her eyes and hated lying to her but said, "It involved sheep."

"Sheep?" Spencer asked. "I didn't know you were interested

in sheep."

"I wasn't until I spoke at length with Painter, my steward, and it seems there is indeed a good market for wool. Cliffside is so vast and not all of the land was being used to farm so I decided to purchase a small flock and see if I could give it a go."

Addie turned to him, a worried look in her eyes. "Should you have come to town so soon after purchasing this flock?"

"Everything is in good hands," he assured her. "One of my tenants—Mr. Haggert—grew up on a sheep station. I have put him in charge of the station." He paused and then added, "I believe you have met his wife."

Her cheeks pinkened and she nodded. "Yes, I called upon her and some other tenants before I came to London."

He noticed she did not share what had happened during that call and he wondered why. Pushing her, he asked, "Did anything unusual happen during your visits to the tenants?"

"No," she said. "I was only distributing baskets of food to those who had need."

Why would Addie hide the fact that she had delivered a child from him? It bothered him greatly but he did not want to discuss it with her in front of Spence and Tessa.

They spoke of inconsequential matters until they arrived at the Martindales' townhouse. The four entered the residence and he couldn't have been prouder to have Addie on his arm for all to see as they joined the receiving line.

"Oh!" Tessa exclaimed. "Is that a new necklace? And bracelet? I did not notice since inside the carriage was dark."

"Yes. They are a wedding gift from His Grace," Addie told her cousin.

"The blue absolutely brings out the color of your eyes, Adalyn," Tessa said. She looked to Everett and asked, "Is that the reason you gave Adalyn sapphires?"

He nodded. "I thought they would suit her."

Eventually, they reached their hosts and Lord and Lady Martindale, whom he had never met, fawned over him excessively.

He hated being a duke for that very reason. Finally extracting them from their hosts, they left the receiving line and entered the ballroom, where a footman handed Addie a programme.

It surprised Everett when she waved the servant away and did not accept it.

"Why did you not take a dance card?" Then he gave her a shy smile and said, "I hope it is because you will reserve all your dances for me."

"No, I will not be dancing this evening," she informed him.

"But you love to dance," he protested.

"I am a married lady now, Your Grace. I will sit with the matrons. Besides, it is rare when a husband and wife dance together."

He wanted to question her about that practice because he had seen Spence and Tessa dance. He knew so few others in Polite Society, however, that Addie might be telling him the truth and this was another of those bizarre, unwritten rules of the *ton*.

"You can dance with Everett once or twice," Tessa urged. "How about the supper dance? You can join us after it."

"I feel I owe it to Mama and Papa to dine with them," Addie said. "They still do not know that I am back in town. When they see me here tonight, Mama will want to catch up and hear about Cliffside."

Everett decided to take charge and said, "Then I will come to you and we shall dance the supper dance and then join your parents afterward."

He left with Spence and they retreated to the card room.

Everett asked, "Is it true husbands and wives do not dance with one another?"

His friend chuckled. "For a majority of the *ton*, that is true. I insist upon dancing with Tessa, however. It is one of my favorite things. To hold her in my arms and move to the music."

Everett played several hands of cards, winning a few, and then he excused himself from the table. He circulated about the room, talking to a few of the people he knew and meeting other gentlemen through introductions. When a footman came in and announced the supper dance would be starting soon, Everett and many of the gentlemen in the card room exited and made their way toward the ballroom.

He scanned the room as he entered and as she had said, Addie sat in a grouping of chairs that included the matrons of Polite Society. He collected her and led her onto the dance floor.

The musicians struck up a waltz and he took her hand in his, placing his other hand against her back, and pulled her closer than he usually did. For a moment, her eyes widened and then the bland look, which seemed to permanently reside on her face now returned. They danced the number together without conversing as he confidently moved her about the floor. When the music ended, he reluctantly released her and tucked her hand through the crook of his arm.

"I saw Mama earlier," she told him. "She knows we will be supping with her and Papa. Louisa and her escort will also join us."

Once in the supper room, they found Lord and Lady Uxbridge and Louisa, who introduced them to a pasty, solemn fellow. The three men left the women at their table and went through the buffet line, returning to join them.

Louisa, whom Everett thought was by far the more reserved of the three cousins, seemed downright animated this evening when compared to Addie. Once more, his wife had become an ice queen, rarely speaking and when doing so, her voice was well modulated and her comments brief. No one at the table seemed to notice anything different about her.

That is, until he caught Louisa's eye. She gave him a questioning look and Everett merely shrugged, not knowing what to say.

The supper ended and he requested to escort Addie back to the ballroom.

"That won't be necessary, Your Grace. Louisa and I have plans to visit the retiring room."

He watched the two women leave and decided he had to act. Glancing about the room, he sought out Spence who was leading Tessa. Finding them, he headed in their direction.

When he reached them, he said, "I need to borrow your wife, Spence."

His friend studied him a moment and then said, "Of course."

Spence took his leave and Everett asked Tessa, "Would you mind if we went out to the terrace? This is a private conversation and I do not wish for anyone to overhear us."

She nodded and he took her back to the ballroom, where they exited through a set of French doors into the night. Only one other couple was present outside and Everett steered Tessa away from them.

"What is on your mind, Everett?"

"I believe you already know, Tessa. It is Addie. I need to know what is wrong with her."

Tessa frowned and it looked as if she hesitated to speak so he added, "I know I am not the man for her. She needed someone as vibrant as she is. I am too quiet and much too sober for her. Yet ever since we wed, she seems like a different person.

"I implore you, Tessa. Guide me. Help me to become the man Addie wants. The man she needs. Because it can't go on as it has been."

"Do you love her, Everett?"

Anguish filled him as he nodded. "More than life itself," he revealed. "I thought I had enough love in my heart for the both of us. I fear I have only made her miserable. That is why I sent her back to town without me. You know how she sparkles, Tessa—and she has not sparkled ever since we made our vows to one another. I thought if she returned to Polite Society, she might become more herself. Yet tonight, she seems so distant. She acts like a woman twice her age. Frustration fills me. I just don't know what to do."

"Normally, I would not meddle in the lives of other people and their relationships," Tessa began, "nor betray any confidence.

However, the two of you have created quite the mess. It all boils down to your list, Everett."

Astonishment filled him. "That bloody list?" he asked. "I don't care about that list one whit. Yes, I made it simply because Addie asked me to do so. At the time, I thought I knew the woman I wanted but my mind has changed. The list is nothing like what I want in a woman. In my wife. In my duchess. The woman I want is Addie. The old Addie. Not the stranger I find myself wed to."

Tessa nodded, understanding in her eyes. "Adalyn believes she is nothing like the woman on your list," she explained.

He chuckled. "She's not. And I am ever grateful for that."

"My cousin wants to please you more than you know, Everett. She is trying to *be* that woman on your list. She is attempting to embody every quality on it to make *you* happy. That is why she is so subdued. She is trying to behave and speak as the Duchess of Camden. *Your* Duchess of Camden." Tessa smiled mischievously. "At least the Duchess of Camden you thought you wanted."

She placed her hand upon his arm and squeezed it. "She has deep feelings for you, Everett. I believe you can have a successful marriage—if you clear up the misunderstandings between you."

Hope sprang within him. "I will make certain that Addie knows exactly how I feel about her. The woman she is. The woman I want."

"When you do, Everett, make certain you address her as Addie," Tessa suggested. "She was deeply wounded when you placed her in the carriage and sent her away. Because you called her Adalyn."

He nodded, understanding filling him. "Thank you, Tessa. You have saved our marriage."

Everett led her back into the ballroom and they parted. He returned outside and found a bench to sit upon, where he tried to think of how and when he would address the problems between Addie and him. It finally came to him. He needed to make a bold statement in order for her to truly believe what he told her.

Returning to the ballroom, he stopped a footman and asked

how many dances were left before the ball ended.

"There are two dances left this evening, Your Grace."

"Thank you," he said, wondering how Lord Martindale's footman knew that Everett was a duke. It was just another of the mysteries of the *ton*.

Everett planned to ask his wife to dance the last number of the evening.

And he needed it to be a waltz.

To guarantee one would be played, he moved to where the musicians sat and waited patiently until they finished the piece they were playing.

Leaning toward a violin player, the closest to him, he asked, "Who is in charge?"

"I am," the man told him, obviously curious that a guest of Lord Martindale's would seek out an orchestra player.

"Will the final song be a waltz?"

"No, that is not what Lord Martindale wishes."

Giving the man his best ducal look, he said, "I am the Duke of Camden and I believe a waltz is what you will play to finish out the evening. Is that understood?"

Nervously, the man nodded his head. "Of course, Your Grace. We will do as you ask."

"Thank you. My duchess and I appreciate your flexibility."

Everett stepped away from the violinist and watched the next to last dance begin, slowly making his way around the edge of the ballroom, his eyes on Addie the entire way. She sat between two women, one he did not know and the other a duchess he had been introduced to previously. Addie sat quietly, nodding occasionally, letting her much older companions do all the talking. It struck him that his wife sat in the exact same manner as the duchess beside her, imitating the duchess' manner.

This would end. Tonight. And Addie would be free to be herself once again.

When the number ended and the dancers left the ballroom floor, he made his way to his wife.

He came to stand in front of her and said, "May I have this final dance, Your Grace?" knowing she would not be churlish and refuse him in front of all the matrons sitting there.

Addie rose. "Certainly, Your Grace."

She extended her hand and he took it, leading her to the very center of the room.

"This is not a waltz," she told him. "Lord Martindale is very old-fashioned and he still believes the waltz to be some newfangled dance. I am told it was only played for the supper dance because his daughter begged for it."

He grinned unabashedly. "I arranged for it to be a waltz," he informed her.

Surprise filled her face as he took her in hand. The music began and he swept her away, his heart racing at what he was about to do. It would pain him to be the center of attention of so many people—but he would do what it took to convince Addie he wanted her exactly as she was. Everett decided to enjoy at least half of the waltz, not knowing if when he finished making his declaration if his wife would ever wish to waltz with him in public again.

Tamping down the apprehension that filled him, he brought them to a halt as other pairs of dancers twirled by them.

"What . . . why are you stopping?" Addie asked, her confusion plain.

Everett captured her hands in his, holding them tightly, afraid she might flee the dance floor.

"I must speak to you, Addie."

"Here?" she squeaked. "Now?"

"Yes. Here. Now," he said.

She regarded him warily and tried to pull her hands from his but he held fast. Couples who had danced around them now stopped, curiosity filling their faces as they looked on.

"I am opening my heart to you, Addie. I trust you will listen to me with an open mind."

Suddenly, the musicians faltered and then came to a halt. In fact, all movement ceased. Every eye in the Martindale ballroom was trained upon them.

"I must tell you first that I hated that blasted list. The moment we finished composing it, I knew it was all wrong. The qualities I placed on it—the kind of woman I thought I wanted to wed—it all changed in that moment."

He swallowed hard, knowing he had to get the rest out, despite the fact that every eye in the ballroom now focused on him. But he would do so.

For her.

"You asked me if I sought love that day. I told you no." Everett paused. "But I lied to you, Addie. I knew from that moment I had already found it. With you."

She began trembling and he released her hands, lightly clasping her waist. Her fingers clutched his coat for support.

"I found what I was looking for in you, Addie. You are everything I wanted and didn't know I needed. I want to hold you forever. Stand by your side and be the joy to your heart. I know I am not the right man for you. That you deserve one much better than I am. But I hope my love for you will convince you that I will do my best to always meet your needs.

"My life began that day we met. I would be nothing without you." He paused, his eyes filling with tears. "Do you think you—"

Everett never finished because Addie jerked hard, pulling him down so that his lips met hers. Her arms went about him and the fiery kiss seared his soul. He enveloped her in his arms and time stood still.

When he finally broke the kiss, he gazed down at her, seeing her love for him reflected in her beautiful blue eyes.

Addie smiled. "I think lists are rubbish," she declared. "And you are the man I yearn for, Ev. I hunger for you and no other. I love you so much. I tried to be what your list required. The perfect duchess. I did my best to be subdued and sober and live up to your ideal woman."

He cradled her face. "You *are* my ideal woman, Addie. You

always will be."

Everett kissed her again tenderly—and only broke the kiss when he became aware of the tittering crowd. He glanced about the ballroom and saw many shocked faces but a few glowed with happy smiles.

"I think we have entertained Polite Society enough for one night," he said lightly. "We will be the subject of gossip for weeks to come."

"Probably months," she corrected, a teasing note in her voice. "Perhaps even years." Then her voice grew gruff. "There go Camden and his duchess. They're besotted with one another, you know."

Then Addie laughed, a sound that freed his soul. He swept her into his arms—and she continued to laugh the entire way as they swept past members of the stunned *ton*.

A footman saw them coming and opened the door and he stepped into the night.

"Shall we stay in town or go home to Cliffside?" he asked.

Tears of happiness glittered in her eyes and she said, "I can be happy anywhere, Ev. As long as I am with you."

EPILOGUE

London—Six weeks later

E VERETT AWOKE. SATISFACTION filled him immediately.
Because Addie lay nestled in his arms.

The past few weeks had been the happiest of his life, with each day full of joy and new explorations. His wife—just as Owen had done when they were boys—was bringing Everett out of his shell. He would never be totally comfortable around groups of strangers but he exuded confidence since he had the love of the most wonderful woman in the *ton*.

It had been hard to voice the words but he had confessed to her how he had tricked her into marriage. Everett had worried that the confession would cause problems between them but Addie had magnanimously forgiven him, even admitting that she was happy he had done so. If not for his actions, they might never have found true happiness together.

He stroked her arm gently, not wanting to wake her but needing to feel the satin of her skin. She stirred and sighed, burrowing deeper against his chest. He lay there contentedly in their bed, knowing every day he awoke it would be beside the woman he loved.

Eventually, she began moving about restlessly, the sign that her slumber was nearing an end. When it did, he felt her lips press against his chest, bringing that rush of desire through him. That hunger that only his duchess could fill.

Everett made love to Addie slowly, taking his time, savoring every touch. Every taste. Every moment. When she cried out in climax, he did the same, burying his face against her throat, feeling her pulse fluttering wildly. He snuggled with her for a few minutes and they talked about how they would leave London today for Cliffside. It was already the third week in June and the heat made the city undesirable to them both. Spence and Tessa were also leaving for the country and would only be about fifteen miles from them so they would be able to visit often.

"I suppose we should rise and dress," Addie said, stroking his cheek before leaning up and kissing his jaw.

"You keep doing that and we will never leave this bed, much less London," he warned.

She moved her hand away. "Oh, I definitely want to leave. Perhaps we can take this up again later. In our carriage."

Everett grinned. "Oh, you are a wicked woman, Duchess."

They had never made love in a carriage. He looked forward to the trip now.

An hour later, they were at the breakfast table, talking about what they would be doing once they returned to Cliffside. First and foremost was a visit to little James Haggert. Everett had told Addie about his visit to see Mrs. Haggert and her babe and how he had promised the woman the two of them would call upon them once they returned to Kent.

Bailey set down the newspaper and Everett began thumbing through it. He would take it with them and read it more carefully later.

Then an item caught his eye and he swore softly under his breath.

"Ev?" Addie asked, her eyes filled with concern. "What's wrong?"

He turned his gaze upon her. "Actually, nothing is wrong at all." Shaking his head, he pointed to the newspaper. "It is an obituary for the Earl of Danbury."

Her nose crinkled in disgust. "Oh, him. I am afraid to say I didn't like him in the least. He ran with a fast circle." She paused. "Oh, I am sorry."

"Because my brother was a part of that circle? I take no offense, Addie. Mervyn was with Lawford—Danbury—when they were both attacked. Mervyn died immediately but I heard Danbury lingered. I hadn't given him any thought."

Understanding filled her face. "That means if Lord Danbury has passed that your friend now succeeds him."

"Yes. Owen Hasbury. We grew up on neighboring estates and just as our older brothers were, we have always been as thick as thieves. We met Spence our first day at school and it was the three of us always. At least until university, where we became good friends with Percy and Win."

"So, Owen will be returning from war. Just as you and Spencer did to assume your older brothers' titles."

"I suppose he must. Owen is a fine officer and a good man. You will like him quite a bit."

She placed her hand over his, despite the presence of the servants in the room. "That may be the case, Your Grace, but I quite like you the best of anyone."

Everett was tempted to lean over and kiss her and then decided why fight temptation? Not when the prize was so rich.

His hand cradled his wife's cheek and he gave her a lingering kiss.

When they parted, he saw the color blooming on her cheeks and felt immense satisfaction that he had put it there.

They finished breakfast and Bailey told him the carriage was awaiting them. As they left the streets of London behind and the traffic thinned as they reached open land, he pulled his wife, his wonderful, outgoing, amazing duchess, into his lap.

With a mischievous smile, Everett asked, "Now, what was this about making love in a carriage?"

Addie beamed at him. "There's always a first time for every-